ALSO BY DARCY COATES

The Haunting of Ashburn House

The Haunting of Blackwood House

The House Next Door

Craven Manor

The Haunting of Rookward House

The Carrow Haunt

Hunted

The Folcroft Ghosts

The Haunting of Gillespie House

Dead Lake

Parasite

Quarter to Midnight

Small Horrors

House of Shadows

House of Shadows

House of Secrets

Craven Manor

Darcy Coates

Poisoned Pen Press

Copyright © 2017, 2020 by Darcy Coates
Cover and internal design © 2020 by Sourcebooks
Cover design by ebooklaunch.com
Cover art by The Book Designers
Cover images © Patryk Kosmider/Shutterstock, komkrit Preechachanwate/Shutterstock, kittirat roekburi/Shutterstock, Lario Tus
Internal images © Freepik

Sourcebooks, Poisoned Pen Press, and the colophon are registered trademarks of Sourcebooks.

All rights reserved. No part of this book may be reproduced in any form or by any electronic or mechanical means including information storage and retrieval systems—except in the case of brief quotations embodied in critical articles or reviews—without permission in writing from its publisher, Sourcebooks.

The characters and events portrayed in this book are fictitious or are used fictitiously. Any similarity to real persons, living or dead, is purely coincidental and not intended by the author.

All brand names and product names used in this book are trademarks, registered trademarks, or trade names of their respective holders. Sourcebooks is not associated with any product or vendor in this book.

Published by Poisoned Pen Press, an imprint of Sourcebooks
P.O. Box 4410, Naperville, Illinois 60567-4410
(630) 961-3900
sourcebooks.com

Originally self-published in 2017 by Black Owl Books.

Library of Congress Cataloging-in-Publication Data

Names: Coates, Darcy, author.
Title: Craven manor / Darcy Coates.
Description: Naperville, Illinois : Poisoned Pen Press, [2019] |
"Originally self-published in 2017 by Black Owl Books"--Title page verso.
Identifiers: LCCN 2019042383 | (trade paperback)
Subjects: GSAFD: Mystery fiction.
Classification: LCC PR9619.4.C628 C73 2019 | DDC 823/.92--dc23
LC record available at https://lccn.loc.gov/2019042383

Printed and bound in the United States of America.
VP 10 9 8 7 6 5 4 3 2 1

CHAPTER 1

DANIEL'S SHOE SCUFFED OVER the hallway runner and dragged up loose threads. He gave it a pitying glance as he turned the corner that led to his cousin's room.

The six-story apartment block was desperate for a bit of care. The thick white paint slathered over the walls had turned yellow where it wasn't already stained from water damage, and two out of his hall's four lights were dead. Daniel doubted it had been an inviting place in its prime, but by the time he'd moved in, it had become a space for the unemployed, the dying, and those with nowhere left to turn.

A house for desperate people. He flexed his shoulders. They ached from a day of scrubbing a casino's bathroom floor. It wasn't a permanent job. Most of Daniel's mornings were spent handing out applications to any business with a Help Wanted sign posted outside, no matter how unappealing the job seemed. When he was really tight for money, he would scout around the town's red district to see if anyone wanted to hire him for the day. He could usually get a few hours of janitorial work in a nightclub, a pub, or one of the down-market hotels. The pay was well below minimum wage, but he wasn't in a position to bargain.

"Daniel! Daniel!" A tiny, wrinkled woman tottered out of her room and waved to him. She'd dressed for the day but seemed to have forgotten that she was still wearing her nightcap. Squinted eyes blinked from behind massive, thick glasses as she held out a china plate. "Daniel, I baked biscuits. Try!"

Some of Daniel's weariness fell away as he met his neighbor at her door. "Thanks, Mrs. Kirshner. That's really sweet."

She only came up to his waist but seemed to swell at his words. "I bake them especially for you, Daniel. Young boy like you needs to eat more."

Daniel took one of the plain brown cookies she held up to him. It was hard and a little dry, but he was ravenous and chewed it quickly. "It's good. One of your recipes?"

"Yes, yes." The tiny woman nudged her glasses a little higher, and her smile flickered. "Normally has cranberries, but…but not today."

"Oh." Daniel's heart sank. He glanced over her to see inside her apartment. Her gray cat, Alonzo, slept on the windowsill. Without curtains, the light through the window cast its glare across the sparse room. He could have sworn she'd owned more furniture when she moved in. A cup of tea sat on the floor next to her chair. The drink was black, even though he knew she preferred it with milk. "Um, Mrs. Kirshner, are you doing all right? I mean, are you getting by?"

"Do not worry, Daniel." She gave his chest a pat. Her hands were tiny and bent with arthritis, but her smile didn't falter. "We are fine. I will call my daughter, yes? She is sending money next week."

Today's Tuesday. A week's a long time to wait. And she never calls her daughter unless things are dire… Daniel dug into his pocket for the twenty dollars he'd earned cleaning the bathrooms. He'd planned for it to go toward dinner that night and lunch the next day, but he really wasn't that hungry, he decided. "Here. It's not much, but it should help until next week."

"Ooh." She made a shushing noise and tried to fold his hand back around the note. "No, no, Daniel's money."

"Really." He laughed and tucked it into the front pocket of her cardigan before she could object any further. "It's payment for all of the biscuits you bake me. Take care, Mrs. Kirshner."

"Good boy, good boy," she crooned, shaking the plate at him. "Have more."

"Thanks." He took a second cookie then waved as she retreated into her home. As she shut the door, he heard her sing a lullaby to her cat. She sounded happy.

Daniel chewed on the cookie as he tilted his head back to stare at the stained ceiling a foot above his head. Down the hallway, a baby began crying. Two men were arguing on the floor below. The light at the end of the hallway—one of the two remaining working bulbs—hissed and flickered.

A house for the desperate…

He exhaled through his nose as he turned toward his cousin's apartment. The cookies would have to do for dinner. If he was lucky, he could pick up a new cash-in-hand cleaning job the following day. Or—he didn't dare hope too much—he might get a reply to one of his applications.

The city was starving for jobs, and any time he walked into an interview, he had to sit alongside at least twenty other candidates waiting for their names to be called. And he had minimal work experience, no qualifications, and no car. His bike got him around the city well enough, but employers expected him to have more reliable transportation.

It was a catch-22. If he could get out of the city, he might have a better chance of finding work, but he would have nowhere to stay. He was lucky to have a roof over his head as it was. His cousin, Kyle, had invited him to stay in his apartment "while he got back onto his feet." That had been six months ago.

Two bronze numbers, 1 and 6, hung on the front of their door. It was technically apartment 616, but no one had bothered to replace the missing digit. Daniel scuffed his shoes on the mat outside while he jimmied his key in the lock. The door scraped open eventually, and Daniel nearly stepped on the white envelope lying on the linoleum floor.

"Dan, that you?"

The voice came from the living room and blended in with the explosions and automatic gunfire of Kyle's video game.

Daniel bent to pick up the envelope. "Yeah, it's me. I wasn't expecting you to be home."

"Boss left early. So I figured I might as well, too." An explosion, then a disappointed mechanical chime signaled that Kyle had lost the game. He swore loudly.

The letter was thick card stock, not the usual flimsy paper the bills came in. It didn't have an address, but Daniel's name had been written on the front in a flowing script. He turned the envelope over. No return address.

The console game played a jingle as a new round began. Daniel shut the door behind himself then drifted into the tiny kitchen as he stared at the letter. Plates and pots sticky with the residue of some rice-based meal filled the sink. Daniel turned on the taps to try to soften the glue-like substance then lifted the envelope's unsealed flap.

He never received mail—and especially not unaddressed, handwritten notes with thick card stock. His first, panicked thought was that it might be an eviction notice, but that made no sense. The apartment was in Kyle's name. Besides, their landlord wouldn't splurge on such decadent paper. He pulled the sheet out and unfolded it.

The letter was short but written in a neat curling script. The lines were all impeccably straight and the words small, seemingly dwarfed by the white space around them. Daniel read it twice before the message sank in.

Mr. Daniel Kane,

I would like to offer you the job of groundskeeper for Craven Manor, starting immediately.

Follow Tilbrook Street until it forks at the dead oak. Turn right and travel on for two miles to reach the property. I look forward to your direct response.

—Bran

Daniel turned the paper over. The reverse was blank. *Is this a joke? If it is, I don't get it.* He'd been desperately waiting for a job offer for months, but the letter was so bizarre that he was having trouble imagining it was serious. *Who gives directions to a property, rather than an address? And why hire me as a groundskeeper, of all things? It's not like I have any experience.*

That wasn't completely true. He'd loved to garden when he lived with his grandmother before her death. They would spend hours in her backyard on the weekends, weeding, pruning, and tending. The space had made him feel safe.

There were no plants around the apartment block. At one time, a tree had been planted in the sidewalk outside, but now only its stump remained. He could sometimes go a full day without seeing any green except for the algae in a drain or an occasional weed struggling out of a crack in the sidewalk. Being paid to work in a garden sounded like a dream.

But it's not a real offer. It can't be. Someone's playing a prank.

The pots were overflowing, so he turned off the tap and moved into the living room. Kyle sat on the couch, seemingly unconcerned that he'd planted himself over the stained section, and bent forward as he stared, fixated, at the TV screen. His character ran through an abandoned warehouse, sniping any enemy infantry that popped up, and occasionally throwing grenades. Daniel cleared his throat, but Kyle didn't respond, so he rested his aching back against the wall and waited for his cousin to finish.

It was hard to believe Kyle had played soccer in college. He'd been a popular guy back then, with bulging muscles and hair the same shade of bronze as Daniel's. He hadn't been good enough to make a career of it after school, though, and had eventually gotten a job with a construction crew. Daniel knew he worked hard, but a diet of soft drinks and greasy takeout had ruined his physique. Fragments of chips dusted the black T-shirt that clung tightly around his midsection, and he'd started to develop fat on his cheeks and the back of his neck. He gnawed at his lower lip as he coaxed his avatar into mowing down another sniper. The game chimed to signal the end of the game. Kyle's team was the victor, and he let out a whoop as he collapsed back.

"Hey," Daniel said and held up the sheet of paper. "Did you leave me this?"

"What the hell is it?" Kyle squinted at the page but didn't leave his couch to get a closer look. "Did you finally get a job?"

"No—I mean, I—"

"Because I've been meaning to talk to you about that. We're going to have to bring in a third roommate." Kyle scratched at his stubble and threw the game controller aside. "I know you pitch in for rent, but utilities are going up next month, and what you give me just isn't cutting it. I already talked to a friend from work. I think he's game."

"Oh." Daniel felt the familiar sinking sensation in his stomach. He slipped an inch down the wall. "But we've only got two bedrooms—"

"Yeah, so he'd have to share with you. I can't risk my sleep being interrupted, y'know? I need to get up early for work."

Kyle rarely left the house before nine, but Daniel bit his tongue on that topic. "A second bed won't fit in my room. There's almost no space as it is."

"Do you have a job? Can you pay me more?" Kyle jutted out his lower lip and lifted his eyebrows. "'Cause if not, we'll both be out on the street."

"I understand. If we need to get a third renter…well, we have to, don't we?" Daniel rubbed his hand across the back of his neck and shrugged. "Could we switch rooms, maybe? Yours is big enough for two beds, and you'd still have privacy in mine."

"Sorry, buddy." He picked up the game controller and began selecting options for a new game. "You know I have too much stuff to fit into that poky space. Hey, can you fetch me a drink from the fridge on your way past?"

Daniel obediently collected a canned soft drink, tossed it to Kyle, then slipped through the apartment's door. His heart pounded, and his palms felt sweaty. The idea of living on the street again—panhandling and digging food out of trash cans the way he had before Kyle found him—made nausea flood his mouth with a metallic flavor.

He stood on the doormat, listening to the crying baby's shrieks echo along the hall. The light flickered, and every flash of light seemed to tighten the nerves inside him.

He ran his thumb over the cool paper, feeling the texture and the weight. Of course it couldn't be one of Kyle's jokes; it was too nuanced and strange. His cousin preferred the flashier, louder variety, like putting firecrackers in Daniel's bed at three in the morning. His sheets were still singed from that one.

But who else would leave this note? Not Mrs. Kirshner. She's too sweet, and her writing isn't this neat. But I don't think anyone else in this apartment block knows my surname.

Daniel practiced folding and unfolding the note. The creases were sharp and precise. He murmured the words to himself. "Offer you the job of groundskeeper…"

The baby's wails finally subsided into hiccups. Daniel tucked the letter into his jeans' pocket and jogged down the stairs to the foyer, where he stored his bike. It was nearing dinnertime, but the sun wouldn't set for another couple of hours, so he had time to at least check whether the property existed.

He lived in a home for desperate people, and desperate people couldn't be choosy.

CHAPTER 2

DANIEL LEANED FORWARD ON his bike and relished the sensation of cold air whipping his hair about his face. Whenever he got out of the city, he liked to pump the pedals as fast as he could and race over the hills and dips. If he found just the right angle, it felt like he was flying.

Surrounded by bird chatter, he turned down Tilbrook Street, following the note's instructions, and found himself in an area he wasn't familiar with. He occasionally passed farmhouses and turnoffs, but no cars disturbed the tranquility of early evening. The farther he biked, the more remote the buildings became, until he was surrounded by only thick pines and strangling vines.

He followed the road's bend. A massive, long-dead oak tree stood at the end of the path. Its branches seemed to extend toward Daniel like gnarled, twisted fingers. His breathing ragged, he slowed as he neared it and stopped in its shadow.

The path took a sharp curve to the left at the oak tree, as though it had hit the obstacle and been forced to go around. The note said to go right. Daniel looked, but there was no sign of any path—just dense, clumpy vegetation.

It was a prank after all. He turned to search behind himself. Uneasiness made the hairs on his arms rise. It wasn't hard to imagine a crime cartel luring a desperate, friendless young adult down a remote road with the promise of a job, only to knock him unconscious with a brick and steal his kidneys. Daniel knew human organs could sell for a lot on the black market; he'd researched it on some of his more desperate nights.

The dirt path was bare, and as far as he could see, nothing lurked among the vegetation on either side. He stepped off his bike, remaining alert, and moved closer to the tree.

Kids and teens had scratched messages into the trunk. Some looked old enough to predate Daniel; none looked recent. Many used the familiar initials and plus sign enveloped in a heart, and one appeared to be a rhyme that had been broken off partway through. And one simply read *Craven Manor* with a tiny arrow pointing to the right.

Daniel turned. There was still no path through the trees. The sun was getting lower, and now that he was no longer moving, he'd begun to feel chilled. *Turn around. Go home.*

He imagined what the evening might hold: lying awake in bed, hungry and frustrated, while he listened to Kyle play his game. He would be bone tired, but the aches in his muscles wouldn't let him sleep for hours. Daniel grimaced.

Walking the bike at his side, he approached the patch of trees and vines where the path should have forked. When he drew close enough, he saw a series of gray shapes embedded in the ground. He scraped his shoe across one to clear the dirt away and found a flat, man-made flagstone. He lifted his eyes and saw more of them leading into the woods. Some poked up at strange angles where tree roots had excised them from the ground. Others had sunk deep into the dirt and were barely visible. He suspected still others lurked out of sight, hidden by time, creating something like a path.

"Well, how about that." Daniel cast one final glance behind himself to make sure he wasn't about to be kidnapped, then he lifted his bike and carried it over the oak tree's massive roots.

He didn't think he was imagining that the air was growing colder. The forest had become dense enough to block out light, and drops of water clung to the plants. They splashed onto him as he brushed past, running under his collar and making him shudder.

The path wove erratically. In some places, trees grew up through the stones, interrupting the path, and Daniel had to hunt around to find where it continued. He didn't like how neglected the trail was. He supposed it was possible that another road approached the manor from a different direction and that the house's owner had simply given him a long-disused shortcut. But he felt vulnerable. The birdcalls seemed distorted, and the trees dwarfed him. Their trunks were so wide that he could have wrapped his arms around them without his fingers touching.

The path tended uphill. Daniel considered leaving his bike and collecting it on the way back, but the idea of losing it in the woods was enough to keep his clammy fingers gripping its handles. Vines and branches kept catching in its wheels, and the path was so rough that he had to carry it more often than not.

Daniel was breathless by the time the forest opened up. The sky had entered the twilight stage when shapes began to lose their color. Already-strained muscles ached from the exertion, but he couldn't repress a grin when he stumbled on a massive wrought-iron gate blocking his path.

So the manor is real. Does that mean the job offer is real, too? For the first time in what felt like months, a spark of hope warmed his insides. Then he stepped closer to the gates, and trepidation returned to extinguish his hope.

The massive iron structure towered over him, with rows of vicious spikes at its top. But it was also incredibly old. Vines grew through and around it, and thick chunks of rust had flaked off the structure. Eroding ground had caused one-half to fall ajar, creating a small gap where he could enter through. Beyond, overgrown tangled gardens obscured the manor. He could glimpse the dark roof, silhouetted against the fading light, a few minutes' walk away.

This has to be the right place, doesn't it? The gates look ancient, though. Words had been inscribed in the metal bar that ran along the center of the gates. Daniel brushed the grime off to read the name: Craven Manor.

He clung to the hope that he was coming from a back path. It didn't matter that the gates were neglected to the point of falling apart if no one ever visited that part of the grounds. And based on the riotous gardens, he suspected no one had been to this corner in a long time.

Strange that the instructions brought me by this route. Even if it's a shorter trip, it's nearly impossible to find.

The gap between the gates was wide enough to squeeze through, but they wouldn't be easy to get back out of. He hesitated—imagining trying to flee while being chased by vicious guard dogs, spit flying from their teeth as they bit at his ankles—and squeezed his lips together.

Desperate people can't be picky.

He rested his bike against the gate then lifted a foot, extended it through the gap, and balanced on a rock just inside the property. He had to brace himself on the rusted metal as he eased through, doing his best not to ruin his clothes, though the grime was staining his hands black. He wouldn't have been surprised if the gate hadn't been touched in more than a century; it looked at least that old.

Vines snagged his foot as he pulled it through, and he stumbled then caught himself on a tree. Visibility diminished as night fell, and Daniel grew nervous about finding his way home. But the letter had said it wanted him to start work immediately. They were clearly desperate for a gardener. If he balked and left, the owner might think he didn't want the job and offer it to someone else.

The flagstone path was clearer inside the property's bounds, but weeds choked the spaces between the stones. Plants spilled beyond their boundaries in uncontrollable tangles, fighting for space. There were nearly as many dead trees as living ones, though many had collapsed and were slowly being turned into compost by tiny insects. Daniel had to clamber over several large fallen logs as he followed the path toward the house.

A deep, prolonged, melancholy cry startled Daniel. A flock of crows perched on a tree near the house, seemingly watching over the building. Two of them took flight as Daniel passed beneath them. Their massive wings made a whirring whistle as they churned the air. He watched them swoop away, the fading light catching in their silky black feathers.

Then he turned toward the house, and the little spark of warm hope he'd been nurturing withered into a dead coal.

Craven Manor was a massive building. Its three stories seemed to have burst out of the ground like an abomination, full of disorderly protrusions and jumbled ledges. More than two dozen black windows overlooked the entryway, which was composed of three broad stone steps leading up to a wooden-arch double door. Pillars supported an awning that could easily shelter twenty people. The stones were all old, worn down, and speckled with green-and-gray lichen. A tower extended from the building's side, rising above the roof's highest peak.

Daniel looked behind himself, as though he might have missed the real house, but he hadn't. The building's size was daunting, and the intricate black stonework was unnerving, but worse than that was its state of disrepair. Many of the windows had cracks or holes in them. A constellation of chips marred the stone walls, which were all stained from decades of rain. The dark-slate roof looked ragged where tiles had fallen. One of the large double doors stood open, but there was no light to be seen inside the building.

Long-dead leaves crunched under his feet as he climbed the worn steps to the front door. The house was clearly abandoned. As he stood, shivering, on the top step, Daniel wondered if he might be the first person to stand there in decades.

Who owns this? And why did they leave it in such bad neglect?

He approached the doors. One of the massive slabs of wood had been left ajar, and it seemed to invite him into the foyer. Daniel's nerves and curiosity warred with each other for a moment, but inquisitiveness won out. He clenched his hands at his side and bent forward, peeking his head through the opening.

The foyer was vast. At least twenty doors lined its walls. At the room's back was a magnificent staircase to the second and third floors. Carpet ran up its center, but it looked even more threadbare than the runner in Daniel's apartment block.

Four old, collapsing chairs were arranged around a fireplace built into the wall on the right, though it was clear the grate hadn't been heated in a long time. The wood in the bracket beside it was dry, waiting to be lit, but had gathered a heavy layer of dust, just like everything else in the space.

Leaves and dirt had blown in through the front door and broken windows. They scattered across the foyer floor and built up in the corners like snowdrifts.

This is bad. Get out. He stood on the threshold, one hand

raised as though to rest it against the open door, but he was still reluctant to touch any part of the house. *No one lives here. No one has for a very long time. Don't linger.*

But something caught Daniel's eye before he could turn away. An envelope rested among the leaves and dirt a few paces away, seemingly placed with great care so as to be visible from the front door. It was identical to the envelope Daniel had received at the apartment, down to the elegantly scrawled "Daniel" across its front.

CHAPTER 3

TURN AWAY. THERE'S SOMETHING *wrong with this place. Get out now, while you still can.*

Daniel took a hesitant step into the building, his attention fixed on the envelope bearing his name. Its crisp white stood out clearly against the browns and blacks surrounding it.

Whatever's happening here isn't right. Don't be a fool. Turn around.

Leaves crunched under his heel. Daniel licked at dry lips. His heart throbbed from stress, but he couldn't ignore the envelope. It waited, deceptively innocent, five paces inside the building. Stepping closer to it made him feel as if he were falling into a deep, black abyss. The light had already been poor, and each pace from the door let the darkness swallow him further.

He reached for the paper. Unlike the floor, the furniture, and the massive chandelier above his head, the envelope wasn't coated in any dust. It, at least, was recent.

Daniel picked it up. The envelope was heavier than the note in his apartment. He sent a final, wary look at the door, half afraid it might slam closed and lock him in the manor, then lifted the unsealed flap to look inside.

The envelope held a letter and two flat, circular objects. Daniel took out the note first. It consisted of two sheets. Like the one inviting him to Craven Manor, the first message was brief and written in a small cursive hand.

Mr. Kane,

Your duties involve keeping the crypt cleaned and maintained and repairing the garden to the best of your abilities. If you require supplies, place a note with your requests on the foyer mantelpiece. The groundskeeper's house in the back corner of the garden is available to you, should you wish to stay there. You will be paid weekly, provided your work is sufficient.

—Bran

Paid weekly… The two round shapes clinked against each other at the base of the envelope. Daniel tipped them into his palm. They were coins, but unlike any currency Daniel had seen before. They were the size of a prune and heavy. A family crest had been minted into their front. He thought they might be gold. *This is my payment?*

The second sheet of paper flopped loose behind the first, and Daniel shuffled it around so that he could read it.

Rules:

- No strangers are allowed onto the property.
- Do not enter the tower.
- Do not leave the groundskeeper's cottage between midnight and dawn. Draw your curtains.
- Keep the door locked. If you hear knocking, do not answer it.

"Okay." The word came out as something close to a whisper. Daniel very carefully folded the sheets and tucked them back into the envelope. "Yeah, no, not a chance."

He was desperate, not insane. The abandoned house, the letters, and the ominous rules all boiled into a whole mess of ain't-touching-that. He'd been reckless to follow the overgrown path to what he now suspected were the property's front gates. It had been even more irresponsible to enter an abandoned building just because he'd seen a note with his name on it. Taking the groundskeeper's position was basically asking to be put on a missing-persons list.

A scraping noise echoed through the building. It seemed to come from one of the upper floors and reverberated in a way that made Daniel shy back. He waited for something to appear at the top of the stairs, but the shadowed, cobweb-shrouded upper halls remained empty.

An animal, maybe? Those crows could probably fit through the broken windows. He was close to certain that he was alone, but his nerves were frayed, and he didn't want to stay long enough to be proven wrong.

He still held the coins in his left hand. They would put some food in his stomach that night, and maybe the next few nights, too. But he wasn't a thief, and he didn't want trouble. He dropped the coins back into the envelope and placed it where he'd found it, on top of the leaf-strewn marble floor. Then he backed up to the open front door, continually scanning the open foyer and upper halls until he'd passed through the exit.

One huge crow remained in the tree near the house's front entry. It looked old; its feathers had taken on a dusty-gray tint, and when it shuffled, its movements were slow. But it watched Daniel like a predator watching its prey as he jogged down the wide, curved front steps.

Daniel moved into the tangled garden as the last hints of day morphed into night. He'd become disoriented and couldn't remember the way to the gate. Flagstones poked out of the earth intermittently, but they seemed to lead in different directions. He chose a path, prayed he'd picked correctly, and pressed between two thorny bushes in search of an escape.

The house stood at his back, seeming to watch him. There were so many windows, all black and cold. If someone really did live inside, they could be watching him, hidden in perfect darkness and surrounded by cobwebs and dust.

That thought was ridiculous. No one could live in that place in its current state. *But then who sent the letter? Why do they want the garden restored?*

The instructions had mentioned a crypt, but Daniel didn't see it as he struggled to find the way out. The structure was either hidden behind the house, or so tangled in plants that it was invisible. He kept pushing forward and stumbled into a small clearing. Marble statues encircled an empty, cracked birdbath. Layers of water stains ran down the statues, giving Daniel the impression that the stone was bleeding. The sculptures depicted women, centaurs, and minotaurs rising out of cracked pillars. Their heads were cast up toward the sky, and their jaws were open in silent screams. Daniel tried not to stare at them.

He hadn't passed any sculptures on his way in. He ran his hands through his hair as he tried not to let the growing panic overwhelm him.

A whirring noise made Daniel yelp and stumble into one of the statues. He clutched the stone and recoiled from a dark shape looming above him.

The flock of crows passed overhead. Their wings were loud—louder than a bird had any right to be—but they were gone within seconds. Daniel sucked in a quick gasp and loosened his hold on the statue. He'd clutched at a Grecian woman pouring water out of a vase as her dress slipped down in a show of tasteful nudity. Grime had collected into the statue's ridges and stained it dark…especially around the eyes. She looked as though she were crying.

As Daniel stepped away from her, his chest painfully tight and his heart throbbing, he caught sight of a tall stone fence between two trees. He followed it to the left, around more thorny bushes and past a dry water feature. The growths were thick, and a metal seat obstructed his path. He climbed over it, heard the metal groan as it was strained, then dropped free onto the other side. The gates came into view, and relief flowed through him, warming his chilled limbs.

He ran the rest of the distance to the gates, leaping over ground cover and not even caring when a dead tree branch snagged his shirt and tore a hole in the sleeve. He reached the metal and shimmied his way through the narrow gap. His bike waited where he'd left it, and he hoisted it over his shoulder without caring about how tired his muscles were.

Daniel threw a final look back at Craven Manor. The trees hid everything except its ragged, dark-slate roof and part of the tower. He knew it had to be his eyes playing tricks on him, but for a second, he imagined something had moved within the tower's window.

"Hey, I'm back." Daniel nudged open the apartment door then spent an extra minute scraping dirt off his shoes before entering. He knew he had to look a mess. He could feel leaves in his hair, and his hands were grimy from feeling through the trees. At least his bike had made the trip unharmed. "You won't believe what happened—"

"Hey."

A stranger was sitting on the living room couch beside Kyle.

His long hair was tied back into a ponytail, and his shirt had sweat stains around the armpits. Both he and Kyle were playing a shooter game, but Kyle paused it as Daniel entered the room.

"Hey, man." Kyle leaned back in his seat and grinned. He looked like he was holding back laughter. Something in his expression made Daniel feel like he was the butt of the joke. "You took your sweet time getting home. We talked about getting a third roommate, right? Meet Fletch."

"Hey," Fletch said again, this time lifting one of his fingers from the controller as a greeting.

"Hi. Uh. Wow." Daniel managed a laugh. "That was quick."

Kyle used the controller to scratch an itch on his chin. "Yeah, he split with his girlfriend, so he'll be staying with us for a while. He's going to take your room. You're fine on the couch, aren't you?"

Daniel opened and closed his mouth several times. Everything seemed to be happening too fast. He was exhausted and hungry, and all he'd wanted to do was get home, have a shower, and crawl into bed. "Actually, I'd really like to keep my room, if that's all right."

"No space for a second bed." Kyle shrugged in a what-can-you-do kind of way. "And Fletch can't stay out here. The streetlamp shines through the kitchen window and would keep him awake."

"Insomnia," Fletch agreed.

"Yeah, so he's got to have the room. His shift at the fish-and-chips shop starts early, so he needs his sleep."

"Hang on." Daniel ran his fingers through his hair, upsetting the leaves, dirt, and a small spider nestled in it. "I thought he was one of your work friends?"

"Yeah, well, I buy lunch from him, don't I?" Kyle slapped Fletch's shoulder then rose and rounded the chair to encroach on Daniel's personal space. "Point is, he's paying his way, so he gets the room."

"But—I am, too." A mixture of desperation and frustration tangled in Daniel's throat, tightening his voice. "I've never been late on a rent payment. Never!"

"But you don't chip in for any of the other stuff. Food, beer, new games. That all costs money. So until you get off your ass and find a job, you've got to take what you can get, yeah?"

The injustice burned. Daniel had never eaten Kyle's food, not even on days he didn't have any of his own. But he knew what his cousin meant: Fletch had money to throw at luxuries that Daniel couldn't afford. Luxuries Kyle would get to partake in.

Kyle clapped the side of his face in a mock caress that made Daniel's blood boil. "If you're real nice to Fletch, he might help get you a job at his place. Washing dishes or something. They're not too fussy about who they hire for that."

"I *have* a job offer." The words were out before he could consider whether they were prudent. "Groundskeeper. Good pay. Accommodation included. So—so—"

Kyle's flabby cheeks pinched up as he tried to keep a laugh inside. "What? *Groundskeeper?* Is that even a real job? You're pulling my leg."

"I'm not. I have the letter!" He pulled it out of his pocket and waved it at Kyle, but his cousin had already turned back to the couch with a flippant "Pfft!"

Fletch pulled a handful of chips out of a bag beside him with one hand and resumed the game with his other. "Oh, and hey, I moved your stuff out of the room, man. It's in the hallway. Sorry for the inconvenience or whatever."

Sorry for the inconvenience or whatever. The words looped through Daniel's mind as he lay awake, staring at their apartment's off-yellow ceiling. He was on the couch, as promised. It was stained with Kyle's vomit from a few months back and wasn't long enough for him to stretch his legs out. The streetlight outside the uncurtained kitchen window glared off the wall beside him, worse than a night-light. *Sorry for the inconvenience...*

He rolled onto his side and clenched his hands under the pillow. He had always managed to scrounge enough for his share of rent. Rent for a room—not just a couch. He'd tried to negotiate a lower monthly payment while Fletch stayed there, but Kyle had been hardball about it. They needed the extra money to pay for utilities.

Utilities and new games. Daniel glowered at the cases lined up beside the TV. Kyle had at least two dozen of them, and a new one seemed to appear once or twice a month.

I can't live like this. But...I have nowhere else to go. Do I?

His defensive words rushed back to him. *I have a job offer.*

That was true, technically. A job offer in a creepy abandoned house, from a man he'd never met, who compensated him in gold coins. But the coins had been real. Daniel had felt their weight in his hand. If the whole event had been a prank or some twisted joke, why had they included the coins when Daniel could have stolen them and run?

That meant he was either being pranked by someone wealthy—like a TV show on a mission to discover just how reckless an unemployed man could get—or the offer was genuine.

Daniel actually managed a laugh, but it quickly died away. *Is it possible it's a real job? No joke and no murderers waiting to harvest my organs? If their purpose was to lure me into a remote area, they'd already achieved it. Why leave the coins? Why not attack me while my guard was down? And if it really is some kind of TV show or something, I should at least get compensated at the end of it, right?*

The fridge rattled as it defrosted itself. Kyle's snores were audible through the thin walls, and the smell of weed drifted out from underneath the door to what had once been Daniel's room. He threw the blanket aside and got up.

Daniel wove his way between the empty chip packets and beer cans to where his possessions had been haphazardly stacked in the hall, and he stuffed his spare clothes and most important keepsakes into a tatty backpack. The clock on the wall said it was five in the morning. The sun would be up soon to light his way to Craven Manor.

CHAPTER 4

MIST PLUMED AROUND DANIEL'S face with every breath. He was shivering, even though he'd taken several extra layers of clothing out of his backpack and bundled them around himself. He hiked along the rocky stone path leading to the manor's gates, carrying his bike and silently cursing himself for his stubbornness.

Even if I get murdered, it's still better than being homeless again. He wiped the back of his hand across his dripping nose and tried not to focus on the memories. Always being hungry. Always being cold. Business owners telling him to move on if he tried to sit under their awning when it rained. The schoolchildren, only a few years younger than he was, who had laughed as they kicked him.

And worst of all, people ignored him. Being homeless made him invisible. People would walk past, wearing thick coats and carrying hot coffees or eating burgers. Their eyes would pass over him as though he were an unattractive part of the scenery.

No one said hello or even made eye contact. And that sense of nonexistence had left him with a permanent fear of being forgotten by the world.

He supposed that was why he let Kyle dictate the rules so often. Kyle had recognized him on the street one afternoon and invited Daniel to share the apartment. Kyle could be stubborn, immature, and pushy, but he'd also paid attention to Daniel when no one else would.

Daniel let his pace slow. As he got closer to the mansion, misgivings crowded into his thoughts again. If it *was* a real job, he had to think the manor's owner was somewhere between eccentric and insane. Even if Bran's intentions weren't outright malicious, the job could still be dangerous.

The bike caught on a root, and he had to stop to wrestle it free. Frowning, he quickened his pace again. Even if the job was dangerous, it came with real money, and he'd been paid up front. He could take the coins to a converter the next day and make plans based on how much they were worth.

Early light shone on the dew collected over the wrought-iron gates. They looked even more tragic in the morning glow, especially now that he could see how magnificent they must have been. The intricate designs worked in iron whispered of old-fashioned aristocracy and decadent homes. Like the day before, he left his bike sitting against the gate and squeezed through the gap. He tried not to shiver as the cold metal chilled his fingers.

He hadn't been able to see the garden in detail the night before, but the whole estate had become like the gate. The space had once been vibrant and elegant, full of carefully maintained exotic specimens, but neglect had let it become something wild and miserable. Dead branches tangled with living. Stubborn plants overpowered their weaker neighbors. Overeager roots and shoots had upended stone garden borders. Daniel pressed his palm to his forehead as he tried to imagine what would need to happen to rein the growth back in.

The crows had settled in trees near the gate, and they sent up a series of mournful calls as Daniel passed under them. He kept an eye on the mansion as he wove through the garden, equal parts hopeful and afraid that its owner had come back during the night, but the windows remained cold.

He followed the fence's edge, wanting to see how large the property was, and found a wooden house nestled between three ancient trees. It wasn't large, but it appeared to have a couple of rooms. Lavender and bushes he couldn't identify crowded around its front door, but the flagstone path leading up to it was clear. He circled around the structure and found a small shed attached to its side. The door hung open, and its rusted hinges shrieked when he pushed on them. The windows were too grimy to let much light in, but he saw a myriad of clay pots, metal watering cans, a wheelbarrow, shears, and a garden hoe clustered between the shelves.

So this is the groundskeeper's cottage. The letter said it was mine. I guess that means it's okay to go inside?

He finished the loop around the building and turned toward

the mansion. From the groundskeeper's cottage, he could see the tower and several of the windows dotting the stone walls. As he watched, a crow descended to settle on the building's roof. He rubbed at the goose bumps growing over his forearms.

Daniel tried to look through the small window set into the cottage's front door, but the interior was too dim for him to make out anything except vague shapes. He took a breath and pulled on the handle. The door scraped open.

The gardener's cottage was significantly cleaner than the main house. A layer of dust rested across the surfaces, but it was thin, not like the intense, muffling coating of dust that filled the mansion. The layout and furniture—a kitchenette to the right, bed to the left, and fireplace straight ahead—were all simple, but looked comfortable and rot-free. The space was nowhere near as decadent as the main house, but it was still infinitely better than the tiny, grimy room he'd been living in at Kyle's.

Daniel placed his backpack beside the bed and began looking through the house. The bedside drawers and wardrobe were empty, but the kitchen cupboards were full. Daniel blinked in shock at the rows of tins and boxes, then he began pulling them out. Cans of vegetables, cookies, tea bags, and even a loaf of bread—they were all fresh. The bread was a couple of days old and just starting to turn stale, but that was nothing Daniel would gripe about. He sent one final, nervous glance toward the open door then tore open the bread bag and stuffed two slices into his mouth. As he chewed, he surveyed the food stocked there. It was enough to keep him well fed for at least a fortnight.

Someone has been to the property recently. Maybe they were even here while I was in the mansion yesterday. But who? The man who signed my letter, Bran? And what kind of name is Bran, anyway?

A new theory occurred, and it felt like a weight lifted off Daniel's chest. Maybe someone had inherited the mansion and wanted to get it livable before moving into it. If they'd hired Daniel for the garden, they might also be employing cleaners for the main house. That still didn't explain everything—like why he'd gotten the job offer through a letter under his door, rather than a more traditional application process—but it made him feel marginally more hopeful.

Daniel carefully restocked the shelves and closed the cabinet doors, then he turned on the taps to get a drink. Nothing came out, but the pipes rattled and groaned as though a large rodent had been trapped in them. Daniel bent down to see if anything was stoppering the tap, one hand poised over the handle to turn it off again, then leaped back as dark, thick liquid spewed into the sink.

He stared at the mess in shock. It was like watching a toxic spill. The ichor splashed up the sink's sides and threatened to clog the drain. But within seconds, the water from the tap turned clear. Daniel let it flow for another minute to wash the gunk down the drain, but he couldn't bring himself to drink it.

Fresh wood, along with a bucket of kindling, had been stacked beside the fireplace. The cabin was dim and chilly, but Daniel didn't want to spend time lighting a fire when the sun would warm the room within a few hours. He left the cottage's door ajar as he stepped back into the garden.

This is mine. The thought was alarming, but as he looked about the tangled overgrowth surrounding him, he realized it was true. He might not own the garden, but it was his to shape and tame. Memories of working beside his grandmother resurfaced. He would dig a hole with his gloved hands, then she would place a new flower into it and hold it steady while he scraped dirt around the roots. Even when the chemotherapy took its toll on her, making it too difficult for her to kneel beside him, she would sit in the shade, giving advice and encouragement as he tended to her plants for her.

His eyes itched. He rubbed the back of his hand over them and set his jaw. The mansion's gardens were nothing like his grandmother's tidy, careful arrangements, but he was starting to relish the idea of working in them.

He wanted to look through his supplies, but the daylight couldn't penetrate the overcast sky, tree cover, and fogged windows of the shed. A lamp and a box of matches on it sat on the desk under the cottage's window, apparently laid out for the exact situation Daniel had encountered. He shook out a match and used it to light the lamp. Once the flame stabilized, he returned to the little shed attached to the house.

The metal door was stuck, and he had to heave on it to wrench it fully open. While the cabin had been cleaned and stocked recently, the shed clearly hadn't seen attention since the mansion had been inhabited. Everything in it was coated in grime and spiderwebs, and the metal implements were all rusted beyond help. Their designs were antiquated, too. Daniel didn't know history well enough to nail down the exact time period, but he'd seen similar tools in movies set during the Regency era.

More than a hundred years—it's unbelievable that this house would be abandoned for so long. But not implausible, looking at how dirty everything is.

He picked through the tools, deciding what he could salvage and what would need to be replaced. In the end, there was very little he could keep. A few of the clay pots were still uncracked, and the shovel had held up better than most of the other tools, but the rest were useless.

Bran said I could ask for new tools by placing a note on the fireplace's mantelpiece. Daniel stepped out of the shed to peer at the manor. As far as he could see, none of its lights had come on. *Does he drop by once a day for messages? Once a week? What if he never comes back? I guess I can buy stuff myself if the coins are worth enough.*

Inside the cottage, Daniel found a notepad and a pen in the desk. He pulled out the chair and was surprised by how heavy it was. He'd grown used to Kyle's house, where everything was a cheap wood or flimsy aluminum. His cottage's furniture was all made from solid timber, and he found he liked it a lot.

He spent a moment with the pen hovering above the paper, wondering if he should include a message thanking Bran for offering him the job or whether that would be weird. He decided to keep the message professional and simple, as Bran had with his. With luck, he might meet his mystery employer within a few days. Speaking to him face-to-face would give Daniel a better sense of what behavior was expected of him.

Bran,

These tools would help with my work.

- *Wheelbarrow*
- *Shears*
- *Saw*
- *Work gloves*
- *Shovel*

He signed his name and folded the paper in half. A half dozen other tools would have been useful, but Daniel didn't want to seem greedy or demanding on the first day. He clutched the paper in one hand and the lamp in the other then began picking his way through the choked gardens.

Crows circled above him, their mournful calls ringing across the estate, as though they were waiting to descend on a corpse and scavenge its flesh. He kept his head ducked and moved as quickly as the environment would let him. He was breathless by the time he climbed the three stairs to the mansion's arched entryway.

Resting a hand on one of the wooden doors, he extended the lamp inside. Its glow struggled to reach the massive foyer's corners, but it was easier to see than it had been the night before. He shifted the lantern, trying to dispel the shadows lingering around the fireplace—and two orange eyes stared back at him.

CHAPTER 5

DANIEL GASPED AND STAGGERED away from the door. His back hit one of the pillars supporting the overhang. He clung to it for a moment, his mind fighting his impulses, then took a cautious step forward.

The eyes had been low, near the marble floor, in the space between the chairs clustered around the fireplace. Daniel leaned through the door's opening, breath suspended, and held the lamp farther ahead of himself. The eyes were gone, and the space where he'd seen them was empty.

"Hello?" His voice echoed through the building, bouncing back from a dozen different angles. He licked his lips as he waited for a response then took another step into the house. "I'm sorry, I didn't mean to intrude—"

A flicker of motion startled him. A liquid shadow moved along the wall beside the fireplace, then the shape resolved itself into a small black cat. Blinking orange eyes, it stared at him.

Daniel released a shaky laugh as the tension seeped from his muscles. "Hey there, little guy. You startled me. I guess I probably scared you, too, huh?"

He crouched and placed the lamp beside him then extended one arm to see if he could coax the cat forward. It wasn't hissing or bristling its tail, which was a good sign, but it also seemed wholly indifferent to his invitation. It sat pin-straight, tail wrapped around its feet, and stared at the wall behind Daniel.

"Shh, shh, I'm a friend." He kept his voice singsong as he crept closer. "I just want to say hello, little cat. Don't be afraid."

He got close enough that a few more steps would let him touch the creature, but it stood and sauntered away. Its tail was down and its ears swiveled slightly in his direction, but it didn't run for shelter. Instead, it stopped near the staircase and resumed its earlier pose, tail wrapped around its feet protectively.

Daniel's heart lurched. When the creature walked, he could see just how thin it was. Bones jutted out in sharp angles, and its ribs were clearly visible under the skin. No one was feeding the cat, and it wasn't catching enough prey to sustain itself. The thought made him sick.

"Just wait here a moment, little guy." He swallowed as he backed away, trying his hardest not to startle the cat. It barely looked at him. "I'll be right back."

He kept his movements slow until he reached the door, then he turned and jogged to the gardener's hut. *The cat isn't flighty, so it must have been someone's pet at one point. It's a long way for a cat to wander from the nearest town, but no one has lived in the mansion in the last couple of decades. How'd it get here?*

He leaped through the cabin's door, skidded on the wooden floor, and turned toward the kitchenette. He remembered seeing a tin of Spam in the cupboard. It wasn't ideal cat food, but it was better than nothing. He found a plate in one of the drawers, wrenched the tin open, and scooped spoonfuls of the slimy pink substance onto the plate.

The journey back to the mansion was slower as he struggled to balance the plate while climbing over dead trees. He began to worry the cat might have wandered off, but as he re-entered the foyer, it was still sitting by the staircase. The lamp's light created a warm glow across its fur, which had probably once been glossy but was rough with age. Its ears twitched toward him, and Daniel smiled.

"Here you go, little guy. I got you something to eat."

He lowered himself close to the ground and extended the plate as he crept forward. The cat made eye contact for half of a second then turned, flicked its tail, and climbed the stairs.

"Wait—come back! Food, kitty, food!"

I sound like an idiot. Daniel couldn't help himself; he grabbed the lamp and followed the cat, plate held out as though that might tempt the creature to stop. It didn't seem afraid, just bored of him, so he followed it around the bend at the top of the stairs and toward the third-floor landing.

Tiny puffs of dust exploded around his feet with every step.

The higher they climbed, the more cobwebs clustered along the railings and architraves. They clung to Daniel's arms when he wasn't being careful, then a large invisible one snagged over his face when he was nearly at the third floor. He stopped, face scrunched up, and tried to brush the threads away without dropping the plate of food or the lamp. By the time he had cleared his eyes, the cat had vanished into the shadows.

"Hello? Little guy?" Daniel craned his neck to see his small companion. The lamp's light didn't reach as far as he would have liked, but it highlighted elaborate molding running along the ceiling and the whirls in the hand-carved balustrades. He peered over the railing and saw the foyer stretched out below him, magnificent in its scope and tragic in its abandonment.

He considered returning to the ground floor and slinking back to the cottage. The letter hadn't forbidden him from exploring the house, but he couldn't shake the feeling that he was intruding on someone else's domain. But the dust under his feet was thick and undisturbed, and he didn't want to give up on the starving cat yet.

"Psst, cat, come back, please." He crept the final six steps to the third-floor landing. The stairs opened into an open area of at least twelve square feet. To his left and right, hallways stretched away until they eventually faded into shadows. Despite their age, the bronze wallpaper and royal-blue carpet looked beautiful. Paintings lined the gallery walls. The halls felt eerily quiet, almost as though they were sleeping.

Straight ahead, a short passageway extended deeper into the

house. Its floor was uncarpeted stones, and it had only one destination: a massive wooden door.

It looked thick—thicker even than the front doors—and the wood was painted tar-black. Daniel, mesmerized, lifted his lamp higher as he crept toward it. Tiny crystals had formed over the stones at the door's base. They sparkled in his lamplight. An emblem had been painted across the wood's black tar in a striking white paint: a circle with a cross running over it. Four massive bolts ran up the door's side. They were all locked, sealing the doorway, but the metal was so rusted that Daniel thought he could break them without much strain.

What is this place?

He quickly realized what he was looking at: the door to the tower. The one the letter explicitly forbade him from opening.

An uneasy groan escaped Daniel's parted lips. He took a step back from the door as chills ran up his arms like tiny spiders. *Do not enter the tower…*

Daniel swallowed and checked over his shoulder to make sure he was alone. Even when he wasn't looking at the door, he could feel its presence: massive, daunting, threatening. *What is Bran keeping up there? It can't be where he's living, surely? If he is, then why are the bolts on the outside?*

Daniel put the lamp down and reached toward the door. He couldn't stop himself. He had no intention of touching any of the four locks, but he wanted to understand the mystery. His fingertips brushed the wood in the center of the painted cross, and he instantly recoiled. Something had thrummed through the wood, like a low electrical current. With it came an immense sense of malaise. Suddenly, he felt as though his whole world were a second away from crumbling, as though the shadows were alive, creeping toward him, their long, cruelly sharp fingers twitching as they stretched toward his throat.

Do not enter the tower…

He snatched up the lamp and dashed to the stairs. Juggling the plate and lamp in one hand, he wiped away the perspiration running into his eyes. His footsteps were like a drum, echoing back from the hundred hidden nooks scattered through the mansion. He felt dwarfed by the building. The air inside was stifling to the point of being suffocating. His lungs worked to suck in oxygen, but it never seemed to be enough. Dizziness crashed through him, and he came to a halt on the second-floor landing, gasping and shaking, while he waited for his vertigo to subside.

The sensation of being suffocated faded, and he realized he'd been hyperventilating. He placed the lamp on the carpeted floor and leaned his back against a dusty bannister. *Get ahold of yourself, Daniel. There's nothing to be afraid of.*

If Bran didn't want him in the tower, well, that was fine by him. He'd watched enough horror movies to know what happened to people who opened doors they weren't supposed to, and his curiosity was no match for his desire to stay alive and keep all of his body parts where they were supposed to be.

As the panic abated, Daniel became more aware of his surroundings. The second-floor landing was similar to the first, with hallways to his left and right, their doors all closed, and their walls swathed in golds and dark, dusty blues. The painting on the wall ahead of him was larger than the others he'd glimpsed—taller than Daniel, even—and it dominated the space. Daniel tilted his head back to absorb the image.

It was a portrait of a girl. She couldn't have been older than eleven or twelve. Blond hair, so light it was almost white, cascaded down her back and curled around her face in delicate wisps. Large blue eyes looked down at Daniel. He frowned as he tried to read the expression; there was curiosity in the eyes, and the cherub-bow lips were quirked up at the corners. But together, the features held an air of vulnerability, even fear perhaps.

Daniel lifted the lamp to bring the details into relief. The girl's pastel-blue dress dated her to the Regency era, possibly slightly before. Her cheeks had a hint of pink, but every other part of her skin was so pale, it was almost ghostly white. Lilies clustered behind her. A brooch had been clasped onto her dress. The motif on the jewelry seemed familiar, but Daniel couldn't place where he'd seen it before.

A gold plaque set into the portrait's frame held a name. Daniel shook his jacket's sleeve over his hand and used it to brush off the dust. *Annalise Myricks.*

"Who were you, Annalise?"

The dress looked expensive. Her hairstyle was simple but well done. Blue eyes, so full of expression and yet so inscrutable, seemed to follow him when he moved.

She must have been important; the painting was massive and

done with a lot of skill. Its frame was gilded and elaborate, and its location seemed intended to give it attention. It would be visible to anyone traversing the stairs, and Daniel also suspected it could be seen from the foyer if he had enough light and stood in the right place.

It was a little strange, though, that she was so young in the painting. Most historical family portraits Daniel had seen featured adults or a whole family clustered together.

Daniel was struck by a sudden need to know more about the family who owned Craven Manor. He put the plate of Spam on the carpet beside the stairs. The note had forbidden him from going into the tower, but it said nothing about the rest of the house. *It would be all right to look in a couple of the rooms, wouldn't it?*

Daniel looked down both sides of the hallway. They seemed to stretch on forever, until his lamplight became too weak to cut through the shadows. He rubbed at the back of his neck, where nervous prickles had grown, then took a hesitant step to the left.

The doors were all tall, made of dark wood, and firmly closed. Daniel turned the handle to the closest room. The metal screeched and fought against him before clicking open. The wooden slab drew outward, and Daniel, feeling deeply uncomfortable, stepped in.

CHAPTER 6

OPULENT, RICH COLORS ASSAULTED Daniel's eyes. Even with the smothering layer of dust, the bright golds and reds were too much for his senses. He'd found a guest room, where a large four-poster bed took up the left-hand side of the space. A bureau with a washbasin sat against the right-hand wall.

Daniel crept through the room. He was careful not to touch any of the antiques as he examined them. Everything seemed to date the building to the same time as the portrait—a little more than two hundred years old. Tightly closed windows had kept moisture from destroying the room, but it still showed its age. The basin was stained, and a long crack ran through it. The bed's mattress had a depression in its center where it had decayed. The long curtains on either side of the large paned window had been attacked by moths until they were little more than rags.

Daniel was drawn toward the view. The glass was smudgy

from generations of built-up grease and dirt, but he could see farther than from the ground. Daniel leaned close and held his breath to stop it from fogging up the panes.

The garden was larger than he'd expected. The tip of what looked like his gardener's cottage stood out to the far left. The plants were tangled and heavy in that section but grew lighter to the right. When he stood on his toes and turned his head, he caught a glimpse of a large stone shape in a copse of pine trees.

Daniel had seen similar peaked stone roofs in cemeteries. There had been one on top of the hill near the place he'd buried his grandmother. Her grave wasn't fancy. Her generosity and hospital bills had taken everything she'd earned in her life, and she'd died poor. Daniel remembered sobbing after the funeral, furious with himself for not having been able to afford anything better than the cheapest coffin.

He left the window, his throat tight and itchy, and returned to the hallway. The thrill of exploring the house was gone. The tall, dark halls had lost their air of mystery and seemed depressive and lonely.

He stopped under Annalise's portrait. On the second viewing, her expression seemed to hold a sheen of terror carefully concealed under a genial mask. He didn't know why her expression bothered him so much, but it wouldn't be something he could quickly forget.

Daniel collected the plate of Spam and took it down to the ground floor. Though the black cat remained elusive, Daniel left the plate between two overstuffed, collapsing wingback chairs near the fireplace. He'd seen the cat there when he'd entered the building, so he hoped it would return and find the food.

In line with the house's aesthetic, the fireplace was oversized and elaborate. Daniel could have lain down in the grate and fit comfortably. A row of decorations ran along its mantelpiece. The candles were all half-melted, and the dead branches had probably once held fir needles. Next to a clock that hadn't ticked in a long time were six metal photograph frames, all highly detailed, and all empty.

Daniel retrieved his note from his pocket and placed it in one of the empty patches near the center of the mantelpiece. The space was cluttered, but everything else was blurred with dust, so his crisp white note stood out clearly.

A shadow moved along the wall near the stairs. Daniel squinted at it, trying to make out shapes among the heavy gloom. A small clot of shadows broke away from the wall and strolled toward him. Daniel grinned as he recognized the cat. "Hey, buddy, came back, did you?"

The cat planted its front paws on the stone and dipped its head and shoulders, stretching its back. The skin moved over sharp bones as though there was nothing in between, and heartache tightened Daniel's throat again. Then the cat straightened and resumed its sentry position a dozen paces away from him, sitting tidily, tail wrapped around its feet.

"Food." Daniel pointed to the plate. "I'm not going to chase you again, but I'll leave this here for you to eat, okay? I'll bring more tomorrow."

He knew the cat couldn't understand him, but the words made him feel better. The cat had probably been a stray for so long that it would never let him get very close, but he could at least feed it and make sure it was comfortable in its twilight years. Its fur hadn't started to gray yet, but its joints seemed stiff, making its movements stilted and slow. A haggardness around its face suggested it had lived a long life.

"Take care, little guy. If Bran drops by, say hello to him for me, okay?" Daniel kept his movements smooth as he backed toward the door. The cat's amber eyes followed him, but it showed no sign of curiosity about the plate he'd left.

Bran's envelope containing Daniel's instructions and payment waited in the leaf litter not far away. Daniel scooped it up and tucked it into his pocket before retreating to the porch.

The crows had gathered in the tree outside the door again. Their mournful caws rose as they saw him, and several shifted warily. The tree was nearly dead. A few stray leaves clung to it, but Daniel suspected it would be gone within a year. The crows were so numerous that they almost appeared like surrogate leaves, dark and ever shifting, as they weighed down the branches. He ducked his head as he passed underneath and waded through the tangle of dead bushes and living, snaking vines.

He'd done his best to memorize the garden's layout from the window, and he pressed through the plants in the direction he remembered seeing the tomb. Bran's letter had instructed him to salvage the garden, but keeping the tomb clean had been listed first, so Daniel assumed that was the priority. He'd already wasted the entire morning poking around the mansion and chasing cats, so he figured it was time to do some work and earn his keep.

He found the copse of pine trees first. They shielded the tomb almost perfectly, and he had to weave between them to find the slate-gray stone façade.

The building was beautiful, even in disrepair. Built entirely out of stone slabs, it was almost large enough to be a small house. The peaked roof was a few feet higher than Daniel's head, and the walls had been carved to create images of plants and animals. The arched entryway led into a six-foot-wide nook where people could shelter. Hints of dark brown suggested a door was set into the back of the nook, but Daniel couldn't get close enough to be sure. Vicious, thorny bushes had overgrown the space, tumbling out of the entryway and clustering around the tomb's sides. Ivy tangled through the bushes, and the plants simultaneously supported and strangled each other.

Daniel ran his fingers through his hair as he examined the mess. It was no wonder Bran wanted it cleared; there was something innately horrible about a person's final resting place being smothered in the ugly, thorny plants. Daniel looked at his hands. He really needed gloves if he didn't want his fingers shredded. But then, he had no idea how quickly Bran would find his note and deliver his supplies.

Find a compromise. He examined the walls. The ivy grew higher than the bushes. Their stems snaked around the intricate carvings on the walls and across the roof and seemed to engulf the crypt. If they had been under control, they might have created a sweet softening effect. But they'd grown so far out of bounds that the effect was suffocating.

Daniel jogged back to his groundskeeper's cottage. Inside the small kitchen, he found a knife and two tea towels. He dropped off the lamp and the envelope with his payment, then he returned to the tomb and wrapped the towels around his fists for protection.

The work was clumsy and awkward, but Daniel managed to gain some height by clambering onto a fallen pine tree to reach the higher vines. Thorns still pricked him, even through the cloths, but he made steady progress cutting the ivy that grew over the tomb's roof. Fistful after fistful of the dark-green leaves shed away from the stone, and Daniel let them fall into a clear patch of ground where he could collect them later.

By the time he'd circled the building and cleared the errant ivy, his hands were raw, and the sun had fallen below the treetops. The knife was hopelessly coated in sap, and Daniel cleaned it on one of the cloths as he stepped back.

Even though he hadn't touched the bushes, the improvement was immense. Daniel grinned at his handiwork, delighted at the way the building had regained some of its dignity without plants weighing its roof down.

The tomb's front was easier to see, too. Carved among the elaborate leaf work, scrolls, and miniature pillars was a name: Annalise Myricks. The emblem above it matched the brooch the girl in the painting had worn.

The date carved beside the name made Daniel's heart suddenly heavy. *1791–1803.* She'd lived to be only twelve years old.

Was she sick? Her portrait had incredibly pale skin, but I'd assumed that was the artist's interpretation of what was fashionable at the time. She died young, but she must have been dearly loved to be immortalized in that painting and this crypt.

He remembered the very slight lift of her lips and the way her eyes had reflected fear. *Did she know she was going to die? Was the painting a deliberate effort to memorialize her before she left earth?*

The sunset was full of bloody reds and glaring golds. Daniel shook the towels off his hands, wrapped the knife in them, and clambered back toward his cottage. He'd intended to return to town before the day was over, but he'd become too consumed in his work and let the sun set.

Daniel stopped outside the groundskeeper's cottage. Compared to the mansion and the gardens, the small tidy building felt comforting. Cozy, even. He rubbed an aching hand over the back of his neck. Having his own room and unlimited food would be nice. It would be even nicer to not have to struggle through the forest again. But even though he could handle Craven Manor during the day, he still felt uneasy about lingering after sunset.

There's caution, and then there's paranoia. You've spent a whole day here with nothing horrible happening. Take a chance. Stay the night.

He nudged his cottage's door open. Without direct sunlight, it felt unnaturally bleak. Daniel hunted for a light switch without luck. He hadn't seen lights anywhere on the property. The house had oil lamps on the wall and fireplaces in most rooms. Daniel suspected it had never been connected to electricity.

He didn't have a fridge, either. That was fine, though. He'd gotten used to drinking his tea and coffee black since Kyle didn't like him using the milk, but it meant any meat or perishables would have to be eaten on the day he bought them.

Desperate people can't be picky.

He snorted a laugh as he knelt in front of the fireplace. Before coming to Craven Manor, he'd felt desperate, always clawing for just enough money to pay rent and eat, running the endless treadmill of job applications and rejections, and feeling that homelessness was always just a misstep away.

Craven Manor had a different atmosphere, however. As he stacked kindling in the fireplace, Daniel tried to put his finger on it. The manor wasn't a cheerful place. It wasn't bright or welcoming. But it felt secure. The last two hundred years hadn't managed to crumble it. Storms could beat at its walls, plants could try to choke it, age could eat at the furniture, but it still stood just as tall and proud.

For all of the property's secrets and intimidating atmosphere, he felt more secure in the cottage than he had at Kyle's apartment. That was a startling revelation. At Kyle's place, he'd always felt like a guest. He might have paid half of the rent and utilities, but his name wasn't on the lease. Even his room hadn't fully been his own. Kyle's guitar, old clothing, and relics from abandoned hobbies cluttered one wall, making the small space even more claustrophobic. But at Craven Manor, Daniel had his own house.

"My own house." He said it out loud, testing the words. He liked the way they sounded. He didn't own the groundskeeper's cottage, but it *felt* like his, as if he had the right to decorate it, to move in new furniture, and to sleep there without fear of being thrown out.

Don't get too attached. He placed a log on top of the blazing kindling and left it to catch fire. The envelope waited on the desk beside the lamp, and Daniel opened it and tipped the contents out. *The coins might still be worthless. The owner could be crazy. You may still wake up in the morning missing a kidney.*

But somehow, the fears felt less real than they had the day before. He'd started to build a mental image of Craven's owner as a recluse who avoided human contact as much as possible. That suited Daniel just fine.

He turned the coins over. The crest on them matched the one in the painting and on the tomb. No wonder it had looked familiar.

A family crest, maybe? I wonder if I could find anyone who recognizes it. This property must have been well known when it was inhabited. The house is large enough that it probably needed a host of maids to maintain it.

Daniel stacked the coins and put them aside. He shook out the two notes, reread them, then left them flat on the table. If the job was legitimate—and he was seriously starting to believe it was—he didn't want to do anything to jeopardize it.

Rules:

- No strangers are allowed onto the property.
- Do not enter the tower.

- Do not leave the groundskeeper's cottage between midnight and dawn. Draw your curtains.
- Keep the door locked. If you hear knocking, do not answer it.

The final rule sounded ominous no matter how he looked at it, but he wasn't in a position to buck against his instructions. He pulled the window's heavy drapes together until no moonlight came through then turned the door's lock. As an extra precaution, he dragged the table's chair under the door handle. If someone really did intend to attack him in the middle of the night, he would at least hear them and have some warning.

Daniel made himself a simple dinner out of the tins in the cupboard and two slices of bread cooked over the fire. He'd barely slept the previous night, and he was sore from the work, so he figured there was no harm in an early bedtime.

He boiled a pot of water over the fire and awkwardly washed himself, then he changed into clean clothes from his bag and crawled into the bed. It was warm and soft, and the crackling fire created a soothing drone that lulled him into a feeling of security.

The happy glow lasted until shortly after midnight, when something started tapping at his door.

CHAPTER 7

DANIEL STARTED UPRIGHT, BLINKING furiously, as the sheets fell away from him. Sleep crowded his mind and made him sluggish, and it took a minute to remember he was no longer at Kyle's.

The knock at the door wasn't a harsh rap, but a soft, curious *tp-tp-tp*. Daniel doubted it would have woken him if his nerves hadn't been wound so tightly from the day before.

He slipped out of bed, and his toes curled as they touched the cold floor. The fire had burned low in its grate. What was left of the glowing embers built layers of shadows across the room's furniture.

Tp-tp-tp. It was a question, an invitation, and a request all in one. Daniel reached toward the door, impulsively wanting to unfasten the lock and see who was outside, but stilled his hand. The clock on his desk read 12:19 a.m. He wasn't allowed to open the door or look through the window until dawn.

Why? Fear slammed into him. The rule had been confusing and even unsettling before, but now, it dripped with malevolence. *Who is it? What doesn't Bran want me to see?*

Daniel's fingers itched to tweak the window's curtain aside. The panes were near the door; all he would need to do was pull the corner back and peek through.

The tapping fell silent. Daniel waited, every muscle tense, then flinched as the tapping shifted to the wall next to the door. He rotated slowly to follow the noise as it ghosted around the cottage. Light knocks grazed over his window. Deeper, slower ones rapped over the space just above the skirting. Daniel tried to swallow, but his tongue was dry and tacky.

Don't be afraid. Your door is locked. Whatever it is can't get in.

He slunk toward the fireplace, afraid of making noise in case it would encourage the entity outside, but desperate for more warmth and light. He propped one of the smaller logs on top of the embers and waited for it to catch.

The tapping sound echoed from the back of his home. It reached as high as the roof, and fresh fear spiked through Daniel's blood. Adrenaline infused him with energy he couldn't spend and made him twitchy. *What could reach the roof? There's no ladder, no fallen trees to climb on. What the hell is out there?*

The knocking had completely circled the building. The final raps, slow and serious, like a final warning, rang out from the front door. Then silence filled the room again.

Daniel stayed crouched on the ground beside the fire. The earlier warmth he'd felt toward Craven Manor had evaporated; all he wanted was for dawn to break through the infernal darkness so that he could leave. The fire didn't feel hot enough to warm his back as shivers ran through him. Every little noise sounded magnified by the night air. Branches creaked in the wind. Insect whirrs were distorted into an alien language. A crow cried out then was silent.

Minutes trickled into hours, and Daniel's exhaustion won out. He collapsed sideways on the rug by the fireplace and dozed fitfully. When he finally shook himself back into wakefulness, dawn's light glossed around the edges of the window's curtains.

It's over. He stumbled to his feet and shook his left leg. It had gone numb where he'd lain on it, and pins and needles dug into him as he hopped toward the window. *Dawn means it's safe... doesn't it?*

He pulled back the corner of the curtain. The stone step outside his door was visible, but no one occupied it. Shadows played with early sunlight among the erratic garden surrounding his house.

Daniel turned his attention toward Craven Manor. The sun was behind it, making it appear solid black, but he could see the tower stretching up higher than the roof. Light glinted off the curved dome. Something moved in its window.

What was that? Daniel pulled the curtains fully apart to clear his view, but the shape in the tower had disappeared. He could have sworn he'd seen something that looked like a woman's silhouette. But no matter how hard he strained, all he could see were the two curtains bordering the glass. They shifted a fraction in the breeze. *Maybe that's all there was? Maybe I saw the curtains move and thought they were a person?*

The explanation wasn't as convincing as he would have liked, but he couldn't see any other answer. No one could be living in the house without disturbing the heavy dust everywhere, and Daniel hadn't seen any tracks other than his own since he'd arrived.

The memory of the door, tall and painted black with the white cross over its front, made him uneasy. He started to turn away from the cottage's window but stopped when he noticed a smudge on it.

The shape was vague and blurred, but it looked like a hand. Daniel squinted as he leaned closer. At the tips of the smudge, he found tiny whorls from a fingerprint.

"Who—" He held his hand up next to it. There was a significant size difference. From palm to fingertips, it was half as large as his.

Is it from the thing that paced around my house last night? He felt physically sick at the idea. But the way the mark was blurred made him think it might not be fresh. *Someone had to visit the cottage to clean it and stock its pantry. The handprint might be from them.*

He rubbed the goose bumps on his exposed arms. He couldn't remember seeing the print the previous day, but he had been rushing through his examination of the cottage. It wasn't too far-fetched to imagine he'd overlooked it.

All right, think logically, Daniel. Are we going to stay?

His gut said to get out. He might not be comfortable at Kyle's, but at least people didn't knock at the door in the early hours of the morning—except for one time, when a drunk man thought it was his apartment and became angry when his key wouldn't fit. Daniel managed to crack a smile at the memory. Kyle had emerged from his room, brandishing a baseball bat. He and the drunk man had yelled at each other through the door until the stranger finally gave up and shambled off.

Daniel's smile faltered. Kyle was rough around the edges, but they were still cousins. Daniel owed him a debt of gratitude for opening up his home. And he'd left Kyle in the middle of the night, without so much as a goodbye.

Then Daniel thought of Fletch, the fast-food worker who had usurped him on a whim. The man probably hadn't meant any harm, but he'd still caused it inadvertently.

I don't want to go back there. Daniel dug through his bag to find the two warmest jackets he owned and layered them over his shirt. *I'll let Kyle know I'm okay, but I won't be moving back in if I can help it.*

He pulled the chair away from the door and unbolted it. Frosty morning air assaulted him and made him shudder despite the extra layers of clothes. As he stood on the doorstep, rubbing his hands together, he became aware of faint noises coming through the trees and disturbing the morning's stillness. The sounds didn't seem organic.

Footsteps? Footsteps and…something being dragged across the ground?

Daniel ran his fingers through his hair in a futile effort to look respectable. It had to be his mystery employer. Who else would visit Craven Manor so close to dawn? Daniel jogged into the garden and did his best to locate the source of the disturbance. The noises became clearer as he drew closer to them, until he broke out of the tangled shrubs and dying trees near Craven Manor's entrance. Daniel slowed into what he hoped looked like a casual stroll.

A young man, not much older than Daniel, was bent over a wheelbarrow beside the stone steps. Shaggy brown hair extended almost to his jacket collar. He was dressed in simple but clean clothes, the kind Daniel associated with people who worked with their hands, and even through the bulky jacket, it was clear he carried some muscle.

The flock of black birds shifted in their tree as Daniel approached. The man was arranging the tools Daniel had requested inside the wheelbarrow, almost like it was a gift basket and presentation was important. Daniel's shoes crunched through a patch of fallen leaves. The man twitched and swiveled in Daniel's direction, his eyes wide and his face tense.

For a moment, the yard was eerily silent. Daniel had the overwhelming sensation that his presence was unwanted, but it was too late to retreat. He swallowed and held out a hand, praying it wouldn't shake. "Hey. Sorry to startle you. Bran, right?"

The other man stared at the offered hand. A twitchy smile created crinkles around his eyes, but the grin didn't feel genuine. Perspiration shone across his forehead. "No…? I, uh, thought you were. You're not Bran? You don't own this place?"

"No. Sorry—I was expecting—" Daniel, feeling lost, cleared his throat, his hand still extended. "I'm the groundskeeper. Newly hired. I've been waiting to meet Bran."

The other man finally relaxed. He flexed his shoulders as a chuckle washed the tenseness away from around his mouth, though it still didn't touch his eyes. "Yikes. Sorry, man. You really startled me. No one was here the last two times I visited, and I didn't expect anyone to be here today, either. I'm Joel, by the way." Joel finally shook Daniel's hand. His grip was firm, if a little clammy.

"Daniel. I guess you haven't met Bran, either?"

"No." Joel scuffed his boot through the fallen leaves. Seeing such a beefy man look frightened was strange, but that was the only way Daniel could describe him. "I work in Arbour's hardware store with my dad. We got contracted to deliver supplies. Dad's not really well enough to bring them himself, so he sends me instead. But..."

Daniel thought he could guess his companion's thoughts. "It's not the most hospitable place, is it?"

Joel nodded furiously as he lowered his voice to a whisper. "It's a damn nightmare. Crows everywhere. A house like something out of a horror movie. And this guy, Bran, we've never even met him. He just sends instructions in letters. Every time I come here, I'm half expecting to get murdered by a crazy axman."

I'm glad I'm not the only one. "But you took the job?"

"We kinda had to." Joel shrugged, and he looked uncomfortable again. "We were maybe a month away from having our business foreclosed when this guy leaves a letter under our door. He wanted us to clean up a cottage and make some deliveries to his house. And in return, he paid us a small fortune—way more than the work was worth. It was so weird; we would have thought it was a prank if he hadn't sent payment up front."

Daniel tilted his head toward the forest behind himself. "You cleaned the cottage?"

"Yeah. This guy, Bran, he said he wanted it livable. And we're supposed to deliver food once a week, along with any other supplies he requests...like this." Joel motioned toward the wheelbarrow. "No specifications about brands or colors or anything, and no way to contact him to ask, so we had to guess."

Inside the barrow were the shears, a saw, a shovel, and the work gloves Daniel had requested the previous day. "They're for me. And they look great. I'm not fussy."

"Well, they're top of the line. We don't want to screw this guy, not when he's paying our rent."

"You got them here fast." Daniel couldn't stop a frown as he glanced from the barrow up to the house. It showed no more life than it had on the day he'd arrived. No lights in the windows. No twitching curtains. No signs of habitation. "I only requested them last night."

"We got Bran's letter under our door this morning. Along with additional payment. He sent more than the stuff is worth, so Dad wanted to make the delivery a priority."

Daniel fished the gold coins out of his pocket. He glanced around, feeling slightly uncomfortable about discussing income with a stranger, but he was too curious to resist. "Does he pay you in these, too?"

"That's it." Joel rolled his shoulders again and scowled at the coins. "Weirdest thing I ever heard of. Like I said, if our business was doing any better, we wouldn't have taken the job. There's something really wrong about the whole thing."

Uneasiness crawled through Daniel's stomach like a fat, hungry insect. He tucked the coins back into his pocket and licked at dry lips.

Joel's expression took on a hint of alarm. "Hey, sorry, please don't repeat any of that to the owner. I didn't mean to complain. We're grateful for the work, really—"

"No, don't worry, I get it. It…it's weird. I'm still trying to get used to it myself."

Joel was silent for a moment as his gaze moved from Daniel, to the gardens, to the house, and back to Daniel. "You're staying here, right?"

"I…" Daniel shrugged. "I guess I am."

"Man." Joel ran a hand over his chin, his eyes still dancing over his surroundings. "I get the heebie-jeebies just visiting. I can't imagine *living* here. Want me to bring you anything else? The letter didn't say anything about running power to the cottage. Just said to make it livable, and I didn't want to presume. But I can bring in a generator and some appliances. A fridge and kettle and stuff."

It was a serious temptation. Daniel didn't technically *need* electrical appliances, but they would make his life a whole lot easier. On the other hand, Bran hadn't given him a budget, and he didn't want to wear his welcome thin by asking for luxury items.

Joel saw his expression and flashed him a tight smile. "It's fine. I won't bill him for them. His original payment will easily cover it."

"If it's not too much trouble—"

"Naw, not at all. I mean, getting the truck through the forest is always an adventure, but I've got to make weekly food deliveries anyway." Joel laughed, and it held only a hint of discomfort. "I'll drop off the generator next time I'm coming by. Fill it with fuel and plug your equipment in. It won't power anything...*this* big"—he waved toward the mansion towering over them, and his smile flickered for an instant before he reaffixed it—"but we've got a model that will power four or five appliances at once."

I could have coffee without boiling water over the fire. Milk won't perish overnight. And I could even have a fan for summer... Staying at Craven Manor long term was starting to look much less problematic. "I'd really appreciate that. You said you drive a truck here. Did you come through the gate? I can barely squeeze through the gap on foot."

"Nah, no gate, but the path's hellishly overgrown." Joel pointed behind himself, toward a section of garden Daniel hadn't explored. "I can only get the truck to about fifty meters away then move everything in by hand."

So Craven Manor does *have a road leading to a different town, after all.* Daniel tried to see the path Joel had taken, but the trees grew too closely together to make it out. A thought occurred, and he shot his companion a quick glance. "When Bran hired you, did he, uh, give you any specific instructions? Any rules?"

"He did. Don't come between midnight and dawn, don't invite anyone else to this place, and don't enter the house."

I was told to stay out of the tower, but Joel has been forbidden from the entire building. There's something in the manor that Bran doesn't want discovered. The unscratchable itch of curiosity returned.

Joel scuffed his boot across the ground again. "Um, anything else you want me to bring you?"

"No, this is great, thanks." Daniel could take a hint. "You can head home. Thanks for dropping this off."

"Absolutely." Joel took a step back then stopped. He glanced from Daniel to the house and back, then made a grumbling noise in the back of his throat. He fished through his pockets and pulled out a pen and paper. "You're here by yourself, right? If anything goes really bad—like, bad enough you need to get out in a hurry—you can call me. I keep this phone beside me all the time, even at night. I…I'm sure there's nothing to worry about. But y'know. Just in case."

Daniel took the slip of paper. It held a cell phone number. He didn't know what to say. He tucked the paper into a pocket and managed a smile. "Thanks."

Joel raised a hand in farewell, but he was already halfway to the bank of trees. "Take care."

Daniel waited until Joel had disappeared among the garden, then he released a breath as he looked at the wheelbarrow. *I should have asked him for a phone. Joel's number isn't much help if I have nothing to call it with.*

Crows cackled as they settled into the tree behind him. The

sun was up, but the thick foliage blocked out much of its light and left Daniel feeling chilled. He rubbed his hands over his arms and tried to look at the situation from an optimistic point of view.

Joel and his father prepared the house for me. That's one mystery answered. Bran apparently prefers being hands-off with his property. I don't mind that, just... I wish the whole thing made a bit more sense.

Joel received letters with instructions, just like Daniel did. And he was being paid in the same gold coins. That wasn't where the similarities ended. Both Joel and Daniel had been too desperate to refuse Bran's offer, no matter how uncomfortable it made them.

It's like he's preying on the vulnerable.

Daniel struggled to dismiss the thought. He ran his hand over the wheelbarrow's handle. His request for gardening equipment had been answered so swiftly that it was disorienting. He didn't know how that was possible when he was seemingly isolated.

Maybe Bran has a security camera or motion sensor installed in the foyer to alert him when I go inside...except Craven Manor doesn't have any electricity to power them. Maybe Bran hired someone to drop by every evening and look for notes. Maybe that's who I heard knocking on my cottage last night.

Crows shuffled above him, their feathers creating a grim rustling. When he looked at them, one cawed softly. They seemed to have gathered around the ancient oversized crow Daniel had seen the day before. Its unrelenting, unblinking stare made Daniel uncomfortable. He picked up the wheelbarrow's handles and began pushing it toward the crypt.

CHAPTER 8

DANIEL COULDN'T STOP CHURNING through the new knowledge as he hiked toward the mausoleum. He'd all but sealed his employment at Craven Manor by accepting Joel's offer of a generator; leaving the house once supplies had been paid for would be a shady move. Daniel squinted up at the tower as he passed under it, but the only thing he saw in its windows was the reflection of the overcast sky.

Maybe I was paranoid over nothing. The taps could have come from a night bird, or maybe even a squirrel. Just because they sounded like a human asking to be let in doesn't mean that's what it was.

The crows exploded out of the tree in a burst of cries and whirring wings. Daniel flinched, but the birds passed over him and vanished into the forest past the fence.

It's a creepy house. But that doesn't mean it's bad. He ran his tongue over his lips. *This could be home. Maybe you can be happy here. Your own bed, supplies delivered at your request...and plenty of nature. Oh boy, is there nature.*

He dropped the wheelbarrow's handles when he reached the crypt. The vines he'd torn off the previous day lay in clumps around the stone building, and Daniel gathered them into the wheelbarrow. He didn't know if the house had a compost pile, but one would need to be set up. By the time he was ready to add new plants to the property, the organic material would have decomposed enough to be good fertilizer. Daniel wondered if Bran's offer to pay for supplies extended to saplings to replace some of the dead trees.

Daniel found a clear patch of ground to dump the severed vines then returned to the mausoleum and strapped on the gloves. Joel hadn't lied when he'd said they were good brands; his hands barely felt the thorns as he clipped branches off and tore the bushes out of the ground. Sadly, the gloves couldn't protect the rest of him. His jeans developed a series of tiny tears, and red scores appeared across his arms. At the same time, the process was cathartic. Every new prick meant fewer of the ugly black shrubs to cluster in the tomb's entryway. Within a few hours, he'd cleared enough to stand inside the shelter.

Daniel paused to admire the space. It had been designed as a place where people could sit to pay their respects to the departed, or even shelter from the rain. Stone benches had been carved into both walls. The tomb's doors were wood, as thick as the house's main doors and carved with leaves and flourishes to match the outside decoration.

He gripped one of the ugly bushes around the door's base. The shrub came up to his shoulders and was hard to get out of the ground. After a series of grunts and muffled swear words, he finally tore it free, but a strange clinking noise joined the sound of his scuffing shoes. Daniel tossed the bush aside. It had been hiding a silver tray and two teacups resting on the ground.

The cups were fine china, with delicate flowers painted in gold around their lips. The tray looked like it had been expensive, but the whole arrangement was coated in grime. Decades of plant growth over them had left a gritty black residue on the china, and a multitude of small bugs had died inside the teacups.

Daniel kicked the bush outside the eave then carefully lifted the tray. The metal had stuck to the stone, and its underside held a layer of red rust. He tried to imagine someone visiting the crypt—a grieving parent, perhaps—to have tea with the dead Annalise. But no scenario he could conjure explained why the cups had been abandoned there.

The malaise that had dogged him since arriving at Craven Manor intensified. It was heavy and tight, like a coat that didn't fit properly, and Daniel couldn't get the tension to leave his shoulders. Leaving the cups in the tomb didn't feel right, so he carried the tray out.

The crows circled above him like vultures. He wondered if that was their routine: spend the mornings in the tree by the house, the afternoons in the forest, scavenging for food, then circle the building before descending into the same tree for the night. He normally loved birds, but the crows showed none of the joy or energy he associated with their feathered cousins.

He climbed the stairs to the house. The door was still open, and the same leaves littered the foyer, but he held still for a moment, listening for signs of life. His paranoia grew as the house echoed every tiny sound back to him. The tree branches scratching against the stone wall, the wind whistling through tiny cracks, even the crackle of leaves being pushed along the foyer floor by errant bursts of wind sounded desperately loud. He braced himself then stepped inside.

Without the lamp, it was hard to see where he was going. Even when he pushed the front door fully open, its light wasn't enough to brighten the foyer. An idea occurred to him, and he crossed to the fireplace. The half-melted candles there were set in old-fashioned bronze holders with curling handles. There were no matches, but he recognized flint hidden among the dead branches and empty picture frames. It only took a few minutes to light one of the wicks.

He unstuck the candle's holder from the mantelpiece and held it ahead of himself. The plate he'd left for the cat was still in the space between two chairs. The pink Spam seemed untouched. Daniel sighed and added the plate to the silver tray. Maybe the cat couldn't recognize Spam as food. *Hopefully Joel's next delivery will include real meat. Poor cat.*

Daniel circled the edge of the foyer and opened doors in the hopes of finding a bathroom or kitchen. The hinges were all stiff from disuse, and he often had to kick drifts of dead leaves away.

The first few doors opened into a ballroom, a dining room, and a magnificent library. Daniel only stayed long enough to see that most of the books were still whole, but that several of their spines were decaying off.

He got lucky with one of the doors hidden beside the staircase. The leaves were thicker there, banked high like snowdrifts, but once he kicked them out of the way and got the door open, he found himself in what appeared to be the staff's quarters. It was a smaller, less opulent dining area. The center of the room was taken up by a table with no less than thirty chairs crowded around it. Doors were set into its walls, and he tried one to the right. It led into what seemed to be a sewing and repair room. An old-fashioned dress lay out on the table, pins stuck around where repairs had been started.

The next door opened into a washroom, where clothes filled large tubs. They'd frozen into strange crumpled shapes, as though they'd been put in there to soak and then were forgotten. Long-dried mildew dotted the fabric. Daniel bent close to see a woman's dress in one tub and white maid uniforms in another.

He retreated to the mess hall and tried its final door. It led into the kitchens, and Daniel's sense of surrealism increased. Pots rested on the stovetop, dry herbs hung from hooks in the ceiling, and a fossilized loaf of bread on the central table was slowly being turned to dust by insects.

The house had been evacuated at short notice. The staff had dropped whatever they were doing and just...left. *Why? What happened that they wouldn't try to salvage anything on the way out?*

He'd intended to wash the cups and tray, but it now occurred to him that the pipes might not work anymore. He turned a tap and waited. A deep, intense grating noise echoed from somewhere below his feet. A moment later, black ichor gushed out of the spout.

Daniel wrinkled his nose at the stench that accompanied the water. It was the same color and consistency as what had come out of his cottage's taps, so he waited for the water to clear. It took several minutes before he felt safe dunking his hands under the stream. He washed the remainder of the ichor down the sink then tipped the uneaten Spam into one of the grimy pots on the stove and submerged everything in water.

He spent a few minutes trying to scrub the gunk off the teacups and tray. It was a hopeless cause, though. His own plate came out fairly clean, but the porcelain and silver had spent too long exposed to the elements for the stains to come off without soap and heated water. He sighed and left them on the counter to dry. If the kitchens had been tidy, he would have put more effort into the dishes. As it was, washing up while surrounded by squalor felt like a Sisyphean task.

Maybe Bran is planning to hire some cleaners once the house's exterior is less of a nightmare to navigate. Daniel raised the candle and tried the kitchen's second door. It led back into the foyer.

He was halfway to the front door when he felt eyes on his back. It took a moment to locate the two amber spheres on the second-floor landing. Daniel moved closer and squinted against the shadows surrounding the cat. It stood directly ahead of

Annalise's portrait. He could barely see the whites of her eyes and a hint of her hesitant smile.

"Hello," Daniel called to the cat. "You didn't eat your food."

The cat's tail twitched, black moving through black. Daniel's eyes ached from trying to see where the cat ended and the gloom began.

"I'll bring you some more soon, okay? Something you might like a little better."

He backed to the door and turned to face the outside world. A chill wind nipped at the holes in his jeans and coat. The coins felt heavy in his pocket. There were still a few hours until sunset, and he had plans for how to spend them.

"Sorry… Are you sure?"

Daniel leaned over the counter of the pawnshop. He was trying to figure out if he'd misheard or if there was simply a mistake. The broker sat opposite, turning one of the coins over in his fingers. Bric-a-brac, secondhand jewelry, and antiques cluttered the surfaces around them and filled the glass case below Daniel's elbows.

"It's a fair price. You won't get better anywhere else." The broker placed the coin flat on the table and pushed it back toward Daniel, a signal that he wanted a decision.

Daniel swallowed. The broker's tone made it sound as though Daniel had complained about how little he'd offered for the coin. He couldn't have been farther from the truth.

The price for one of the coins would cover a month of rent and food, with enough left over for a decent bottle of wine. Daniel's fingers had gone numb. He hoped his face didn't look as shell-shocked as he felt. "Um. Sure. That's fine. Uh, could I have a couple of envelopes, too?"

"Absolutely." The broker, a short man with smile lines around his mouth, pulled out his receipt book. "If you get any more of those coins, bring them to me first, okay? You'll have a hard time selling them elsewhere, being a collector's item and all. But I know people who will want them, and I can get you a good price."

When Daniel left the store, he was still in shock. The money in his pocket was more than he'd ever had at one time before. And the mysterious Bran had promised him more if he kept working at Craven Manor. Up until the moment the broker gave him the quote, Daniel had half expected the coins would be worthless. But they weren't. He was rich...by his standards, at least.

He'd traded one of the coins but kept the other safely in a zipped pocket in case of emergencies. The pawnbroker's store was across the street from Kyle's apartment, and Daniel waited until he was inside the lobby before taking the money out and dividing it into portions.

Forty dollars went back into his pocket. With Bran supplying food and shelter, he wouldn't need much cash, but he knew it would be smart to have some on hand. Two hundred went into a second envelope to help Kyle with the rent until he could find a new roommate. The rest was tucked into the second envelope, and Daniel held it close to his chest as he jogged up the stairs.

The light flickered at the end of the hallway. It had grown worse in the two days Daniel had been away. The carpet seemed to be growing barer, too. Daniel stopped outside Mrs. Kirshner's room. When he bent his ear to the wood, he could hear her cooing to her cat in German. He slipped the envelope under her door.

Daniel followed the hall until he reached the lonely and discolored 16 hung from Kyle's door. He still had his key, but it seemed rude to use it. He didn't live there anymore, after all. Instead, he knocked. The door cracked open a moment later, then Daniel was gasping as Kyle slapped his back.

"There you are! I was afraid you'd gone and died in a gutter somewhere." Kyle was wearing an old sweatshirt and had let his stubble grow to an unruly stage, but he looked happy.

Daniel laughed and let himself be dragged inside. "Sorry, I should have left a note. I moved into the groundskeeper's cottage."

Kyle squinted at him.

"Remember? The job I told you about—tending to a house's garden?"

"You kidding me? I thought that was a joke." Kyle shook his head as he looked Daniel up and down. "So what's the deal? You moving back in? Fletch's girlfriend took him back, so you can have your room again."

Daniel hesitated for only a second. "Actually, I'm going to stay there. It's a good job. It pays well. Here." He held out the envelope. "Two hundred to cover the next few weeks of rent. Do you think you can find someone else to share with before then?"

"Maybe." Kyle pulled out the cash and thumbed through it, counting it, then tucked it into his back pocket. His grin stretched plump cheeks. "Wow, look at you. Real job. Real money. You're finally growing up, huh? Come on, let me buy you a beer. It's the least I can do. I want you to tell me all about this job."

CHAPTER 9

KYLE LOUNGED BESIDE DANIEL at the bar's counter. It was a busy night, and a cloud of chatter surrounded them. A soccer game played on the TV suspended from the ceiling, and every few minutes, whoops and cheers drowned out their words as the local team scored.

The beer was going to Daniel's head. He couldn't remember how many he'd drunk, only that it was a lot, and both he and his cousin were slurring their words. Kyle had bought him a hearty meal and was paying for the drinks, and he seemed to be in good humor.

"So, so, hang on, the place is really empty?" Kyle nursed a beer, sloshing the liquid inside its bottle. "You're all by your lonesome up there?"

"Just me, the cat, and the birds." Daniel tried to laugh, but it came out as a giggle. The lights were very bright. "And the guy who delivers food, but he only comes once a week."

"That's bonkers, man." Kyle shook his head like it was the funniest thing he'd ever heard. "Absolutely nuts. But he's paying you okay, isn't he?"

"Yeah. Check this out." Daniel retrieved the coin from his pocket and passed it to Kyle. "That's what my wage looks like. How weird is that?"

Kyle's face scrunched up as he turned the coin over. "Is this gold? What is he, a pirate?"

"I know, right?" Daniel put his bottle back onto the counter. A quiet voice in the back of his mind said he was being careless, but he was too giddy to pay it much attention. "As far as I can guess, they were minted back when the house was occupied. Late Georgian era or maybe Regency era."

"When's that?"

"Late seventeen hundreds or early eighteen hundreds." Daniel bent forward to point to the seal on the coin. "That same emblem is on the tomb in the yard and worn by people in the house's paintings. It's probably the family crest."

"Hey, I know that." The bartender had approached unseen to place two fresh beers at their sides. He was squinting at the coin. "My grandfather had one of those."

"No way!" Kyle's voice had risen in volume, and he seemed to be barely containing his laughter. "Did your grandpa get hired as a ground-person too?"

The bartender's high coif and stringy beard reminded Daniel of a yak. He glanced down his bar, but all of the patrons were engaged in chatter and still had full drinks. The bartender leaned far over the thick wooden counter, his eyes narrowed, and spoke in a tone so soft that Daniel could barely understand him. "Nah. My grandfather's great-grandfather was a physician. He was employed by the Myricks family."

The name sparked the coal of curiosity in Daniel. He scooted nearer. "Physician? Did he treat Annalise Myricks? Do you know why she died?"

The bartender snickered at Daniel's eagerness. "I never met him. He died, like, an eternity ago. But my grandfather was a historian and collected his great-grandpa's journals and trinkets. My parents would take me to visit him as a kid, and he'd always talk forever, telling story after story about our forefathers. He was half-senile, and everything he said sounded like a wheeze, but he loved talking about his physician great-grandfather and the crazy family on the hill. The mother was bonkers, apparently. Paranoid and obsessive-compulsive. He used to read passages from the physician's journal, and it was the kind of stuff that would give you nightmares."

The barkeep scrunched his face up and squinted at an invisible book as he imitated his grandfather. "I would have *loved* to give her some electroshock treatment. Any other woman would have been put in an asylum for the ravings she spouted, but she was rich up to her eyeballs, and rich people were untouchable."

Daniel could picture the old patriarch clearly, with a worn, haggard face, spittle escaping his chapped lips as he recited memorized passages from the book. A fireplace would cast deep shadows in the crevices of his creased face, and his eyes, half-blind with cataracts, would rove across the room.

"She didn't want treatment herself, afraid I might curse her with my medicine. She wouldn't let anyone touch her. But she did let me treat her child, the poor mite."

"Annalise?" Daniel pressed.

The barkeep broke his pantomime to shrug. "Like I said, I haven't heard the stories since I was a kid, but that name sounds about right."

"Do you know what was wrong with her?"

"Yeah." The barkeep rubbed a tattooed hand over his beard. "That was Pawpaw's favorite part of the story. She had this condition that made her skin blister in the sun. He called her a 'moon child.' Of course, these days they have a proper name for the disease, something complex beginning with an *X*. Point was, she couldn't be allowed near any kind of sunlight. She spent her days locked up in their mansion, thick curtains covering all of the windows, and was only allowed out at night."

Daniel blinked and saw the portrait in his mind's eye. She'd been impossibly pale, the kind of paleness that came from never seeing the sun. "How did she die?"

"No clue, bud." The barkeep shrugged. "Pawpaw's journals said he tried things to help her, all kinds of crazy experimental treatments, but nothing worked. After a few years, the mother sent him away in a fit of fury and told him to never return."

Kyle squinted up at the bearded man. "You seriously called him Pawpaw? What, did he die of embarrassment?"

"Shut up! I loved my Pawpaw." The barkeep glowered at Kyle then flipped a cloth over his shoulder and marched to the other end of the bar.

"Why'd you have to say that?" Daniel hissed.

"Come on, he's a pretentious twit. Enjoy your beer."

Daniel picked up his bottle but didn't drink any. His mind was swirling. He tried to imagine what it might feel like to be trapped inside during the day, closeted behind heavy blackout curtains, never allowed to see the sun or to feel its rays on his skin for fear it would blister into agonizing scabs. Would prolonged exposure have killed Annalise? He didn't like to think about the girl's end. Daniel ran a hand over his face.

"Hey, what? The douche didn't upset you, did he?" Kyle snickered and tapped Daniel's knee with his bottle. "You should tell his pawpaw to stop repeating those ghoulish stories."

"It's not that," Daniel lied. "I just… I need to be heading back. I didn't mean to stay out this late."

"All right. Hang on a minute. I've got something to ask first. D'you think you could get me a job at your mansion? Put in a good word for your buddy?"

Daniel's buzz was starting to fade, but dizziness persisted. He licked his lips. "I would if I could, but I don't think he's looking for new employees. His instructions specifically said not to invite anyone else to the house."

"Come on, help me out here. Haven't I been good to you? We're blood, you and I." Kyle's eyes narrowed. "Or are you going to drop me now that you've got a cushy gig trimming grass?"

"We…we're not blood. Cousins by marriage." The dizziness was getting worse. Daniel rubbed at his forehead, trying to clear his mind. "And I don't trim grass. It's a lot of work. The place is a mess."

Kyle drained the last of his beer then slammed the empty bottle onto the counter. "Look, man, I'll level with you. I need a new job. My boss is riding my ass constantly, and the pay is trash. I know you earned more than what you gave me tonight, and a job like that could set me up for life. All I'm saying is, I saved you from the streets. You *owe* me."

"I…I…" The lights were far, far too bright. Daniel stood, and the vertigo rushed through him like a wave. "I'll talk to him. Write him a letter. But I can't promise anything, okay?"

Kyle slapped his shoulder, his grin back in place. "Attaboy. You and me, we've got to stick together, don't we? Go and see what strings you can pull for your buddy."

The night air was chill, but Daniel appreciated the sting on his skin. It helped chase the fog out of his mind and give him purpose. He tucked his hands into his pockets as he and Kyle strode toward the apartment, Kyle chatting about the new game he'd bought.

Something's not right. His fingers wiggled in the pockets, but they were empty. Daniel pulled up short. "Kyle! The coin's gone."

"Huh?" Kyle squinted at him. "Whatcha mean?"

"The coin—I gave it to you to look at. What happened to it?"

"I put in on the bar. What? You didn't pick it up?"

Daniel dashed back to the stocky brick building on the corner of the street. The bar was packed. He could only pray no one had taken the coin in the couple of minutes he'd been gone.

The vertigo was a serious liability as he wove through the crowd to reach the section of the bar he'd been sitting at. The seats where he and Kyle had been sitting were still empty, but the coin was nowhere to be seen. Daniel scanned the wooden slab and the nearby ground, feeling helpless frustration rise in his chest, then waved to the barkeeper. The bearded man shot him a sour glare but grudgingly approached.

"Did you see my coin?" Daniel fanned his fingers over the bar to emphasize the empty space. "It was right here. Did you find it and take it to keep it safe?"

"Sorry, buddy." The barkeep shrugged, but his expression seemed genuinely regretful.

Daniel hovered there, the sting of loss and burn of humiliation warring for precedence. A hand clapped his shoulder, and he turned to meet Kyle's grim smile.

"Not here?"

"No, gone."

"What a bummer." Kyle shrugged. "I'd offer to buy you a drink, but I guess I already did."

"Don't joke. This is serious." Daniel scanned the crowd, looking for flashes of gold among the glinting bottles and glasses the patrons held. His heart sank in tandem with his shoulders. Whoever had taken it must have pocketed it.

Kyle slung an arm across Daniel's shoulders. Together, they walked back outside, into the night.

Daniel exhaled and watched the plume of condensation evaporate. "What time is it?"

"Just on eleven, buddy. Want to go somewhere for round two?"

"Can't." Daniel extracted himself from the embrace. "I've got to get back. Curfew."

As he jogged down the street to collect his bike, he heard Kyle call after him. "Don't forget to ask about that job!"

I shouldn't have made that promise. Daniel scowled to himself as he tugged the bike along the bendy, unstable flagstones of the road to Craven Manor. *Bran might actually hire him. Best-case scenario, Kyle's behavior will taint me by association. Worst case, I might actually lose my job.*

Kyle wasn't a hard worker. He did enough to cover himself when his boss was around, but Daniel had seen how his cousin behaved when he wasn't being watched. His forty-minute lunch break would stretch into two or three hours of sipping beer in the shade and cracking jokes with his friends. At the manor, with zero accountability, Daniel doubted Kyle would do anything.

You should have known better, idiot. He saw what you earned. That was why he took you out for the beers. He never does anything like that without expecting a favor in return.

The bike caught on a root, and Daniel had to kneel to untangle it. When he straightened, he'd lost track of which direction he'd been traveling. The mossy ground between the roots and shrubs was void of flagstones.

He twisted, searching behind himself, and felt a ping of dread. He was already cutting his curfew close; what happened if he wasn't inside his cottage before midnight?

You can't have strayed far from the path. He paced back the way he thought he'd come, head and shoulders bent as he scanned the ground for hints of gray. The trees all looked alien in the moonlight. Animals chattered nearby but fell silent when he drew too close. The fear sharpened, and Daniel increased his pace, moving as quickly as the bike would let him. The dozy pall the alcohol had cast over him had thoroughly faded, but the clarity only increased his anxiety.

Then his shoe hit something firm. Daniel scraped the dirt away and sucked in a breath as he saw stone. He hunted around it, digging through the leaf litter and the loam until he discovered another, then a third. They gave him a direction. He followed it, and soon the path resolved itself. His relief was immense, but he knew he'd lost a lot of time.

It was eleven when I left the pub. It takes just under an hour to reach Craven Manor. But I was dawdling, stuck in my thoughts. What if it's already after midnight? Does Bran have any way of knowing I got home late? I need to buy a watch with my next payment.

The rusted gates were visible through the trees. Daniel broke into a jog then smothered a curse as his bike stuck in another shrub. He shook it free and sprinted the last few feet.

The moon washed its blue light across the gardens and the manor's roof. It looked deceptively peaceful. Daniel left his bike beside the gate and squeezed through the gap. There were no clanging bells or sirens at his intrusion, but he still felt guilty as he slunk through the trees. Dead branches grazed his arms and neck as he wove past them. They reminded Daniel of brittle fingers scrabbling at his skin. His heart flipped unpleasantly.

A wail echoed through the garden. Daniel looked up at the crow perched above him. He recognized it as the old oversized bird that normally lurked by the house's front. He'd disturbed it, and it ruffled its feathers as though affronted.

"Sorry," Daniel whispered.

Its beady eye followed him as he passed its tree, then it shook its feathers out and launched into the air. Its wing beats were slower than its companions' but harsher, as though fighting against the air. Daniel watched it until it disappeared over Craven Manor's rooftop.

Hurry. Get inside. Lock the door. It might not be too late.

He staggered into the ring of statues. The half-nude ladies and centaurs seemed less carefree than before. Although their poses were relaxed—arms thrown overhead, feet dancing—their gazes were accusatory, and the stains running through their garments seemed harsher.

Daniel hated the way their eyes followed him. He slipped past them, toward where he knew his cottage was hidden. He caught a flicker of motion in the corner of his eyes. He could have sworn he'd seen something moving through the trees—

Don't linger. Get to your house.

An awful sense of dread descended over him. The hairs rose across the backs of his arms. His mouth felt horribly dry. His palms sweaty, he flexed the fingers as he broke into a run.

Someone's following me.

Paranoia hit him like a sledgehammer. He couldn't stop turning his head, hunting for movement among the dead branches and strangling vines, convinced he had company but unable to see it. His cottage was just ahead. Moonlight glittered on the windows like a beacon.

And yet the thing behind him was gaining. He couldn't hear it or see it, but he could feel it. And it grew closer with every step, fixated and inexorable.

He hit the cabin's wall hard enough to force the breath out of him. The door's handle was jammed. He twisted it, panicking that he'd been locked out of his home for missing the curfew, but then it screeched as it turned. His feet tripped over the entrance, and Daniel tumbled onto the wooden floor. He swiveled to close the door, and his heart missed a beat. A figure stood just outside the threshold, its glassy eyes locked onto him.

CHAPTER 10

DANIEL GAPED. THE WORLD seemed to slow, unraveling, until he was trapped in that moment. He lay on his back, one hand stretched toward the door that was just out of reach and the other pressed against the wooden floor. His sweaty fingers rubbed through the grit and dust. His brain, stunned into stupidity, latched on to the texture. His floor needed sweeping. That was real. Mundane. Easy to believe.

Unlike the phantom outside his door.

She was there and not, tangible and a delusion, all at the same time. He could see her. He could see *through* her. The black gnarled trees at her back were as perfectly clear as she was.

His lips parted, but he managed only a whisper. "Annalise."

She'd lost her color. The blond in her hair was gone, along with the flush across her cheeks and the pastels in her dress. It had all been converted into the phantom white. When she moved, the image rippled and threatened to vanish, like trying to hold on to a Magic Eye solution. Her curls drifted behind her as though she were suspended in water. Her eyes were missing both pupil and iris.

She stepped forward. Her dress and hair seemed to float with the motion. One of her hands reached toward him.

Fear broke through Daniel's shock. He lunged toward the door and forced it closed. The latch bounced then caught with a reassuring click. Daniel forced a shaking breath down his throat as he leaned the side of his head against the wood to listen.

The outside world was perfectly silent. No insects chirped. No birds shifted in the trees. If not for his own ragged breathing, Daniel might have thought he'd gone deaf.

Then came a soft *tp, tp, tp* on the other side of the door.

Daniel crept backward, away from the door, and pressed a hand across his mouth to silence the noises that wanted to escape.

Tp, tp, tp. The knocks were harder. More demanding. Daniel's eyes burned as he flicked them from the door to the window and back. He hadn't pulled the curtains. Patches of stars were visible between the canopy.

The rules said the curtains had to be shut. Will something bad happen if they're not?

Daniel crept toward the window and used the desk to pull himself to his feet. He gripped the thick cloth, but didn't pull it.

The rational part of his mind was already scrambling to come up with an explanation for what he'd seen. His eyes had been playing tricks on him. She'd been a wisp of smoke, a tapping branch. A parting gift from the alcohol.

But his heart wasn't as easily convinced. Daniel's cheek bumped the glass as he leaned against the window and squinted toward the front step. He could see patches of bare earth, the stone step before his front door, and the tangled branches surrounding his home. Nothing moved among them. The rational part of his mind started screaming louder, claiming victory over the phantoms. And yet the insects still weren't chirping.

Daniel swallowed around the lump in his throat. He raised a hand, hesitated, then rapped a knuckle against the glass.

He counted his heartbeats. His breath misted over the cold pane. Seconds passed, and he began to think he was alone. Then came *tp, tp, tp* right beside his head.

He jolted back as Annalise materialized on the other side of the glass. Empty eyes stared into his. Her tapping fingers pressed to the window, leaving a smudge on the glass. The corners of her mouth twitched up into a hint of a smile. Daniel blinked, and the girl was gone.

Daniel bit the inside of his cheek, willing himself not to be sick, as he drew the curtains. He was clammy and shaking.

The tapping didn't return for the rest of the night. Daniel kept his curtains closed and door locked, and after sitting up for a restless hour, he crawled into bed and tried to sleep. His nerves were too keyed up to let him fall into any kind of deep rest. Annalise might not have been tapping on his door, but Daniel was certain she was still outside his home, waiting.

When he startled awake for what felt like the hundredth time, Daniel gave up on sleep and rose to start the fire. The earliest hints of morning lit the gap under his front door. He sat on the fireside rug, his hands clasped around a mug of black tea, and watched the flames.

Ghosts are real. It was still hard to wrap his head around the new knowledge. Daniel had seen supposed video evidence and read real-life accounts of paranormal activity, but in every one of those cases, it had been easy to dismiss them as a coincidence if they were too subtle, or a hoax if they were too clear. But after he'd glimpsed the spirit outside the window, even the rational part of his mind had abandoned its objections.

He'd never seen a ghost before Annalise. Did that mean ghosts were incredibly uncommon? Was Annalise special in some way? Or was there something about Craven Manor that made her linger after death?

His mind spiraled in circles, hunting for answers that didn't exist, until exhaustion finally pulled him under. When he next opened his eyes, the sun was high enough to force a sliver of gold under the edge of the curtains. He'd knocked his cup over, and the dregs of his tea had spilled across the wooden floor, so Daniel rose to find a towel.

I'm staying, aren't I?

He mopped up the spilled liquid then crossed to the sink and rinsed the cloth. As long as he stayed in the groundskeeper's cottage, he would be in close proximity to a ghost. He searched his soul for negative emotions like disgust or fear, but they weren't present. Annalise's spirit didn't seem malevolent. She'd answered his knock on the window, and she'd smiled. She hadn't tried to come inside. He'd been frightened when she chased him through the garden, but that could be explained as a child playing. She was only twelve, after all.

So I stay. I finish clearing her tomb, then I make the rest of the garden a little more habitable.

His mysterious host, Bran, had to know about the ghost. That was why he wanted the mausoleum cleaned even though the house wasn't occupied. It was for Annalise's sake, to give her some comfort after death.

Daniel left the cloth to dry on the sink and opened the cottage's door. He remained alert for any sign of the ghost, but the patch outside his home was clear. Birds bickered. Insects hummed. Annalise had retreated for the day.

Does she live in her crypt? That would seem logical, but… Daniel looked toward the tower protruding from Craven Manor. He could barely see its curtains. When he stared hard enough, he began to imagine he saw a face behind the glass, obscured by the shadows.

Bran's letter told me to lock my door and close my window at night so that I wouldn't see Annalise. It also forbade me from opening the tower door… Does she stay there during the day?

Daniel tilted his head and strained to see through the tower window, but it was too far away to be sure of what lurked behind it. He might have seen a piece of furniture, a shimmer of light on a wall, or even an optical illusion playing across the glass. He turned away and followed the overgrown path through the gardens. *Whatever lives there—Annalise or otherwise—Bran doesn't want me to pry. So I won't. I'll keep my head down and do my job.*

It felt surreal to go back to work after having his worldview shaken, but he knew exercise could help quiet his buzzing mind. Daniel felt a small rush of pride when the tomb came into sight. He'd done a lot to improve it during his two days there. The hideous thorny bushes were gone from the entrance, and the vines were charming rather than suffocating. Daniel scoped around the area, pulling out the remaining smaller bushes he hadn't gotten the first day, and assessed what still needed to be done.

The tomb's walls could use a scrub, but that would need a bucket and some kind of nontoxic detergent. He would have to request them next time he spoke to Joel, the deliveryman.

Daniel scanned the area. The tomb would have been a two-minute walk from the house under normal circumstances, but with the garden overgrown as badly as it was, the trip easily took ten.

I'm supposed to fix the garden as much as I can. Why not work outward from the crypt? I can clear pathways to both the house and my cottage, and tame the surrounding areas in stages.

Daniel retrieved the shovel and began plotting out sections of ground to clear. The path wouldn't be straight because in some areas, the vegetation grew so thick that it would have taken weeks to remove it. Traces of original pathways and design elements were still visible among the plants. Daniel plotted a route that took advantage of them.

He used the shovel to excise leaf litter and smaller plants out of his chosen trail. Most came out easily and were heaped in piles to be carted away with the wheelbarrow, but some of the weeds stuck so badly that he needed to dig them out.

"Come on, stupid thing." Daniel grunted as he alternately pulled on and hacked at the roots of a particularly stubborn plant. Its leaves tore off in shreds, but its root system was tougher than he'd expected. Daniel was no stranger to hard labor, but his muscles were starting to tire.

He heaved back, and the plant exploded out of the ground and showered dirt across the scene like confetti. Daniel, laughing, used the back of his gloved hand to clear specks off his face. He threw the plant aside and went back to check that no bulbs remained.

Something off-white protruded from the hole. Daniel frowned at it as he tugged broken roots out of the loamy earth. It was a strange shape but deep enough underground that he could cover it up again. *A rock?*

Just to make sure, he rapped his knuckles on the shape—and recoiled. It felt wrong. Whatever he'd touched wasn't stone. It had felt hollow.

Daniel dropped the roots and began scooping the dirt away from the object. The ground wasn't as compacted in that part of the garden as he'd found in other areas, which meant it hadn't been part of the original path. He kept digging, slowly unearthing more of the shape. It was vaguely round and about the size of a soccer ball. Fissures ran across it. The off-white shade had been stained by the earth, and as Daniel dug deeper, he found a hole in its side.

His hands had turned numb, but he didn't stop scraping the soil away from the object. He gripped its top and gave it a tug, and a human skull emerged from the ground.

CHAPTER 11

DANIEL HELD UP THE skull as waves of nausea rose through his stomach. Its jaw had fallen off and remained buried in the loamy earth, leaving just the cranium's empty eyes and its row of upper teeth to leer at Daniel.

He dropped the skull. Its cracks widened as the bone thudded into the earth.

Is it Annalise's skull? Is this the reason her spirit isn't at rest? He turned to where the weeds blocked his view of the mausoleum. *That makes no sense. Why did Bran want me to tend to the crypt if there's no body inside?*

Sweat coated Daniel. He used his forearm to wipe it off his face. The skull was too large to belong to a child. It was nearly as big as Daniel's head.

This came from an adult, then. Someone who died on the property.

His breathing was rougher than the exertion warranted, and

every nerve in his body screamed to move away from the bones, but Daniel repressed his instincts as he bent over the hole. Part of the lower jaw protruded from the dirt. It was no more than a foot deep, which meant the grave—if it had been a grave—was shallow. He thought it was possible the body had been left on top of the ground and had, over the last two hundred years, gradually sunk into the earth or been covered by sediment during heavy rains. He looked behind himself. White bone crested out of the earth in multiple places. Weeds had grown around it and hidden it well, but he recognized a knee and part of a rib.

He stood and shifted his weight from foot to foot in an effort to relieve some of his tension. His gloves had protected his fingers from actually touching the bone, but he still rubbed them together as though there were traces of death that needed to be removed.

Calm down, and think it through. There was already a crypt on the property. Maybe it was surrounded by a forgotten graveyard, and he'd simply stumbled on one of the bodies buried there.

He rotated as he placed his location. He was still close to the wall, no more than forty meters from the crypt. It would be a logical place to have a cemetery.

Families buried people on their property all the time back then. This isn't anything extraordinary.

Except it was. Even accounting for two centuries of erosion, the grave was shallow. There was no tombstone in sight, not even a marker, and no sign of other graves.

Paranoia spread through Daniel's veins like liquid fire. He tore off the gloves and began pacing. *This was a secret grave. I'm sure whoever buried this body didn't want it found again. What could that mean? Murder?*

"Damn it." His tongue was dry. The house loomed over the trees, and the late-afternoon sun made its shadow extend just shy of where Daniel stood. In another half hour, it would swallow him.

Do I need to call the police? The letter said not to allow strangers onto the property, but if there's a murder involved, I have to tell someone, don't I?

He tried to picture what that would lead to. Would they dig through the garden, searching for more bones? What if they found them? What if the ground underneath Daniel's feet was littered with long-rotted corpses?

Calm down. He leaned his back against a tree trunk and rubbed his palms over his closed eyes. Slow breaths didn't do much to calm his racing heart, but they did help clear his head. *Think it through, Daniel, and don't do anything hasty. This isn't some recent death where a killer needs to be apprehended and grieving families are seeking peace.* The bones had been buried for more than two hundred years. They were too fragile to be any more recent than that. Which shifted the scene from an unsolved crime to something like archaeology.

From where he stood, he could see the skull's cap. The smudged dirt and dark fissures were clearly visible. *It will still need to be reported, even if no action is taken. There might still be a great-grandchild out there who wishes they knew what happened to their ancestor. And it deserves a proper burial. The only question is—should I leave a note for Bran and wait on his advice or go to the police directly?*

His attention drifted from Craven's slate roof to its tower, and his composure crumbled. A face glared down at him through the blurred glass. With no light inside the room, barely any features were visible except for a pale face and a long-fingered hand pressed to the window.

Daniel's blood turned cold, and the fading sunlight wasn't enough to warm him. The figure was only visible for a second, but then it turned and faded into the room.

It couldn't have been Annalise's ghost. The previous night, she'd been close to invisible—almost like a wisp of evaporating fog. But the shape in the tower looked solid.

Does someone really live here, after all? It was nearly impossible to believe. The dust had been too thick and the lightless hallways too dark. But what other explanation was there?

He gave the bones a final, lingering stare then pushed away from the trunk and marched toward the house.

The crows had settled around the entrance again. There were more of them; fresh visitors clung to the stone ledges and the nearby trees. Their attention felt heavy, as though the dozens of eyes trained on him carried weight. Daniel kept his head down as he jogged up the stone steps and entered the foyer.

He looked for signs that someone had disturbed the space, but couldn't find any. The crumbling chairs were still covered in grime. There were no new paths in the slowly decaying leaves scattered across the floor. Flecks of dust floated in the air, but not enough to suggest someone had passed through recently.

It seems impossible, but I know I'm not alone. Daniel lifted his chin. "Bran! I want to talk."

His voice reverberated through the manor's countless empty chambers. Daniel let the words hang in the air for a moment, then he called again. "I found the bones in the garden! If you can't explain them, I'll need to report them to the police."

His only answer came from muffled echoes. He shuffled his feet. Nerves and wavering conviction made his voice crack.

"Bran, or whoever lives here, I'm grateful for the job. But I can't ignore a skeleton. I either need to hear something from you, or I'll have to call in outsiders."

He waited in the foyer until he began to feel foolish. Noises floated to him—the sound of creaking wood, the hollow whistle of wind forcing its way between gaps in the stones—and beneath it all was a sound so subtle that he couldn't separate it from his imagination: fingernails scratching on wood. But no footsteps, and no words.

He's not going to answer. Daniel scuffed his shoe across the marble, disturbing dead leaves in its path, then backed toward the door.

Something crumpled under his shoe. It didn't have the normal brittleness of the dead leaves, and Daniel lifted his foot. He'd stepped on a white envelope that had been left on the entryway's top step, the place he'd walked over just minutes before. Daniel picked it up and looked about himself. He searched for movement among the gardens, but the only disturbance came from the murder of crows lurking above him. He flipped up the envelope's flap and pulled out the paper.

Bury the bones, please. I cannot stand to look at them.

You seek answers. Join me for supper in the dining room at seven tonight.

—Bran

Daniel returned the note to the envelope as he shuffled down the stairs. A sense of dread had returned, and it made his eyes water and the hairs across his arms prickle. *This proves it. As improbable as it seems, I'm not alone at Craven Manor. He's been watching me. Through the windows? Among the trees? There's no way to know. But he was here, meters away from me, and I didn't hear or see him. It's unnatural.*

He tucked the letter into his pocket and increased his pace as he lurched into the gardens. Bran wanted him to bury the bones. That felt wrong, but Daniel had to remind himself that the bones were old. Reburying them wouldn't make him an accomplice or a criminal. And if Bran's answers didn't satisfy him, the remains could always be uninterred.

The unmarked grave wasn't difficult to find. Daniel had left debris scattered around the scene. The weed he'd pulled out hung to one side, its roots slowly drying in the sun. His gloves lay on the ground. And the hole was dark and raw, like a still-bleeding wound in the ground. The white bones stood out in stark contrast against the loamy earth.

The grave wasn't deep—only a few inches of earth covered the bones. Daniel raised a shovelful of soil to pour over the bare skull, but unease stilled his hand. He hated the idea of leaving the skeleton exposed. He could heap dirt over the exposed bones, but it would only wash away. Whoever this person had been in life, they deserved a proper grave. He scooped out a clear patch of ground near the skull and began digging a new hole.

Block after block of ground came out under the pressure of his shovel. The first foot was easy, but after that, Daniel began to encounter stones. They slowed his progress but didn't stop it.

Without help, he couldn't dig far enough to create a genuine six-foot hole—but he got it to at least four feet. It wasn't wide, but the bones didn't have any flesh clinging to them that would require more space.

From freelance janitor to groundskeeper and now undertaker. You're really moving up in the world, Daniel.

He wiped the back of his hand across his forehead as he considered the logistics of moving the bones. If the skull was anything to go by, the rest of the skeleton would be too fragile to remove in little pieces. It would be easier to shift it over in blocks.

He noted the space the bones protruded from then traced the area where he thought the body might be resting. Weedy grass grew over it, and he cleared the plants away before beginning his dig.

The first thing he found was a rib bone. He adjusted his angle and kept digging past it until he also found a hip bone, then a shin. Finally, when he was certain his marks encircled the entire body, he dug down and levered the bones out in square-foot-sized chunks.

Just like a jigsaw puzzle. He lowered three ribs and an upper arm bone into the new grave. *Keep the pieces in order. Don't let them get scrambled.*

It took more than an hour to transfer the whole skeleton, moving as carefully as he could to make sure he hadn't left any parts behind. By the time he began filling the new hole, the sun was setting.

All right. I either did a really good job giving a body a dignified burial, or disturbed a century-old crime scene. A hysterical giggle escaped him as he tamped down the earth. The sense of dread refused to abate. His instinct was to trust Bran. Except for some bizarre requests and odd behaviors, the man hadn't caused him any harm. But it was impossible to stop doubt from creeping in.

He didn't have a tombstone, but a few minutes of searching found a long-dead branch that was shaped like a very wonky cross. Daniel snapped it off its tree and thrust it into the earth at the grave's head. It was still a far cry from the crypt's elegant dignity, but it was better than nothing.

Crows cawed in the distance as they settled around Craven Manor for the night. Daniel jogged to his cottage and let himself inside. The clock above his fireplace said it was already after seven, so he hurried to wash as well as he could in the sink and change into fresh clothes before making the return trip back to the dark mansion.

Its front door hung open, and Daniel entered under the watchful eyes of a multitude of somber birds. The space was just as empty and desolate as it had been earlier. Daniel ran his hands through his hair, trying to make sure he looked at least a little presentable, then approached the fireplace. He stopped by the ancient furniture and waited for his host to appear. Instead, a door farther into the foyer drew open with a slow, prolonged creak.

Daniel didn't move for several moments. Light came through the doorway to illuminate the cobwebs clustered around its frame. They looked almost like a halo, both delicate and threatening.

Move. Don't keep him waiting. Daniel forced his feet to work. They carried him as far as the tile before the doorway then stopped.

A sense of unreality washed through him. The dining room was lit with lamps spaced along the walls and on candelabras in the center of the table. A crackling fireplace dominated the room's closest wall. Three large wingback chairs were spaced around it, and the bright flames sent twisting shadows rollicking up the wood-paneled walls.

The massive table stretched the length of the room. Daniel imagined at least forty guests could sit around it without bumping elbows. Heavy dust coated the surface. Only one place had been set—the seat at the head of the table, closest to the fireplace. A bowl was filled with steaming soup, and a plate beside it held a bread roll and butter.

Is this what he meant by dinner? I'd assumed we'd be eating together. Daniel snuck a look behind himself, but the foyer remained deserted. "Bran? Sir?"

Did I arrive too late? Did he give up and leave?

Curiosity pulled Daniel toward the table. The bowl was clean and modern. The soup looked like some kind of minestrone. But they'd been placed on top of the powdery dust thick enough to obscure the wood's color.

The door slammed closed. Daniel flinched and swiveled toward it, but no one had followed him into the room.

A voice rasped from one of the wingback chairs by the fireplace: "Sit."

CHAPTER 12

DANIEL DID AS HE was told, fumbling to pull the chair out from the head of the table and slip into it. The voice was unlike anything he'd ever heard. It was cracked and dry, as though it had been stolen from a man on his deathbed. But at the same time, there was enormous force inside the word, the kind that told Daniel it would be dangerous to cross its instructions.

"Enjoy your dinner, Mr. Kane."

The words made Daniel shudder. He clenched his hands in his lap and hazarded a glance around the back of his chair. "Will you be joining me?"

"Not tonight. I do not have much of an appetite."

The voice came from the central fireplace chair. Its high back and flared sides perfectly hid the occupant. He and Daniel sat back-to-back, less than five feet apart but blind to each other. The idea of creeping around the chair's side to see his mysterious host's face flittered through Daniel's mind, but he didn't dare follow through. The voice didn't invite games.

The spoon and butter knife had been laid on top of a clean napkin to keep them off the dust, but Daniel still had to hide a grimace as he picked them up. He dipped the spoon into the soup and gave it an experimental stir but didn't drink any. "You're Bran, aren't you?"

"Correct." The chair's leather creaked as the man shifted.

Daniel had been developing the idea since he'd entered the room that he might be talking to a ghost, but the noise killed that theory. Ghosts—at least the kind of ghost Daniel had heard about—didn't have any weight to exert on their surroundings.

"You have questions," Bran said. "Ask."

Daniel's spoon looped around the bowl again. His mind was churning with requests and doubts, and his tongue felt rubbery as he tried to phrase them. "Those bones… Do you know who they belonged to?"

"Yes. You found Eliza Myricks. She was Annalise's mother."

Daniel drew a sharp breath. He looked behind himself again, hungry to catch a glimpse of Bran, but his companion remained hidden. "I heard—" He caught himself. *Would it be rude to repeat what the bartender said? Will he think I've been gossiping about the house?*

"Continue." The cracked, guttural voice was curt but not hostile.

Daniel licked dry lips. "I heard she was paranoid. Bordering on insane."

A strange hacking, gasping sound came from the chair. It sounded like choking, and Daniel dropped his spoon as he prepared to stand. Then he realized what the sound was. Bran was *laughing*.

"That is correct." A bleak mirth infused the words and gave them life but not in a way that warmed Daniel. "She was a cruel, changeable woman. Young Annalise bore the brunt of her erraticism, and it ultimately killed the child."

Daniel frowned at his soup. "Her grave was shallow. And it didn't have any headstone."

"Yes. She was interred by her sole surviving relative, her son. He was not strong enough to bury her deep, but left the grave unmarked deliberately. He did not believe she had earned a Christian burial. I agreed with him enough to leave her body undisturbed."

"Oh." Daniel felt a twinge of discomfort and lifted a spoonful of the soup to distract himself. "I shouldn't have dug her up. I didn't know she was there, and I was trying to clear a path—"

"That is forgivable. As was your trespassing beyond your curfew last night."

The tone wasn't harsh, but it held an undercurrent of resignation that made Daniel cringe. "Sorry. It won't happen again."

"As I said, forgivable."

Desperate to shift the discussion back to safer ground, Daniel cleared his throat. "The soup is delicious. Thank you."

"I had the store owner prepare it." Bran exhaled as he shifted restlessly. "Do not be reticent about your requests if you require improvements to your living arrangements. I am not concerned about the finances."

"Oh! Right. Thank you. You've been really generous." When Bran didn't respond, Daniel brought another spoonful of the soup up to his lips. His mind was cluttered with questions, but he felt too unsafe to be pushy about them. He tried one of the less antagonistic angles. "Craven Manor is a beautiful building. Did you inherit it or buy it?"

"I inherited. My surname is Myricks."

So he's related to Annalise. That could explain the interest in helping her ghost. "I thought this place was empty when I first arrived. Have you lived here for long?"

"Some time, yes, though I do not spend all of my hours in the house." Bran's shoe scraped across the rug as he adjusted his position again. Daniel suspected something was causing him discomfort—possibly arthritis or a kind of chronic pain.

He had one more pressing question but struggled to find an easy way to bring it up. He broke the bread roll in half and painted it with butter as he gathered his thoughts. "I'm guessing Annalise is the reason you wanted me to lock my door and shut the window after midnight. You didn't want me to know the manor is, uh..." There was no tactful way to say it. "Haunted."

"Hah." Again, the raspy, grating laugh put Daniel's nerves on edge. "You are correct. Annalise can become curious. Though you seem to have accepted her presence with considerable grace."

Daniel managed an awkward shrug, even though he knew Bran wouldn't see it. "I've always been open to the idea of ghosts.

I've never seen one before, though." He tore pieces off the roll. "Is there anything I should...or could...be doing to help her?"

"Her state is intractable. There is no help to offer, save for preserving the places she is fond of. Her crypt. Her gardens." Bran paused, and again, the leather seat creaked. "You are aware of her condition?"

"The sun allergy? Yeah."

"During life, she was unable to leave the house during the day but thrived under the moonlight. From what I understand, the gardens were her sanctuary. While inside the house, she was smothered by her mother's will. But Eliza Myricks did not like venturing into the gardens. So the outside world became a sanctuary to the girl. That is a mentality she has preserved in death, it seems."

"Her ghost doesn't come into the house?"

"No, never."

Daniel was crumbling the half-eaten bread between his fingers. "She doesn't live in the tower?"

It took Bran a second to answer. When he did, he sounded tired. "No. I do not mind your straying through the manor, but stay away from the tower. That is one rule that, if broken, would be unforgiveable."

The image of the figure standing at the window flitted through Daniel's mind. *Is it where Bran lives? But if so, why are the locks on the door's outside? He couldn't be hiding someone else in the tower, could he?*

Daniel sensed he didn't have long left to speak with the house's owner. He latched on to one question that had been disturbing him since he'd seen the girl's crypt. "How did Annalise die? Did you say her mother did something to her?"

"Yes. Eliza Myricks's insanity spiraled deeper with every passing year. When Annalise's doctor tried to offer Eliza some medicine, he was summarily dismissed. One of her brooches went missing, and she chased the entire staff out of the building with a knife. You may have seen their unfinished work scattered through this wretched house. Finally, when it was just her and Annalise trapped together, the weight of her paranoia rested on the child. She began to imagine Annalise was a witch and that the aversion to sunlight was a sign from heaven that the girl was unholy."

Daniel waited, a full spoon hovering above the bowl, for Bran to continue, but the only sounds came from the crackling fireplace and the occasional hiss of a candle.

Then Bran sighed, and a deep, overwhelming weariness infused his rasping voice. "She burned Annalise on a pyre."

The spoon, still full, dropped back into his bowl. Daniel pressed a hand over his mouth. He pictured the girl in the painting, wide eyes and the hint of a smile, with terror infused under the surface. "That's horrible."

"It was. And I believe it is the reason Annalise has not been able to find rest. Violent deaths in this area tend to leave marks. If you will excuse me, I will bid you good night, Mr. Kane. I find I have grown weary."

The door creaked. Daniel hadn't even heard the man rise, but he swiveled to watch him leave. He was just in time to see the back of a dark coat disappear through the doorway and into the foyer's oppressive gloom. "Wait! There's one last thing—a cat lives here—it's very thin—"

"Do not mind the cat. It cares for itself." The voice had grown faint, and its echoes bounced so badly that Daniel couldn't tell which direction Bran had taken. He rose out of his chair and went to the foyer door, but his companion had already disappeared.

"Okay. Good night. And, uh, thank you for taking the time to talk to me." Daniel rested a hand on the open door and exhaled. Talking with Bran had been one of the most stressful experiences of his recent life.

At least he gave me some answers. Poor Annalise. Burned alive—I can't imagine how horrific that must have been.

The warm soup and bread roll waited for him in the dining room, but Daniel had lost his appetite. He collected the plates and bowl then went to the kitchen to wash them. He didn't want to leave the cleaning up to Bran. He hadn't been able to place his employer's age, but he certainly wasn't young, and just a few minutes of speaking had exhausted him.

As he rinsed the last of the crumbs off his plate, his thoughts drifted back to the tower. Bran hadn't given him an answer about who lived up there, although Daniel was sure he'd seen a face through the window.

It's all so strange. Bran isn't a ghost, and yet he lives in a house that is, essentially, unlivable. No electricity, water hasn't been run through the taps in years, no garbage collection. And no grocery deliveries until Joel was hired shortly before I was.

Bran had said he didn't spend all of his hours in the house. For all Daniel knew, he might walk in from town every day. Or he could even have another building on the property, though Daniel suspected he would have found it by then.

All the towels in the kitchen were decayed, so Daniel shook the plates and cutlery until they were mostly dry. He tried not to think about the cooks and maids being chased out of the room by their knife-wielding mistress.

What would she have looked like? Would her hair be fine and light, like Annalise's? Was she also tall and thin? When transferring bones into the new grave, he'd seen scraps of clothing tangled in the dirt. It might have been the decay dying them black, but Daniel could very easily imagine the demented woman clothing herself in dark colors. It would have matched her décor style. The house held an air of elegance and refinery, but in a cold, unkind way, as though it judged every person to step through its doors and could show a level of malicious spite toward anyone it deemed unworthy.

Daniel went back to the dining room, unfolded the napkin, and placed the still-wet plates and cutlery onto it. He wasn't sure if the plates belonged to Bran or to Joel, but either way, they were ready for collection.

The fireplace where Bran had sat was dead and cold, as though it had never been lit in the first place. Daniel gave it a wary glance then blew out all of the candles in the room except for one of the candelabras from the table's center. Night had set in, and clouds choked the moon, so he hoped Bran wouldn't mind him borrowing a light.

As he passed through the foyer, he felt eyes following him. He scanned the shadows and found the cat near the ancient chairs. It sat pin-straight, its tail tucked around its bony paws, as his candlelight reflected off unblinking eyes.

"Why aren't you eating, little buddy?" Daniel stopped a few feet away from the cat and knelt to speak to it. "Bran said not to worry about you, but that doesn't seem right. You're too thin."

The cat stared at him, unmoving. He held a hand out as an invitation for pettings, but it ignored the offer. *Maybe it has some digestive problem. It could be on a very specific diet. After the concern Bran has shown toward Annalise, I can't imagine he would neglect a cat like this.*

A shiver ran through the animal, and it shuffled its paws and tail even more tightly together. Daniel had the benefit of a jacket, but even with his layers, he could feel how cold the air was. And it would only get worse as the night progressed.

"Bran?" He raised his voice to be heard through the building. "Bran, your cat's cold. Is it—I mean—would you let me light a fire for it, please?"

His words echoed back at him then died out. He stayed crouched by the cat for a moment, and when a response didn't come, he shuffled toward the stack of kindling left beside the fireplace.

"He didn't say no, so that's basically a yes, right?" Daniel grinned at the cat. Its ears twitched in his direction, though it refused to turn its head. "Yeah, I reckon it is."

Daniel brushed dust off the kindling, stacked it in the grate, and struggled with the flint to get it lit. The cat didn't move until heat started to emanate from the fire, then it rose and crept closer to the flames.

"You're so thin, little buddy," Daniel whispered. He reached out to run a hand over the cat's head. Its hackles rose, and its jaws parted in a furious hiss. Daniel withdrew his hand. "Okay. No touching. I understand."

He sat beside the cat for a few minutes, enjoying the fire's warmth and the animal's company. The cat mellowed under the heat, and its amber eyes drifted into a contended squint. The tail unfurled from around its paws and twitched lazily at its side.

"Bran should really take better care of you," Daniel murmured. "He's such a strange person. In every aspect. I mean, the guy's named after a breakfast cereal, for crying out loud."

The cat didn't show any appreciation of Daniel's humor, though it did blink at the flames lazily.

At the back of his mind, Daniel was aware that time was passing. He didn't want a repeat of the previous night. Bran had seemed relatively unfazed by the after-hours trespassing, but Daniel didn't want to push his luck. He got to his feet slowly to avoid disturbing the cat, then fetched his candlestick and slipped through the open door.

Shifting feathers told him the crows lurked, unseen, above his head. He looked up, but all he could make out were layers of black. Crows, dead branches, and night sky jumbled into a colorless kaleidoscope, and he shivered as he hurried through the garden. A speck of rain hit his cheek, followed by another tapping on his forearm, and Daniel exhaled in relief as he slipped into his cottage and locked the door.

Sleep came easily that night, but his dreams were unsettling. He pictured himself dragging bones out of the earth, only there were too many to belong to just one body. Skulls, femurs, and endless ribs broke free from the soil. He threw them behind himself and dug deeper. They were never-ending. Soon, he was on his stomach, arms stretched deep into the abyss he'd carved in the ground, and still, the brittle human remains went deeper.

Daniel snorted as he woke and rolled onto his side. A low-level stress headache pulsed behind his temple. He rubbed a hand across his face and shivered; he'd been too tired to light a fire before going to bed, and the cottage was frigid.

Something scrabbled at the wooden door. Daniel rubbed sleep out of his eyes. He'd been expecting to hear more of Annalise's questioning taps, but this held none of her previous patience or curiosity. It sounded like fingers on wood, drawn over the same place again and again until the nails were worn down to stubs and the flesh was bleeding. It spoke of mindless terror. An all-consuming urgency.

Daniel threw his covers away and pulled boots over his chilled feet. He went to the door and touched his palm against the wood. It shuddered as the clawing increased in speed and harshness. He backed away.

The sound refused to stop. Its echoes surrounded him until he began to feel as though he would never escape them. Scared by the thought of what he might see but helpless to do anything else, he crossed to the window and pulled back the curtain.

The scrabbling ceased immediately. Daniel held his breath as he bent closer to the glass. The space outside the front door was empty. He frowned. "Then what—"

A hand slammed into the glass near his face. Daniel gasped as he jerked away from it. Annalise appeared there, her sightless eyes bulging and her hair coursing around her face as though a harsh wind whipped at it.

Her mask of sweet civility had broken. In its place was raw dread. Her lips stretched open, and every muscle in her face twitched as she tried to scream. It was the expression of a drowning person, someone so mad with terror that they would kill to gain one single gulp of air.

Daniel couldn't look away. *What happened to her?*

Annalise beat her open palm against the window once then threw the hand back to point to Craven Manor. Daniel squinted as he approached the window, and fear squeezed at his thundering heart. A fire's glow was visible over the trees.

WHEN I LEFT THE *mansion, the only light came from the fire I'd lit in the foyer. Did it catch on the furniture? Has it spread? Have I burned Craven Manor to the ground?*

Daniel's mouth was too dry to speak. He looked back at Annalise. She clutched at the window, her fingers scrabbling uselessly against the glass and her eyes round with sick fear. Then, in a heartbeat, she vanished. Daniel pressed a hand to the place he'd last seen her touch. It felt like ice.

Daniel didn't have a cell phone, and no landline ran to the manor. He could race to town, but it would take at least half an hour to get there, and even then, the fire trucks wouldn't be able to get through the forest. *How much would be left of Craven Manor by the time they reached it? A handful of embers decorating its charred hull, most likely.*

A new thought hit him. *Did Bran spend the night in the house?*

The man was elderly and frail, and the mansion vast. There was no guarantee that he would have been able to get himself out.

Please, please, let it not be too late. Daniel snatched his coat off the hook beside the door as he dashed outside. Spits of rain hit him, but there weren't enough to put out a fire. He prayed the clouds would give up their burden in earnest before the house was consumed.

How will I even find him inside that labyrinth? Or the cat, for that matter—the place seems to go on forever. I could spend hours in it and not see every room.

He shook his head to clear the panic and focused on the golden glow cast across the treetops. It wasn't too bright. The fire might still be small. If it was contained to one or two rooms, he might even be able to put it out. And the walls were built out of stone, which would slow the flames' spread.

Daniel burst into the patch of clear ground ahead of Craven's entryway. His momentum stalled. There was no sign of smoke pluming into the sky, and no bitter tang of charcoal in the air. The windows were intact. He couldn't hear the snapping roar of uncontrolled flames.

And yet half of the building was lit up. Everywhere he looked, golden light poured out of the windows. It illuminated the crows in the tree. They were shuffling and bickering with discomfort.

"What…" *Is Bran lighting every lamp in the house? What for? And if there's no fire, why was Annalise so frantic?*

His urgency replaced with caution, Daniel climbed the steps to the entryway. The foyer door stood open as always, inviting him inside.

The fire in the hearth had been allowed to die into coals. There was no sign of the little black cat. But the sconces around the wall had been lit. They bathed the area in a level of definition Daniel had never seen before. Cobwebs seemed to glimmer, and the massive chandelier helped refract some of the glow into sparkling lights across the ceiling.

Annalise's portrait surveyed the scene from the top of the stairs. She was fully illuminated, and he found it hard to look away from the muted panic in her eyes.

Noises came from higher in the building. Daniel approached the stairs and hesitated with his fingers resting on the dust-smothered bannister. They weren't the house's normal sounds. He heard footsteps followed by doors banging open. The sound of objects hitting the floor. Then more quick, heavy footsteps.

Daniel began to climb. Annalise's eyes never left him, and he had to force himself to look away. When he reached the landing, he found the hallways' lights had been lit. Their doors were propped open, and more of the candlelight flooded out of them. Daniel had grown used to seeing the building closed up and silent, like a shrine to a long-dead family. In a strange way, it was physically distressing to see the light bring all of its faults and neglect into such sharp relief.

The clattering, scraping clamor continued along the third-floor hallway. Daniel turned toward the second flight of stairs, wet his lips, and called, "Hello!"

The sounds ceased. Daniel hung in suspense for a moment then called again, "Bran? Is everything all right?"

Pounding steps moved along the hallway, then a face, flushed and sweaty with exertion, appeared at the top of the stairs. "Ha!" Kyle crowed. "You finally made it!"

He struck a pose at the top of the stairs, one hand planted on his hip and the other extended in a flourish.

"Wha—what are you doing here?" Daniel felt as though his world might collapse. He moved up a stair but stopped before he could get any closer. Kyle carried a satchel on his side, as well as a backpack, and he'd worn dark clothes.

Kyle's face scrunched up. "Come on, are you really that dumb? I've come to have a poke around. See if there are any souvenirs I like."

Oh no. No, no, no. Daniel's eyes darted to the backpack and satchel. They were half full. "You can't take this stuff. Put it on the ground and leave."

Kyle's smiled dropped, and his face darkened. "I knew you were going to be a pain in the ass about this. I could see it in your face last night; you weren't really going to ask your buddy Mr. Pen Pal about getting me a job, were you?"

"I-I will! I was going to write him a letter!"

The slant of Kyle's eyes suggested he didn't believe Daniel. "I thought we were friends. But friends are supposed to look out for each other."

"Friends don't steal from other friends' employers," Daniel hissed. He took another step closer. "I'm not playing around. You need to get out of here. Right now."

Kyle made a scoffing noise then spat a globule of phlegm

onto the floor. "You said it yourself. This place is abandoned. Its owner is AWOL. Who cares if a bit of stuff goes missing? He should thank me for clearing out some of his trash. Pretty much everything here is garbage, anyway."

Daniel felt physically sick. He rubbed sweaty palms against his jeans. "The house isn't abandoned. I met the owner, and he really lives here. Please, you can't let him find you."

For a second, his cousin's cockiness wavered. Then Kyle glanced along the hallway, and the smug grin was back in place. "Bull. No one lives here. It looks like something out of a kids' Halloween attraction with all of its spiders and broken furniture."

"I'm telling the truth." Another step. He was close enough to smell the hint of alcohol hanging around Kyle. "We had dinner. Bran told me about the house; he's one of the original family's descendants. This is theft, and I know you're not a thief. Please, just leave. You'll get me fired—or jailed."

"I always thought you were a sneak, Dan." Kyle adjusted the satchel as his lips twisted into a grimace. "Always looking for a leg up. Always trying to find something to squeeze out of people. I bet you've been selling stuff out of this house yourself, haven't you? That's where all your money came from. It's not some weird old geezer who hired you to trim his garden. You found an empty house, decided to take the loot for yourself, and cooked up some cock-and-bull story to throw me off the scent. And I wouldn't have ever figured it out if I hadn't followed you."

Kyle hadn't shown such a level of meanness in months, not since the last time he'd spent a weekend binge drinking. Daniel studied his cousin's stance and saw it was slightly off-center. Kyle wasn't completely wasted, but he hadn't come to the mansion sober, either.

"You seriously followed me?"

"Psheah, last night. You were drunk off your ass and staggering all over the place, so I thought I'd keep an eye on you and make sure you got home okay. Only thing is you got lost in that stupid forest. It took me ages to find my way out again."

I thought I heard leaves crunching. I can't believe he stalked me here. It can't have been from altruism, either—otherwise he would have walked alongside me. Which means he followed me to find out where the house was.

Daniel climbed the last two steps and took Kyle's arm. "You need to get out of here before Bran finds you. And you need to leave me and my job alone."

Kyle's face was expressionless. For a second, Daniel thought he might comply with the demands. Then he threw his body weight into Daniel and charged him into the nearest wall.

Daniel's skull hit the red wallpaper, and he heard a crack. Pain shot through his head, sparking from the back and into the left temple. His vision turned blurry, and he barely noticed that the wind had been forced out of him as he crumpled to the floor.

"Tell me where it is," Kyle hissed. He knelt at Daniel's side and ran his hand over his hair in a mock caress. Daniel tried to recoil, but Kyle fixed on a fistful of hair and tightened his grip until the pain multiplied.

"Stop—"

"The gold coins, Daniel. Same as the one you were flaunting last night. I know there has to be more of them."

"Not—no—" He tried to roll onto his back, but Kyle's grip kept his head planted into the decayed rug. Dust filled his nose and stung his eyes. "I don't—Bran gave them to me—"

"You're a pathetic liar, Dan." Kyle pushed away.

Daniel lifted a hand to his head. It felt as though someone had started a fire that licked across his skull. When he took his fingers away, he saw a smear of red on them.

Kyle had stopped at the top of the landing and was staring down the stone pathway opposite. His eyes narrowed as he glanced up and down the tar-black door at its end. "What's through there?"

"Don't."

His cousin's lips curled into a crooked smile. "They wouldn't lock it if there wasn't something valuable inside, right? Hang tight, buddy. This won't take long."

Daniel rocked to his knees. His vision blurred, and he planted a hand on the wall beside himself to keep steady. "Kyle, no! I won't forgive you for this!"

"Sure you will. I'll split the loot fifty-fifty with you. How about that?" Kyle's singsong voice floated down the hallway. Daniel heard a heavy metallic clang that sounded like a boot hitting one of the rusted bolts. "It's more than you did for me."

"Stop! We can't open that door." He tried to get his feet underneath himself, but they collapsed and plunged him back to the carpet. The fire across his head burned. He heard a second heavy clang followed by a third and what sounded like broken metal being thrown aside.

As Daniel tried to blink the blurred lights out of his eyes, he became aware that he wasn't alone. A presence had entered the hallway behind him. It was something that was intended to be felt rather than seen, and its strength was enough to send a shudder through him. He instinctively knew who it was. *Bran.* Daniel tried to stand again. "Kyle! Get out, damn you!"

A fourth clang and a muffled curse came from the tower door. Something moved past Daniel. It looked like a shadow flitting across his fuzzy vision, and it disappeared down the stone passageway before he could fix on it.

Kyle choked then screamed. It was a horrific noise. Daniel fought the vertigo as he tried to reach his cousin. He staggered into the wall but managed to remain upright.

There was movement. Something tall and dark wrenched his cousin out of the hallway. Daniel had a half-second impression of Kyle's face, contorted in shock and fear, as he grappled with the arms around his neck. They passed Daniel in a flash and disappeared through one of the open bedroom doorways. Daniel lurched after them, but the door slammed in his face. "Kyle!"

He could hear sounds of a struggle inside the bedroom, with Kyle spitting curses and sharp yelps of pain. Daniel grabbed the door handle and tried to turn it, but it was locked. Kyle screamed again. Glass smashed. And then silence.

The door drifted open as though its latch had never caught. Daniel stared into the bedroom, shock and fear thundering through him and drenching him in cold sweat. Rich browns and reds shone under their coating of dust, as the lamps illuminated the room's furniture. Cupboard doors and drawers hung open from Kyle's earlier scavenging.

Daniel's own pale face stared back at him from a cracked mirror opposite the bed. A trickle of blood ran from his temple. He touched his finger to it as he stepped into the room.

Kyle was gone. As was Bran. The window had been broken. Jagged shards of glass ringed the hole. Daniel moved closer and saw a smear of red on one of the glass fragments.

Breathing was impossible. His vision was still blurry, but it had become further distorted by fear-induced tears. Daniel passed his head through the hole in the glass and looked downward. Kyle's body lay three floors below, cradled in a mess of dead bushes.

CHAPTER 14

"NO, NO, NO, NO, *no.*" Daniel's heart thumped, skipped a beat, then thumped again. He pressed a hand to his chest. He felt dizzy and sick, but he couldn't stop staring at his cousin's still form in the garden below.

Dull pain radiated through his fingers. He realized too late that he'd rested his hand on the windowsill, over shards of broken glass, and blood trickled down to drip off his wrist. He pulled his hand back and clenched it.

Bran was nowhere to be seen. The curtains rolled inward as a cold wind slipped through the window. Shadows gathered in the room's corners, impervious to both the lamplight and the moonlight. There was no motion or sound, not even breathing.

This can't be real. Daniel's legs were unsteady as he stumbled into the hallway and toward the stairs. He was dripping blood onto the carpet but was barely aware of the pain in his hand. He felt as though he'd been sucked into a horrible, otherworldly nightmare, the kind that would leave him with phobias even decades later. It was almost inconceivable to think that he was awake.

Leaves skittered across the tile foyer floor as he ran through them. He was breathless, but not from exertion. His chest felt as though someone had wrapped an enormous rubber band around it, and every inhalation was fighting against that resistance.

Daniel leaped down the porch's steps. He'd misjudged the distance, and his feet skidded out from under him. He hit the ground, pushed away from it, regained his footing, and raced around the house's exterior.

As a child, Daniel had gone to school with a boy called Adrian. The boy's father worked with the police and apparently shared a lot of stories with his son. Adrian liked to shock the other children with them during lunch.

According to Adrian, his father had attended a lot of suicides, especially for people who had leaped from the tops of buildings. He'd called them "jumpers." The name had seemed painfully flippant to Daniel, almost as if it were intended as a joke.

He remembered Adrian beckoning everyone at his cafeteria table closer, a gap-toothed grin promising dark secrets beyond what their imaginations could handle. He'd said the jumpers didn't stay whole when they hit the sidewalk. They burst like water balloons. Blood and brain matter would spray all over the sidewalk. The council had to use industrial hoses to clean the matter off.

The image of a human popping had always hung with Daniel. Maybe it had stayed with Adrian, too; he himself had leaped from a building a few weeks before his eighteenth birthday. Logically, Daniel knew depression or anxiety could target anyone, but he couldn't stop from thinking that the policeman's nightmare-fuel stories had never left Adrian's head. They would have crammed themselves in there, growing bigger and blacker with every passing year, until death looked like the only escape.

Popped like a water balloon. Daniel tasted bile. He wanted to scream. He never should have shown Kyle the coin, never even given him money. He'd wanted to share his luck with the man who had helped him. But Kyle had paid a horrific price.

Daniel slowed as he neared the scene, gasping against the rubber-band sensation. He felt numb all over; not even the cuts on his hand hurt anymore. The broken window was visible three floors above. Glass fragments had been thrown across the weed-choked ground, and one crunched under Daniel's shoe. It took him a moment to find Kyle's body.

He wasn't lying on the ground like Daniel had expected. There was no halo of blood, no popped human balloon. He'd crashed into a tangle of half-dead shrubs, and even after he'd crushed them, they still held him nearly three feet off the ground.

The bushes were thorny, though. Daniel struggled through them to reach his friend. He was faintly aware of scratches, but it was easy to ignore them as he reached between the tangles to touch Kyle's cheek.

He was warm. Daniel had to remind himself that Kyle had fallen only a few minutes before, so warmth was no guarantee of life. And the lack of response wasn't a good sign.

Kyle lay on his back, his head thrown to one side. Blood dripped from cuts across his arm, face, and torso where the glass had sliced him. The bushes cradled him awkwardly.

Daniel moved his hand lower to feel for a pulse in Kyle's neck. His fingers were numb with shock, and his mind was so frantic that he couldn't differentiate reality from what he *wanted* to feel. Desperate, he rose onto his toes and held his hand an inch above Kyle's open mouth. Warm, moist breath ghosted over his fingers.

He's still alive. Daniel stepped back as giddiness and fresh adrenaline made him unsteady. *It's a borderline miracle.*

The broken window seemed impossibly high. The overgrown bushes were probably the only thing that had saved Kyle from sharing Adrian's fate.

Focus, Daniel. He's alive, but you don't know for how much longer. Blood continued to drip from Kyle's arm and face. He needed medical attention…but Daniel had no phone. He could run to town, but that meant leaving Kyle alone—and not just alone, but alone with Bran, who had thrown him through a window. It would take him half an hour to get to town, even if he ran. That was an unacceptably long time to leave his friend bleeding.

Wait, Kyle owns a cell phone. Did he bring it with him?

Daniel pushed forward again, fighting through the brittle branches, and searched Kyle's pockets as carefully as his shaking fingers allowed. There was a solid lump in the back of the man's jeans. Daniel fished inside the pocket and pulled out the phone. He thanked his lucky stars that Kyle hadn't left it at home.

He dialed the emergency help number with shaking fingers

but stopped before putting the call through. They would ask for his address, and he didn't even know it. Telling them to "turn right at the old oak" would be useless, doubly so when the path couldn't fit an ambulance and the intermittent paving stones were near invisible at night.

But other than myself and Bran, no one else knows how to get to the house. Daniel's head snapped up. *Wait, that's not true—there's Joel.*

Daniel erased the emergency help number with one hand and hunted through his jacket's pockets with the other. He'd tucked the note there when the deliveryman had given it to him, and Joel had promised that he kept his phone next to him at night. He also had a truck that could get most of the way to Craven Manor.

Daniel stayed at Kyle's side, surrounded by the thicket and listening to the dripping blood, as he pressed the phone to his ear and prayed he was making the right choice.

Daniel sat in the hospital waiting room. He felt lost. He'd been diagnosed with a mild concussion, and the cuts on his hand had been stitched. He was officially discharged under instructions to rest, drink a lot of water, and return to the hospital if dizziness or nausea came back. But even though he was free to go, he stayed for Kyle.

The doctors had gone over his cousin's case notes with him.

They said his spinal column was intact. He would have scars from the lacerations. Scans showed he had some minor bleeding into his brain, but it had stopped by the time he reached the hospital. They had made the call not to perform surgery.

Daniel couldn't remember what he'd told the nurses when they asked what had caused the accident. They'd found the alcohol in Kyle's system and seemed to assume he'd fallen during a drunken stunt.

After Daniel had called him, it had taken a disheveled and bleary-eyed Joel thirty minutes to jog into sight. Between them, they had moved Kyle—who was, by then, half-aware and moaning—into the back of Joel's pickup truck. It had taken another twenty minutes to get to the hospital.

"*We're not sure what the bleeding will have done to his brain. There might be some damage.*" Daniel cradled his head in his hands as he ran through the doctor's words. The waiting room's lights were impossibly bright and made his migraine tenfold worse.

And because he was alone, all he had to do was think.

Bran had tried to kill Kyle. There was no way he could have thrown a man out of a window and realistically expected him to live. The intent had been murder. That knowledge was forcing Daniel to reassess everything he'd thought he knew about the man—not just the assumption that Bran was ultimately well meaning, but also the man's age and physical capabilities. Daniel wasn't small, but Kyle could beat him in a fight. Working construction had built up his cousin's muscles and endurance. And yet Bran had dragged him around like a rag doll.

But he sounded so frail. Was he faking? Daniel dug his fingers into his hair. The scalp still ached from where Kyle had gripped him. The memory of the assault was fresh in his mind, though he wasn't sure what to make of it. He and Kyle had always been friends—at least, that was what he'd thought. How could his cousin turn on him so suddenly and violently? Daniel hadn't lied to him or cheated him, and it stung that Kyle held so little trust in him.

It must have been the alcohol. He's not like this normally. Something got into him and bothered him—the stress of needing a new roommate, maybe—and he went out drinking. One thing led to another, and he ended up at Craven Manor in a bad mood and with his inhibitions removed.

The idea all made sense, except for one detail. Kyle had tried to follow him to the mansion the night before. That suggested premeditation.

The bustle had grown too much. Quick voices, intermittent beeps, and crying children crowded Daniel's mind. He stood, gathered his blood-speckled jacket, and stepped through the automatic doors.

Dawn was still an hour or two away. The air was cold enough to make his skin ache, but he couldn't bring himself to wear the bloodied jacket. Instead, he folded his arms around himself and began walking.

He regretted sending Joel away. The deliveryman had feigned liveliness as he sat next to Daniel in the waiting room, but Daniel could tell the missed sleep was hurting him. He'd sent him home after giving a promise to call if he needed help. Daniel still didn't have his own phone, though, and Kyle's phone was now tucked into the cupboard beside the sedated man's bed.

Daniel walked without having a direction. The streets were empty except for the occasional delivery van and a bakery's employee putting out a sign advertising early breakfast. Daniel stared at the sign then stepped into the café to buy breakfast with one of the twenty-dollar bills he'd tucked into his jacket pocket. He didn't feel hungry, but he knew the dizziness and headache would get worse without food. As he ate, he thought.

Kyle's apartment is only twenty minutes away from here. I still have the key. I could stay there for a few days while he's in the hospital and put some distance between myself and Craven Manor.

Daniel frowned as he chewed on a piece of toast. The thought was tempting, but would Kyle be angry? Technically, Daniel had paid Kyle for that month of rent. And he'd saved his life. Kyle couldn't object to Daniel staying there while he was in the hospital, could he?

It would give him somewhere to go other than the manor. He wasn't sure he wanted to go back there too quickly. Bran may have been provoked—Kyle was trespassing, stealing, and trying to open the one door Bran clearly wanted to keep shut—but Daniel was still alarmed by how quickly he'd turned to violence.

For that matter, Daniel wasn't sure if he was *welcome* back. He'd officially broken two of the three rules: don't stray outside after midnight and no strangers on the property. And Kyle had come very close to breaking the third rule: opening the tower door. *For all I know, Bran could throw me out of a window, too, if I try to go back to that place.*

That made his decision for him. Daniel paid for the breakfast, left the warmth of the bakery, and set up a brisk pace as he worked his way back to their apartment.

Scarce hints of sunrise lightened the horizon as he pushed on the apartment block's squeaky main door. The linoleum on the narrow stairs complained as he climbed them. His feet were still unsteady despite the food, and Daniel had to use the rail to keep his balance. It was sticky with years of grime, and loose bolts made it wobbly. He was back in the home for desperate people.

Why did Kyle have to come to Craven Manor? Daniel turned the stairwell's corner and continued climbing. Snores drifted through a door to his left. Someone else had apparently fallen asleep with the TV left on, and a laugh track played over indiscernible voices. *It was a good job. I enjoyed it. I felt like I was making a difference, even in a small way.*

The bronze 16 marking Kyle's apartment glinted in the flickering light. Daniel fished his key out of his jacket and pressed it into the lock. The door was always stiff, so when the key didn't immediately turn, Daniel fell to his usual routine of jiggling and twisting the metal. It took him a minute to realize the key wasn't just stuck. It didn't fit. Rather than the usual stained metal Daniel had become so used to, the lock was a shiny new silver. He withdrew the key and swallowed.

Kyle changed the locks on me.

Daniel tried to squash the feelings of hurt. Maybe the change hadn't been intended to keep him out. Fletch, the friend from the fast-food shop, had only stayed a day before moving on; maybe Kyle changed the locks to keep *him* out.

But deep down, he knew that wasn't true. Kyle didn't *have* a third copy of the key, so Fletch would have had to wait for Kyle to open the door, just like Daniel had during his first weeks at the apartment, until Kyle got around to making a duplicate. The locks had been switched to stop Daniel from re-entering the home.

When did it happen? Yesterday, the day after I told him about my job and showed him the coin? Or earlier, after I originally left?

Daniel turned and rested his back against the door. He ran a hand over his mouth. No matter the motive or the timing, it left him with nowhere to live.

Nowhere except Craven Manor.

He swore under his breath. He was left with no choice except to return, and he couldn't give Bran time to cool off, either. There would be no chance to send him letters of apology or to wait for an invitation back... Not unless he spent a few days homeless, and that wasn't an option.

He wasn't going back onto the streets. Because if he did, he was scared he would never leave them again.

CHAPTER 15

DANIEL CAME TO A stop outside Craven Manor's gates. He was breathless from the weight of the two canvas bags he carried, and grateful the day wasn't too warm. Even without a jacket, he was sweaty and overheated.

He felt as though he'd lived half a lifetime in the previous twenty-four hours. Discovering the skull, the bizarre dinner, then Kyle's attempted theft and hospitalization all swirled into a confusing array of images and emotions in his weary mind.

It took a lot of coordination to squirm through the gates. The bags were heavy and unwieldy. The rusted metal caught on his jeans, and he stumbled then corrected himself. Craven Manor's peaked roof was visible over the treetops, and the silhouette of a large crow was perched on its highest tiles.

Part of him expected to be confronted, maybe even chased away, as he wove through the overgrown gardens. Seeing the grounds cloaked in their usual sedentary calm was more than a little disorienting. It gave Daniel the impression that Craven Manor was trapped in a bubble, wholly concerned with only its own affairs and indifferent to the rest of the world.

He brushed away a curtain of gray vines and stepped into the small patch of clear ground around the mansion's entrance. The crows waited for him. He didn't think it was his imagination that they looked ruffled and offended as they huddled together. *I'm not the only one missing sleep.*

The front door was still open. Daniel wished he could take that as a sign of welcome, but he knew it was just the way Craven Manor was. Its door stayed open through storms and sleet, and Daniel's presence wouldn't change that.

He climbed the broad stone steps. An eddy of wind swept leaves ahead of him. He stopped just inside the door and scanned the floor and fireplace mantel for a letter. There wasn't any.

"Bran, I'm so sorry." He swallowed then spoke a little more loudly. "Kyle never should have come here. And…and I never should have told him about the house. It wasn't right."

He'd become so used to his host's silence that it wasn't surprising when the echoing words went unanswered. Daniel wished he had some way of knowing Bran had heard him. Maybe the mansion's owner had hidden himself away in some solitary corner of the house. He might even have left the house entirely. But Daniel prayed Bran had heard and that the silence meant he hadn't wholly rejected the apology.

The cat held its usual spot in front of the fireplace. It was shivering and refused to meet Daniel's eyes. The noise and commotion must have terrified it. Daniel made small, comforting noises as he crept toward the cat. "It's okay, little guy. You're safe. He won't be coming back."

There was enough kindling beside the fireplace that Daniel could start a new fire. He built it quickly—practice had made him more proficient at using the flint—and waited for the flames to catch on to one of the larger logs. The cat refused to turn but stayed with its back to the warmth. It shuffled its paws a little closer together, and a fresh tremor ran through it. Daniel wished he could cuddle it, but he knew that would only upset it more. Giving it a warm environment was the best he could do.

Daniel went back to his cloth bags and opened one. With the last of his wages, he'd bought three pots of white lilies from the town's garden center. He'd tried to match the species to the flowers he'd seen in Annalise's portrait.

One pot went onto the fireplace's mantel, between the partially melted candles. Daniel arranged it the best he could. The mirror above the mantel was fogged and had a long crack running through the glass, but it still highlighted some of the flowers and helped make the plant look fuller.

Daniel left the other two lilies on the floor and returned outside, where dark, pendulous clouds continued to mask the sky and created an imitation of twilight. Daniel circled the mansion and found the place where Kyle had landed. The plants had been partially crushed in the impact, and broken branches held spots of congealed sap.

He shouldn't have survived the fall. Daniel couldn't tear his eyes away from the bushes. *Three floors, and only these plants to cushion him. He's one of the luckiest men I know.*

Before carrying Kyle to the pickup truck, Daniel and Joel had unfastened his satchel and backpack and left them on the ground. The bags were only half-filled, but they still felt heavy. Daniel carried them back into the foyer and placed them on the fireplace's rug. The cat continued to shiver. Unable to give it further comfort, he settled for feeding a fresh log onto the fire then unzipped the backpack.

Kyle had been looking for anything valuable, but he didn't seem to have found much for all the searching he'd done. Some of the items he'd taken were the empty photo frames from above the fireplace. Daniel lifted them out, examined them for damage, and gave them a quick dust with his sleeve before placing them into the empty gaps between the dead branches, candles, and clock. He couldn't remember their order but hoped he'd managed okay. Even though they didn't hold any pictures or paintings, someone must have cared about them enough to keep them on display.

Most of the other stolen items weren't as easily identifiable. The candelabrum Kyle had taken was one of hundreds scattered through the house, and Daniel didn't know which room he'd snatched it from. He eventually placed it on the dining room table, near where he'd had dinner the night before. The tabletop was still dusty except for a small patch where Daniel's plate and napkin had smudged it away.

The rest of Kyle's stash amounted to three necklaces, a pair of diamond earrings, and two hairbrushes. They must have come from one of the bedrooms. Daniel didn't feel wholly right about going deeper into the house, and for a second, he considered leaving the jewels in the foyer. But that seemed even more disrespectful. Daniel glanced between the leaf-littered ground and the grand staircase and finally resolved on searching for the room.

The stairs groaned as he climbed them. The house had returned to its usual wash of shadows; either Bran had extinguished the lamps and candles Kyle had lit, or they had burned themselves out during the night. Annalise's portrait watched his motions, but the eyes looked no less fearful than they had the night before.

Daniel turned left on the first landing and looked inside the closest guest room. Kyle had pulled bureau drawers open and thrown their contents over the floor. Daniel tightened his lips, then he hoisted the satchel over his shoulder and began righting the drawers.

The room didn't hold much—just spare linens and a set of dresses that had decayed into rags. The smell of rotting fabric made Daniel sneeze as he tucked the last of the items away and closed the drawers. He went through the other open doors, righting overturned furniture and packing scattered blankets back into their cupboards.

Kyle had torn apart most of rooms on that floor. Daniel was surprised at the thoroughness; his cousin must have been in the house for at least an hour before Annalise woke him.

Partway through straightening the fourth room, he began to wonder how much he was actually helping. The cloths were all rags, and most of the furniture was collapsing, too. If anyone wanted to inhabit Craven Manor, most of its insides would need to be thrown out.

But Bran still lives here…even if it's just part-time. He seems to care about the house. Seeing it torn apart like this is going to smart, even if the items are worthless.

Daniel worked through the floor methodically. Glimpses through collapsing curtains showed him different views of the garden. Daniel found himself appreciating the property more and more. Trees and vines pressed close to the glass, but he thought its garden must have been designed thoughtfully to provide every room with an attractive view.

Once he'd righted as much as he could on the second floor, Daniel turned toward the third with growing reluctance. He'd begun to suspect he knew where the jewels had come from.

Bran had said Eliza Myricks had been so paranoid that she'd chased her staff out of the house. She certainly wouldn't have had guests, in that case, and Annalise was too young to own such jewelry. They must have been Eliza's.

Daniel bypassed the hall that led to the tower's door and turned right. Only two doors hung open there; the first was the room Kyle had been thrown out of, and the second led him into a woman's opulent bedchamber.

He had no doubt who had owned the room. Eliza Myricks had commissioned a painting of herself, which hung on the wall above her bed. As large as Annalise's, the portrait was no less striking. Daniel approached it cautiously.

She looked like a proud woman. High cheekbones and full lips gave the impression of beauty, but a tightness around her eyes and brows hinted at viciousness. She posed like a queen, seated, hands clasped in her lap and her head inclined slightly toward the viewer. Her black hair had been tied into an elegant knot. The only hint of resemblance between her and her daughter was the paleness of their skin.

Daniel looked into the satchel he held. An elaborate diamond necklace inside matched the jewels Eliza wore in her portrait. He turned toward the bureau and found gaps in the dust.

"I'm sorry." He spoke to the shadows as he replaced the necklaces, earrings, and hairbrushes. Eliza's eyes seemed to bore into his back as her visage judged him silently. Kyle had gotten only as far as her second drawer before he'd been interrupted, and Daniel put things back into their places as best he could.

Poor Annalise. Eliza must have been a difficult parent to please.

Daniel briefly wondered if he would find Annalise's room somewhere on the third floor, but he'd already overstepped his bounds more than he was comfortable with. The satchel and backpack were empty, so he threw them over his shoulder and returned to the hallway, shutting Eliza's door behind himself.

Only one area of damage remained, and it was the one Daniel had been most nervous about approaching. He squared his shoulders as he returned to the landing, then he faced the stone passageway that led to the tower's door.

CHAPTER 16

KYLE HADN'T SUCCEEDED IN breaking open the door, but he'd gotten close. Three of the four locks lay in a heap on the floor, and the wood they'd been bolted to was splintered. The final bolt, a narrow bronze shape, had been kicked until two of its screws came out. It hung in place, but only barely. Daniel could have pulled it off with his bare hands.

Daniel approached the structure. A barely audible sound came from behind the wood. It reminded him of the noise Annalise had made at his door the previous night. Fingernails dragging across wood.

His throat tightened. Underneath the scrabbling was an urgent gasping noise. Daniel frowned as he bent closer, breath held, and grazed the tips of his fingers over the door.

He could feel the scrape of nails against wood as something scrabbled to get out. His eyes drifted toward the broken locks littering the ground. They were frozen with rust. *No one's opened this door in over a hundred years. Whatever is inside the tower isn't alive anymore.*

A wheezing whine escaped the being on the other side of the door. The scrabbling grew louder. He could feel the trajectory; the nails scraped from a space just above his head down to waist length, over and over and over again, as they tried to dig their way free.

The strange crystals he'd noticed the first time he saw the door still sparkled on the ground, but they weren't as neat as they had been. It took him a second to realize what had happened: Kyle had scuffed them in his efforts to break through the door. Instead of running in a clear line along the wood's base, the delicate structures had been broken and smudged.

Another whine floated through the wood. Daniel pulled away. Shivering, he folded his arms around himself then jogged back down the hallway and into the closest room. He found a chair beside the bed. It was made of wood, and its structure was still sound, so he carried it back down the stone hallway and placed it so that its back was jammed below the door's handle. It was a sad substitute for a real lock, but he hoped it would help.

Bran was prepared to kill to keep whatever is in the tower inside. I'll have to trust that there's a good reason for that.

As Daniel moved down the stairs to the foyer, he rolled a word around in his mind. *Trust.* He'd trusted Kyle, and his cousin had taken advantage of it and tried to destroy Daniel's new life for the sake of personal gain. Kyle was his cousin, a man he'd thought was his friend, and had been his roommate for six months. Bran was a stranger, a man whose face he'd never seen. Daniel prayed he wasn't being a fool for putting his trust in his peculiar, dangerous employer.

The cat had left its seat by the fire. Daniel scanned the foyer for it, but it must have either gone upstairs or found somewhere to hide. He placed an extra log on the flames to give the cat some warmth if it returned, then he left Kyle's satchel and backpack folded neatly by the door.

"Bran, again, I'm sorry for what happened. If there's anything I can do to make this right, tell me. Or, uh, write a note or something." He felt like a fool, yelling into the seemingly deserted house. This time, he didn't even wait for a reply before picking up the cloth bag of potted lilies and moving into the garden.

His progress on the path between the manor and Annalise's grave hadn't gotten far, but days of walking between them had begun to wear a patch in the weeds, making it easier to find his way. He felt tired down to his bones, but he wanted to do one more thing before returning to the cottage. The ground outside the crypt was bare without the thorny bushes he'd torn away, and he wanted to fill it with something beautiful.

He knelt in the soft ground around the stones and dug holes with his bare hands. He separated the lilies out of their pots, working the roots free gently, and tucked them into their new homes.

"This will look nice." He sat on his heels to admire the result. The lush lilies and dark ivy contrasted beautifully, and the effect would only improve as the plants grew.

A hint of color came from inside the crypt's seating area, and

Daniel rose to investigate it. Someone had placed a small bouquet of wildflowers below the door set into the back of the alcove. They were delicate and fragile, and the bunch held no more than five stems, but Daniel was moved by the sight. *Clearing this area wasn't just for Annalise's sake. Bran must visit her.*

He backed out of the tomb and entered the path leading back to the cottage. It was still early afternoon, but exhaustion and stress compounded on each other until he felt ready to drop. He washed quickly at his sink but couldn't muster the energy to light a fire before he fell into bed.

Tp, tp, tp.

Daniel groaned and rolled over. His neck and shoulders were stiff, and a throbbing headache pulsed behind his temple. It was hard to tell the time with the curtains blocking out the moon's angle, but he guessed there were still a few hours before morning. He'd slept a long while and felt dozy enough to fall back under.

Tp, tp, tp.

He sat upright as the noise and its significance penetrated his sleep-fogged mind. *Annalise.* He rolled out of bed, hunted for his shoes in the dark, then gave up and tiptoed across the cold floor to reach the window. He pulled the curtain back and found Annalise on the other side.

She was fainter than she'd been the night before, but at least there was no trace of the blind terror she'd worn. Colorless eyes stared up at Daniel, and her lips twitched into a mischievous smile. Then she sprang away, dancing between the trees, her long hair and dress floating behind her as though she'd been suspended into a world without gravity. The girl hid behind a tree. Long pale fingers crept around the edge of the trunk, followed by one side of her face as she peeked at him. Then she leaped away again. He thought she might be laughing.

Daniel grinned. "Came to say hello, did you? I hope you liked the flowers."

She darted in and out of the trees, sometimes drawing near before dancing away again. Daniel watched for a few minutes then went to light his fire and boil a cup of something warm. He guessed Annalise wanted to play and was trying to lure him into a game of hide-and-seek, but he wasn't sure Bran would approve of it, so he stayed in his cottage and contented himself with watching her through the window.

Who would have thought I'd live in a haunted garden…and not mind? Daniel rubbed his bare feet together to get some warmth into them as he sat beside the window. Annalise skirted around the house, occasionally tapping on the walls to tell him where she was. When she came close to the window, Daniel tapped back and was rewarded with a delighted grin. She pressed one hand against the glass, and Daniel watched in fascination as tiny splinters of frost spread away from her touch.

"You like Bran, don't you?" Daniel wasn't sure if she could hear or understand him, but he wanted to try communicating with more than just knocking.

The girl bit her lip and nodded. The motion was unguarded, and Daniel sipped at his drink. "You were frightened for him last night, weren't you? You were afraid he might be hurt."

The ghost tilted her head and squeezed her lips together.

He tried again. "Last night, when you woke me, you were scared that a stranger was in the house. You didn't like him."

Again, Annalise failed to give him an affirmative response. The joy had faded from her face, though, as though a bad memory had dispelled the happy energy. Daniel felt guilty for killing her playful delight. A theory had started to grow, though, and he pursued it.

"Or…were you afraid of what the man might do?" Daniel put his mug aside. "Were you scared he was going to open a door? Didn't you want him going into the tower?"

A glimpse of the previous night's terror flashed through the girl's eyes. She looked over her shoulder, toward the tower above the house, and Daniel followed her gaze.

Someone had lit a candle in Craven Manor's tower. Through the pale glow, he could see a figure pacing past the window, back and forward, back and forward, with even, measured steps. Suddenly, it stopped and turned, and he knew it was looking toward his cottage. A sickening sense of dread curled through his stomach.

"Who is it, Annalise?" He turned toward the girl, but she'd vanished. He was alone with the silhouette in the window, two strangers watching each other. Daniel tried to swallow, but the muscles in his throat didn't want to work. Instead, he yanked the curtain back into place to block the phantom's view.

It needs to stay trapped in the tower. Shivers had set in, and Daniel dragged his chair across the room to sit in front of the fire. He could feel the heat on his limbs, but it didn't permeate far and left his core thoroughly frozen. He remembered the fingers scratching at the door, back and forth, incessant and desperate. Daniel didn't like to think about what sort of creature needed four bolts to be contained…or what would happen since only one was left.

He stayed huddled over the fire until early dawn shed its rays across the closed curtains and his aching limbs and throbbing head pulled him back into sleep. He slipped in and out of consciousness, half falling out of his chair. When he finally shook himself out of his stupor, he found a note had been slid under his door.

CHAPTER 17

DANIEL PUSHED OUT OF his chair. He hadn't heard anyone approach the door, but he already knew who the note was from. The thick envelope and small neat letters spelling Daniel's name identified his employer like a fingerprint.

Though he could be my ex-employer by now. Daniel ran his fingers across his chin as he picked up the letter. It was weighty but held a single sheet of paper.

Daniel fished the note out. Heartache dropped his shoulders before he even read the words. There was no way a letter that short—only ten words—could be anything except a brusque dismissal.

He blinked blurred, stinging eyes as he struggled to read the tight cursive. When he finished, he read it again, confusion and doubt making him certain he'd misunderstood some part of it. Except there wasn't enough to misunderstand.

Mr. Kane,

Scatter salt across the tower door's threshold.

—Bran

Daniel blinked, pinched the bridge of his nose, then read the message a fourth time in case his eyes were playing tricks on him. *This is it? He's not even going to mention Kyle's robbery? No warnings, no recriminations, no forgiveness… Just a task that makes no sense?*

He wasn't going to complain. He still had his job, as far as he could tell, though it felt painfully precarious. He wished Bran had elaborated even just a little bit. Was he still planning to fire Daniel, but wanted to do it face-to-face? Or was his employer ignoring the invasion entirely?

Daniel made to slide the note back into its envelope, but it still held some weight. He squeezed the pocket open and found two gold coins inside.

No way. This means he really does intend to keep me, right? He'd already paid me for my first week here, now these must be the wages for the upcoming seven days. And he didn't even garnish them… How about that.

Daniel reverently placed the note on the desk before changing into warmer clothes and pulling on his boots. Despite the throbbing head and broken sleep, he felt invigorated.

He jogged to Craven Manor and didn't even care as drips of

freezing water fell off the branches and trickled through his hair. He leaped up the steps and into the foyer. His good mood was probably influencing his opinion, but the cobweb-coated space seemed a little less depressing than normal.

The black cat occupied its place by the fire. Only charcoal remained, but a hint of warmth still radiated from the hearth, and the cat was pressed as close as it could without sitting in the grate. It was curled into a tight little ball as it tried to conserve heat.

It might not like the food, but I can still curry its favor with warmth. Daniel knelt beside the cat and relit the fire. The cat peeked its eyes open to watch him but didn't try to move away.

"There we go, little guy." Daniel's fingers itched to scratch its head, but he resisted. *Baby steps.* "Your owner has let me live another day. He wants me to salt a door, which seems like a strange thing to do, but I'd gladly throw some pepper on it, as well, if he asked me to. Only problem—I have no idea if they keep salt in this place. I bet *you'd* know where to find it, wouldn't you?"

The cat's bones rippled under the fur as it adjusted its position. Daniel tried to smile, but the expression felt flat. He'd grown fond of the cat, but its malnourished state still disturbed him. It wasn't young. He'd heard that sometimes animals deliberately starved themselves when they grew too old, and he prayed that wasn't what was happening.

If I see Bran again, I'll talk to him about it. Maybe he'll let me take the cat to a vet.

Daniel stayed until the fire was strong enough to be left untended, then he lit a candle from the mantelpiece and went to look for salt.

In a worst-case scenario, he could bike to town, exchange one of the new coins for cash, and pick up a bag from the store. But it would save a lot of time if Craven Manor already had some.

He started his search in the most likely candidate, the kitchens. He found bags of weevil-devoured flour and oats, a bag of sugar, and small boxes of desiccated tea leaves, plus countless jars of preserves. Curious, he picked up one of the bottles. Its label had faded into illegibility, and when he swished it, an array of vague shapes swirled through a dark-amber liquid. They could have been severed toes for all he knew, and he put them back on the shelf.

The kitchens didn't hold any trace of salt, and Daniel spent a few minutes checking the surrounding rooms—the mess hall, the washing room, and the dining room—without luck.

He was resigned to walking to town when he caught sight of a narrow door in the back of the mess hall. He opened it, expecting to find a cupboard, and instead stepped into a small room filled with burlap sacks. Dark ink had been used to write SALT across their fronts, and Daniel lifted his eyebrows. There were half a dozen bags in the room, and each one was about as large as his torso.

That's a lot of salt. Maybe it snows during winter, and they used it to clear the road. Or maybe they just like really, really salty food.

He fetched a rusted knife from the kitchens and sliced a hole in the top of one of the bags. A crust had formed where moisture had leaked through the porous material, but once he broke through it, he found the salt underneath was still soft. He collected a saucepan that had survived the centuries of neglect and shoveled handfuls of salt into it.

Bran's request had been vague enough to make Daniel nervous. He worked best with explicit instructions that he could follow to the letter. Telling him to scatter salt across the tower's threshold left him with all sorts of questions, such as how much, where exactly, and the most obvious one—why? He erred on the side of caution and brought half a saucepan of the grainy substance.

Daniel held the saucepan in one hand and a candle in his other as he climbed the stairs. Shadows were progressing over the walls as morning transformed to afternoon. Darkness had fallen over Annalise's portrait again, and all Daniel could see of the image were the wide whites of her eyes.

He slowed as he reached the third floor's landing. Straight ahead were the short stone walkway and the black door with its broken locks and white cross. Even from where he stood at the top of the stairs, he could hear the scraping, scrabbling noise coming from the other side of the wood. The sense of foreboding crashed over him and tightened his chest until it was hard to draw air.

It will be fine. Go and season the door, just like regular people do all the time.

He stepped closer. The scraping had taken on a different cadence from the night before; it now held the cracking undertones of splintering wood. Daniel had a sudden mental image of the door being chipped down millimeter by millimeter by the unseen being's nails. How long until it dug through the door? And what would happen when it did?

He half ran the final three steps to the door. Desperation to do his job and get away from the nauseating hallway overwhelmed him.

He dropped to his knees and looked down. The line of glittering crystal formations was still visible in the low light, and realization clicked into place. Someone had poured salt there decades before, but moisture had melted it and re-formed it into the elaborate crystal structures. That gave him a guideline for his work, at least.

He dunked his hand into the salt and pulled out a fistful. Starting on the left side of the door, he dribbled a thick, unbroken line from the wall and across the passageway, trying to get it as close as he could to the base of the tar-black door.

The scratching noise changed. It became faster, harsher, fiercer. Hairs rose across the back of Daniel's neck as he ran his salt line to the opposite wall. He didn't stop until the white grains butted up against the stone, but he still held some of the powder in his fist. On an impulse, he threw it at the door.

The salt scattered against the dark wood, and a loud, gurgling, wailing sound emanated from behind it. Daniel pressed his hands against his ears to block it out, but the macabre scream had gotten inside his skull. He felt as though he would never escape from it. The noise was angry and grieving, and the emotions in it made him want to cower into a ball.

Then it faded, and the stone hallway was silent again. Daniel found he was panting. He knelt there for several minutes, waiting for the scratching to start up again, but the tower remained silent.

"Mr. Kane."

Daniel startled at his name and twisted to look behind himself. His candle lit only the few feet around him, but at the end of the hallway, in the juncture where the stairs' landing split into the hallways, he thought he could see a silhouette. "Hello?"

"Come and speak in my office. The room at the end of the hallway." The voice was too distinct to mistake. Bran's crackling, gasping voice sounded worse when magnified by the empty halls.

The silhouette turned and stepped out of sight.

Daniel's throat was too dry for his answer to be louder than a whisper. "Okay." Clutching his candle, he rose onto unsteady legs and trotted back to the crossroads. He couldn't see Bran. Daniel took a bracing breath then turned left, the direction Bran had vanished into.

Craven Manor's hallways seemed to extend for miles. Daniel knew it was only his racing pulse and stress that made them seem endless, but it was hard not to feel dwarfed by the patterned walls that squeezed on either side. In his candle's light, the open door at the end of the hall looked like an abyss. Even when he reached its threshold, his light couldn't penetrate more than a patch of the long-decayed rug covering the room's wooden floor. "Bran?"

"Enter."

He stepped inside and flinched as the door glided shut behind him. He didn't think it was his imagination that the candle had lost strength inside Bran's study. He caught glimpses of a bookcase full of rotting volumes on one wall and a cold fireplace on the other. A massive window—easily two arm-spans wide—took up the opposite wall, but its heavy drapes were drawn, blocking out the light. Daniel still couldn't see Bran.

"Light the fire. Then sit."

The words came out of the darkest corner of the room. When Daniel stared at it, he thought he saw the glint of two eyes. He quickly turned away and knelt on the hearth. His fingers shook. Even with bone-dry kindling and practice using flint, he struggled to start a fire.

"Ease your mind." The cracked voice hadn't lost its formality, but the tone sounded a fraction softer. "This discussion is for your benefit."

"Terrific," Daniel managed.

The kindling caught. He waited until the flames were large enough, then he placed a thin log on top. The two wingback chairs on the fireside rug were a long way through the decomposition process, but Bran had told him to sit, and Daniel still had concerns about how easily his body might sail through the massive window. He shuffled backward into one of the chairs.

A floorboard creaked as Bran paced behind him. Daniel dared to glance around the side of the chair, but the fire's light couldn't stretch any farther than his candle had.

Unnatural shadows. He shuddered and turned back to the flames. *There's something not right with this room.*

"I wish to speak with you on several topics," Bran said. "But most pressingly, the entity in the tower."

Daniel licked dry lips. "What is it?"

"My burden. My curse." Bran had drawn close without Daniel realizing. A change of tension in the chair's fabric told him Bran had placed his hand on its back. "Eliza Myricks."

CHAPTER 18

DANIEL WANTED TO TILT his head back to see the fingers resting on the fabric above his head, but he resisted the temptation. Every nerve in his body felt twitchy with anxiety, and he had to curl his toes to keep his legs still. "I was starting to suspect it might be. Is she a ghost, too?"

"Hmm." Wood creaked as the hand moved away. "I am not certain. She is not alive, at any rate."

Curiosity ate at him, but Daniel forced himself to exercise patience as he waited for his companion to continue. Bran paced the room twice before he spoke again.

"Eliza Myricks believed evil spirits stalked her. Salt has long been used to cleanse ground and ward off bad spirits, and Eliza stored immense quantities in her private pantry and used it liberally. When she became paranoid that Annalise was a witch, she tried to force the girl to eat it. Annalise became sick as she tried to swallow the salt, and that was when Eliza chose to burn her to death."

Nausea rose alongside the horror, and Daniel pressed a hand over his mouth.

"When Eliza Myricks perished, she did not leave the earth, but stayed behind as a twisted version of herself. Ironically, salt now works to keep her sealed in her tower. I am concerned about the door's durability since your friend tried to open it, but it seems to be holding. For now."

"Again, I'm really, really sorry about what happened."

"As am I. It was not my intention to harm your companion, but he broke through the window during the struggle, and I could not stop his fall."

"You weren't…trying to kill him?"

"No. Simply remove him from the vicinity of the tower. It is vital that the door remains sealed."

"I can buy some new locks."

"The locks were unique. Their manner of preparation cannot be reproduced." Bran's voice was emotionless, but his feet continued to carry him across the floor in slow, even loops. "What is done is done. You were careless but not malicious. I trust you will learn from the experience, so we will not dwell on it."

"You're not…" Daniel tried to find a more appropriate word but settled for "Angry?"

"I have lived for some time now, Mr. Kane, and it has given me appreciation for how insignificant many of our daily trials are. You will not find me lacking in patience."

Again, Daniel tried to look around the back of his chair. The fire had grown, but so had the shadows. They warred through the room, and contrary to nature, the shadows were winning. "You're dead, aren't you?"

The words escaped him before he could stop them. Bran chuckled, and the rasping noise drew goose bumps across Daniel's flesh.

"I am not a ghost, if that is what you are wondering. But I am not alive, either."

"What are you, then?"

Bran was silent for so long that Daniel began to imagine he'd disappeared. But then the man said, "Open the curtains, if you wish."

A queasy dread filled Daniel as he crossed to the massive window. Its curtains were stiff with age and thick enough to block out every hint of sunlight. He gripped one-half and dragged it back. Blinding light raced through the shadows and highlighted the clouds of dust he'd inadvertently shaken out of the fabric. He pulled back the second curtain, and finally, the room and its contents were laid bare to see.

A large mahogany table, ringed with three chairs and covered with thick dust, stood to one side. The space above the fireplace had been invisible in the earlier shadows, but Daniel saw empty picture frames hung there. The volumes filling the bookcase looked expensive; most had gold on their spines or were bound in thick leather.

A man stood in front of the desk, facing Daniel. He wore a charcoal vest and long black coat, both looking as though they dated to the early 1800s. Black hair was swept back from his temple and curled at the base of his neck. His face was long, like the fingers clasped ahead of himself, and his lips were thin.

Daniel swallowed an involuntary gasp. He battled with his fear and won, but only just barely, as he pressed his back against the window.

In some ways, Bran appeared to be a young man—no older than thirty—but in others, he was ancient. Dark shadows underlined his eyes, which were heavy-lidded and dull. His lips were cracked, his cheeks sunken. He had no wrinkles or creases that came with age, but his skin was paper-thin, ashen gray, and mapped entirely with black veins. It gave the impression that his skin was cracked like parchment.

The lips twitched with bleak humor. "I have not aged well, have I?"

"I—no—that's not—" Daniel bit his tongue before he could say anything stupid. He couldn't stop from staring, even though he knew it wasn't polite. It took a moment to drag his scattered thoughts back together. "You said Eliza Myricks was buried by her sole surviving relative. That was you, wasn't it?"

The head tilted in a graceful nod, and Bran's hair shifted as though weightless, much like Annalise's did. "Correct. You have been curious about my family's history, and I feel the time has come that I must share it with you. Eliza Myricks was my mother, much as I rue the fact. I did not know her well. She sent me to a boarding school when I was eight and refused to take me back between terms. For more than a decade, I was moved from institution to institution—largely based on my mother's whims, as she decided an establishment was ungodly and would corrupt my mind—and I only saw her twice during my adolescence."

Bran moved away from the table and started pacing again. It struck Daniel as something like a compulsive habit.

"When I completed my education at age twenty and returned home, I was alarmed to find Annalise, my younger sister, no longer lived in the house. I asked my mother what had happened to her. She insisted I had never *had* a younger sister."

He laughed, and the wheezing, gasping noise seemed to struggle out of his throat. "I went through the whole mansion looking for proof that Annalise had lived here. I had only been eight the last time I saw her, but I refused to believe she was a figment of my imagination. My mother had been scrupulous about removing signs of her life, though. Every picture frame that had once contained a painting of her was barren. Her bedroom had been turned into a washroom. She had been erased, totally and completely."

Daniel couldn't bring himself to leave the window. The sun was insipid and filtered through a century of grime caked to the glass, but it felt safe. It protected him from the shadows that seemed to sprout from Bran like a dozen discordant spider legs. As Bran grew angrier, the shadows became darker and longer. Some flitted across the floor, others crawled up the walls, and one dared to creep up toward the fireplace's grate. When it touched the flames, they began dying with a series of pained hisses.

"It took me weeks to find my sister, and when I did, the discovery was not joyous. Charred bones had been heaped into a pail in the tower. And the final trace of Annalise overlooked it—a portrait Eliza had commissioned just months before the girl's death. It was too large for her to easily burn alongside Annalise's clothes and possessions. So Eliza had hung it above my sister's bones in our tower, the one part of the house she always kept locked."

He held out his hands, seeming to examine them for flaws, then squeezed them so tightly that the fingers made cracking noises. "I will not conceal the truth from you. I killed my mother that day."

Daniel was surprised to see a hint of grief in Bran's eyes. "How?"

"She was in the garden. She was raving; paranoia and grief had made her mad. But her insanity was not pardon, and I did not show her any mercy. I approached from behind, took up a rock, and cracked her skull." He drew a breath then let it out slowly. "The gardener's tools were nearby. I dug her a shallow grave beside where she had fallen, pushed her unholy corpse into it, and buried her."

"But she didn't stay dead."

"No." The grief transformed into a bitter smile. "As I said during our dinner, things that die here have a tendency to linger."

Daniel tore his eyes away from Bran and fixed them on the fire. The rogue shadow had retreated from it, and the flames were recovering. "So you used the salt to trap her in the tower. But she's still trying to get out, even two hundred years later?"

"That is correct. She has never rested. I do not know if she ever will. I chose to stay in the manor and do what I could to contain her. I used not just salt, but also bolts that belonged to the church she had once knelt in. They seemed to work."

Bran crossed to stand beside Daniel and looked out into the garden. His features tightened with weariness. "I soon found I was not alone in the manor. Once I had interred my sister's bones in the family crypt and carved her name over the door, I began to see her spirit running through the garden at night. I would sit with her and talk for hours. She cannot speak, but she finds ways to make her opinions known."

Daniel managed a smile as he followed Bran's gaze toward the crypt. "I know what you mean. She woke me to tell me Kyle was in the house."

"Hm. And moving closer to the tower door." His cracked lips tightened. "Above all else, Annalise fears her mother. She watches the tower from the gardens. And Eliza watches the gardens from her tower. Even in death, they cannot be free of each other."

He didn't want to stare, but Daniel found his attention continuously drawn back to Bran's mapped, paper-thin skin and near-weightless hair. "Do you think you'll ever die? Properly, I mean?"

"I do not know. I always expected to, but days blended into months and finally years, and one day, I realized I could not remember the last time I ate." He lifted his hands. The veins were worse on them, especially around the fingertips, which were nearly black. "I have become more shadow than human. It became harder and harder to maintain my house and my garden. One evening, I carried a tray of tea out to Annalise's crypt, as was our habit, but when dawn came, I had no strength left to lift the tray and return it to the house." Bran clenched his hands and dropped them to his side. "I can still lift light objects. Pens. Letters. Small flowers. In times of stress, I can exert some of my former strength, but not as much as I once possessed. I have faded. Perhaps eventually, I will fade entirely and cease to exist in any realm. But for now, I still have use of this form, and a couple others besides."

Daniel frowned. "Sorry—I was following right up until that last part. Other forms? Like the shadows?"

"Yes." Bran's heavy eyelids fluttered. "And others. My mother's insanity, Annalise's sensitivity to light, and my own peculiar condition share their roots in our ancestors. We came from a line of disgraced kings and queens. Severe inbreeding left many of them with deformities and abnormalities."

"Do you think that's why you and Eliza are still alive, even after death?"

"Perhaps." His face was unnaturally serene, as though it had been carved out of stone. "My mother's paranoia centered around Annalise being a witch, but it was not my sister she should have been concerned about. As more of my body fades and is replaced by the shadows, I have learned to shape them. Mold them."

Daniel had been staring at the window as Bran talked. When his companion fell silent, he turned. Bran was no longer in the room. In his place, an oversized, tattered crow perched on the back of the closest chair. Daniel's mouth fell open, but no noise came out.

The crow king—the same ancient bird that had watched Daniel move in and out of the house—hopped to the edge of its chair. Its movements were stilted, suggesting an immense age. It spread its wings with a deep whirring noise and dove toward the ground.

The bird never landed. Instead, the bone-thin cat thudded into the carpet. Its amber eyes stared into Daniel's as the scruffy creature paced past him.

"No." Daniel's mind threw up a blanket objection to what he was seeing. He staggered away from the animal and pressed his palms into his closed eyelids. "I'm going crazy."

"No more than I have during this last century."

Daniel removed his hands from his eyes, and Bran stood before him once again. His skin was a shade paler, and the shadows around his eyes were a fraction deeper. He spread his arms in a shrug. "Some of our ancestors—the early Vikings, the kings and queens before their disgrace—called themselves shape-shifters. This is a trait I appear to have inherited."

"Okay." Daniel's mouth agreed, but he found himself shaking his head. "Shape-shifter. Sure."

Bran's cracked lips stretched into a smile. "It is not a gift I possessed during life. As the years moved on and I began to feel less human and more shadow, I found my form malleable. Shadows are more liquid than solid, after all. I pour myself into a fresh mold. It is not magic, and it is not alarming. It just…is."

"I'm glad *you* don't find it alarming, but…" Daniel felt heat rush across his face as he remembered all of the embarrassing things he'd cooed to the cat. "Oh. Oh no. I'm so sorry."

"For what?" Bran began pacing again.

"For trying to pet you." The heat increased until Daniel felt as if his face might be glowing. "For making that joke about you being named after cereal."

Rasping laughter filled the room. Bran clasped his hands behind himself as he turned to loop around the desk again. "Do not apologize. You have a compassionate soul. I cannot eat, but...I have rather enjoyed the fires."

"Okay." The word escaped as a squeak.

"Do you know why I chose you to tend to our garden?" Bran tilted his head as he regarded Daniel. "I would not have invited just anyone onto our property. I wanted someone who would place others' needs ahead of their own. One day, while I was in the town, I found a man sitting on the street. He had no home, no money, nothing of his own except a dirty blanket and a sandwich someone had given him. When he saw me, he pulled the meat out of the bread and offered it to me. I knew I had found my helper."

"I—" Daniel frowned. He was sure he would have remembered giving someone his food, especially a person who looked as distinctive as Bran. Then it clicked. "The dog!"

Bran smirked.

The coal-black mutt had been so skinny that Daniel had been shocked it was still walking. It had glanced at his sandwich as it passed him on the street. Daniel had been hungry, but not so hungry that he could forgive himself for letting the animal starve. He'd pulled the steak out of the sandwich and held it out to the dog. The mutt had carried it off, tail wagging, while Daniel contented himself with the leftover bread.

"That was only a couple of days before Kyle found me," he remembered.

"When I had arranged your accommodation and returned with your letter, you were gone. I traveled into town often, searching for you, but time does not behave for me the way it used to. It blurs together now. It must have been several weeks before I found you again."

"Six months." Daniel gave an awkward shrug. "You found me in the end, though, right?"

"Yes." Bran paused by the window for a second before resuming his path around the desk. "There have been…mistakes, but your intentions are sound. You have cared for Annalise, though she is no longer alive. I am more shadow than human, but you do not fear me. And you complete the tasks I request of you. I am once again able to sit with my sister in her crypt."

Daniel felt uncomfortable saying it, but he forced the words out. "I like it here. I like the job. I think I'd be happy if I got to do it for a while longer."

"That suits me, as well, Mr. Kane."

"You can call me Daniel. If you want."

Bran didn't respond, and Daniel looked up from the flames to see he was, once again, alone in the room.

CHAPTER 19

DANIEL BLEW OUT HIS candle then thrust his hands into his pockets as he left Bran's study. The hallway still seemed to dwarf him, its myriad of identical doors robbing his sense of space and time. Reaching the stairs was a relief.

As he descended to the foyer, he spotted the cat sitting beside what was left of the fire he'd kindled earlier that day. A sense of surrealism washed over him. He knew the cat was Bran, but to his eyes, it was still a regular cat—one he wanted to pet and feed and chatter to. Addressing it formally felt ridiculous, but he managed a stiff nod. "Bran."

The cat blinked once. Bran had said he appreciated the fires, so Daniel shuffled up to the embers. "I'll, uh, get that for you." He ground a new log into the coals and waited as it heated and caught. The cat sat beside him, silent and detached, as the flames lit its amber eyes. Daniel cleared his throat. "I should get back to work, I suppose."

He waited for Bran to shift into his human form to say goodbye, but he didn't. Maybe being a cat was less tiring, or maybe Bran had gone so long without human contact that social norms no longer bothered him. The situation was too surreal for Daniel, though, and he hurried into the garden.

This is going to take some effort to get used to. Once he'd ventured far enough to be away from the crows' watchful eyes, a hysterical laugh slipped out of him. If he hadn't seen Bran change form with his own eyes, he would have thought it was some elaborate prank. He didn't even know what to call what he'd seen. *Shape-shifter. Skinwalker. Were-cat?*

It didn't take long to reach Annalise's crypt. The ground around the lilies had started to dry out and wilt the plants, so he followed the trail toward the cottage to fetch some water.

How must it feel to live for decades past your expiration but fade a little more with every year? Daniel thought, in some ways, it might actually be worse than death. Bran had been trapped in the aging, decaying building, with only a mute ghost for company and a dead woman he hated scrabbling at her door. It was a recipe for insanity.

Daniel didn't have a watering can, so he filled up a pot with water from the tap. He'd told Bran he would be happy to continue on in the job, and that was the honest truth. A small kernel of worry continued to dig at him—worry that Bran had been lying when he'd said he hadn't intended to hurt Kyle—but Daniel was mostly successful in repressing it. He wanted to trust his unusual host.

Lost in thought, he completed the trek back to the lilies and gently sloshed water around the plants. His mind was still tangled around Kyle. Without a phone, Daniel had no way of checking up on his cousin's condition or talking to him.

How much did he see?

He hadn't considered that question before, and it created knots in his stomach. He let the last of the water fall out of the pot as he straightened and turned toward the tower.

Is Kyle going to remember what happened, or will it be lost in the haze of drunkenness? He hadn't been at blackout levels, and the fall would be hard to forget…

Kyle's personality made him a wild card. He would either forget everything or lock on to the memory with the same level of obsession he showed when playing video games.

Will it be a problem if he does *remember?* There was no light inside the tower, but Daniel thought he could see the woman inside, pressed close to the glass. He turned away and marched toward his cottage. *Will Kyle go to the police? Would anyone believe him if he told them a man made out of shadow tossed him through a window? Even describing the house—an ancient, crumbling manor forgotten in the forest—would cause skepticism. And the doctors were already concerned about what the fall might have done to his mind.*

Daniel dropped the empty pot onto the crypt's bench. Intense tiredness suddenly hit him, and he sagged onto the seat.

Kyle might never have full use of his brain again…because of me. Daniel had told him about the house and showed him the gold. He should have known Kyle would want some for himself. *And what if he tells people about Bran and the house and they really do think he's having delusions? Will he be put into a mental institute, his freedom stripped away, and kept on heavy sedation?*

Daniel had intended to have dinner when he returned to the cottage, but at that point, he felt too sick. If Kyle suffered—if his life was ruined—it would be because of Daniel's carelessness.

I all but invited him into the dragon's lair. His eyes burned, and he scuffed his feet across the crypt's stone floor. If he tried to protect Kyle by corroborating his story, that would mean betraying Bran—or worse, being locked up and sedated himself. There *had to be a solution that resulted in no harm to anyone.*

He might be able to convince Kyle he'd imagined the whole event or that it was a prank gone wrong. Kyle would hate him for what had happened, but hatred was better than being diagnosed with delusions.

Daniel needed to speak with Kyle and assess where his mind was. It was still possible his cousin didn't remember any of the evening. Amnesia, drunkenness, or even the assumption that the memories had been a dream could save the situation. And if not… Daniel would have to play it by ear.

The hospital's visiting hours were over for the day. Daniel would have to wait until the next morning to speak to Kyle privately. He could only cross his fingers that Kyle hadn't already shared his story with the nurses.

Daniel went to bed early that night, but nerves kept him awake until well after midnight. Annalise came to tap at his door again, and he got up to greet her. He stood by the window and watched her dart between the trees, her long, fine hair floating like a wave behind her. The shadows were too heavy to see clearly, but Daniel thought he glimpsed a large, disheveled crow in the pine above his house.

Morning took an eternity to arrive. Even after losing sleep, Daniel was awake for the first rays of light glinting over the treetops. He bundled himself in layers to keep warm then went to the manor before leaving for town.

Bran deserved an explanation of where Daniel was going and why, but he still felt like an idiot as he unpacked the situation to the black cat in front of the fireplace. Bran listened, occasionally blinking, but didn't show any alarm or shift into his human form. Daniel hoped that was a sign of approval. He said goodbye and slipped back into the chilly morning.

Even though he kept his pace leisurely as he walked into town, Daniel arrived before visiting hours. So he took the opportunity to exchange one of his new gold coins for cash at the pawnbroker, then he spent the next twenty minutes wandering the streets.

He felt intensely self-conscious with a small fortune tucked into his pocket, but his clothes were ill-fitting and tatty enough that no one gave him a second glance. He passed stores full of fresh, mud-free jeans and clean hoodies, but it still felt too soon to spend money on what had been classified as frivolities barely a week before.

The smells wafting from the bakery were too good to resist, though. Daniel slid into one of the seats and wolfed down a fried breakfast. He tipped well then spent the final half hour loitering outside the hospital. As soon as the clock hung from the building's tower ticked over to ten, he entered the building and asked after his cousin.

The nurse, a dimpled woman who looked as though she hadn't slept in twenty hours, read the case notes for him. Kyle had woken the previous day. His cognitive abilities didn't seem impaired, but the doctors wanted to keep him for at least another few days to monitor him. The news was an intense relief. Kyle hadn't suffered permanent impairment, and the doctors wouldn't be reporting his condition favorably if he'd talked about the mansion in the forest. The nurse gave Daniel a ward and room number, and he jogged up the stairs rather than wait for the elevator.

Kyle had a room to himself, and as Daniel entered, the smell of antiseptic and bleach assaulted his nose. The blinds on the small window were half-turned to reduce the sun's glare. Kyle was sitting up in bed, a tray with a cookie and a cup of tea above his knees and his phone in hand.

Daniel couldn't help searching for changes in his cousin. Kyle's skin was a shade grayer and had lost its usual flush. His eyelids drooped, and his jowls seemed slacker than normal. The stiff white hospital gown didn't suit him.

"Hey," Daniel said. He hovered in the doorway, still not certain whether his visit would be welcomed.

"You came at last, huh?" Kyle tossed his phone onto the tray next to his tea. He didn't smile, but there wasn't any trace of anger in his expression, either. "D'you want a cookie? They taste like garbage."

Daniel wasn't hungry, but he didn't want to reject any olive branches, either. "I'd love one. Thanks." He shuffled into the seat beside Kyle and accepted the plastic-wrapped cookie. He turned the package over and pretended to be interested in the branding. "How're you feeling?"

"Like I got thrown through a window." At last, Kyle's mouth twitched into a smile, but the expression didn't look honest. He held up his left arm, which was swaddled in bandages. "They say it'll scar."

The phrase "I'm sorry" nearly left Daniel's mouth, but he caught himself. The fall hadn't been his fault, and apologizing would be both an admission of guilt and an acknowledgment of what had happened. He didn't want Kyle to start going down that path. It would be best for everyone—including Kyle—if he stayed ignorant. "That sucks."

"It sure does." Kyle shuffled a little farther up his bed and rested his head back on the pillow propped behind him. "You got yourself into a messed-up situation with that house. If you want my advice, you should get out before something like this happens to you, too."

Daniel felt his heart kick up a notch, but he kept his face serene. When he spoke, his voice barely wavered. "What do you mean?"

"You're probably hoping I didn't see anything. Or that I

assumed I dreamed it. Or that you can convince me it was some kind of delusion." Kyle's eyes hardened as they scanned Daniel's face. "But I know what I saw. Bran Myricks, supposedly dead for two hundred years, hauled me through that house."

Daniel tried to laugh, but the noise didn't come out right.

"His face was rotting." Kyle's voice remained flat. There was no flicker of fear or anger in his expression, just set inevitability. It was unnerving. "Gray like a ghoul, all sunken and lumpy, nothing between the skin and the bones. He's dead—he's got to be—but he's not staying in his grave, is he?"

Daniel's throat was too tight to swallow. "Are you sure you didn't make a mistake? You were drunk—"

Kyle picked up the phone. He tapped it twice then held it up for Daniel to see. It showed a portrait, drawn in a style similar to Annalise's. In it, Bran's skin was supple and healthy, but the lidded eyes, long nose, and black hair swept away from the temples were unmistakable.

"No. Bran Myricks died in 1805 when a plague passed through the village." Kyle's mouth twisted. "Only the bastard didn't stay dead."

CHAPTER 20

DANIEL FLICKED HIS EYES from the portrait on the phone to Kyle's face. His heart hammered against his ribs at a painful tempo. "Have you told anyone about this?"

"What, you mean the nurses? Hell no." Kyle pulled his phone back close to his chest. "I'm not a moron. They wouldn't believe me. But you do, because you've seen the exact same thing I have. You accepted a job from a walking corpse."

Daniel clasped his hands in his lap and leaned back in his chair. He tried to keep his voice level, but he sensed his cousin had the upper hand, and Daniel was scared of how he might use it. "That's why you can't return to the house. It's not safe for you there. You understand that, right?"

"It's not safe for anyone there." Kyle's eyes narrowed. "You're planning on going back, aren't you?"

"That's not important right now."

"Hell. You've *already* been back. That's why you're visiting me now, isn't it? To try to protect that murderer?" Kyle pressed his thumb and forefinger into the bridge of his nose. "You're such a moron."

"I had nowhere else to stay." Daniel hadn't meant to snap, but the words left him more harshly than intended. He cleared his throat and continued in a softer voice. "You changed the lock on your apartment."

"Whatever. I'll give you a new key. Just don't go back to the madman's house, okay?"

A sense of wariness drew over Daniel. "Why do you want me to stay away? So you can go back yourself when you're out of the hospital? Bran has been nothing but polite and considerate to me. He just doesn't like people digging through his stuff and stealing his family's heirlooms."

"Haven't you been listening?" Kyle slapped an open hand onto the tray. Tea sloshed out of the mug and pooled on the plastic. "He's a murderer! Insanity ran through the whole damn family, and it infected his brain worst of all. It won't take him much to snap."

"You're lying."

Kyle snorted and snatched up his phone. He swiped a finger across the screen and began reading. "He got shipped from school to school when his fellow students mysteriously died. He was always implicated, but there was never enough proof, so they just moved him on to be someone else's problem. After he returned to the family home, he only maintained peace for two weeks before bludgeoning his mother to death in their garden. Following her murder, he traveled to the nearest town and slaughtered anyone he encountered in a rage of bloodlust." Kyle lowered the phone. "Those were peasants. Women and kids, Dan. People who had done nothing wrong."

Daniel couldn't feel his fingers. He tried to see the article Kyle was reading from, but the phone's text was too small. "Yes, he killed his mother. She'd murdered his younger sister, so he killed her. But he wouldn't have attacked innocents. He's not..."

"Oh boy. He's told you a wonderfully sanitized version of what happened, hasn't he?" Kyle threw his head back in a cackling laugh. "His *mother* didn't kill the sister. His mother had spent her life trying to protect the girl. The mansion was a short walk from a small village, and the townspeople were superstitious up to their eyeballs. One year, a famine hit them hard. So they decided a witch was cursing them. And who was the most likely candidate for being a witch? The little rich girl who blistered in the sun. So they dragged her down to the churchyard and burned her."

Daniel's head rushed. He pressed his hands to his temples, trying to still it. He remembered Bran's expressions from the previous day. He'd looked crushed with grief when telling the story about his mother and sister. "You've got it wrong. The mother was deranged and unstable. She killed her daughter."

"Nuh-uh." Kyle wiggled the phone, eyebrows lifted. "I've been doing a lot of reading. This history site says Eliza Myricks was shy and chronically anxious. But she doted on her family, and even overcame her phobia of doctors to invite one into the house to treat Annalise."

Timid. Riddled with phobias. Spending her life trying to protect Annalise. Daniel tried to mesh this image of Eliza with the one he'd built over the previous days. He thought of the fingers scratching at the tower door and the quiet, gasping breaths.

"A person like that would be incredibly easy to manipulate by a strong-willed psychopath, don't you think?" Kyle's smile sent shivers through Daniel. "Someone like Bran."

His mouth was dry, but swirling his tongue through it didn't moisten it. "If you're so certain that's what happened, prove it. You said he attacked a town. Which one? Here, or Arbour?"

"Neither. It's called Flinton. It's a ghost town now. Just a short walk through the forest. The Myricks family's wealth made it thrive...until Bran attacked them, of course." Kyle rubbed a finger over the phone's case. "Apparently, it was pretty brutal. He unleashed some kind of curse on them, and no one was spared. Can you imagine that, Dan? Innocents slaughtered because of the sins of a few town elders. Like I said, he's a psychopath."

Daniel didn't know where to turn. *I can't trust Kyle. I can't trust Bran. How am I supposed to know what's the truth?* "I've never heard of Flinton before. And I'm pretty sure I would have, after living here my whole life. Can I have a look at that article on your phone?"

"I have an easier way to prove it." Kyle's smirk was infuriating. "Look at the coins he gave you. The family must have minted them or something, because they've got a map on the back. It doesn't just show the house, but the town, as well. I wouldn't lie to you, Daniel. We're basically like brothers. We need to stick together, don't we?"

Daniel blinked at his cousin as if seeing him for the first time. "The coins—"

"I'll be out of my job for a while once they release me from the hospital. It'll probably take a few months of recuperation, I guess." He shrugged and grimaced. "But I've been thinking. You can come back and stay with me. Sell off those coins the creep gave you. We can live off of them while I get better and you look for a new job. Depending on what they're worth, we could get you some nicer things. A new TV, maybe."

Daniel stood. Anger had settled deep in his stomach, but it wasn't the burning, fiery type he'd experienced before. It felt heavy and cold, like a solid block of ice, the kind that would take months to melt. "Kyle, how do you know there's a map on the back of the coins?"

The man's mouth tightened.

"You stole it, didn't you?" He tightened his fists until his fingers shook from the strain. "I thought I'd lost it in the pub, but you'd pocketed it."

"You're going to be a pedant about this, are you?" Kyle grimaced. "Can't you see I'm trying to help you? Or is your head too far up your ass?"

Daniel had never wanted to hit someone as much as Kyle's smug face seemed to invite it. He squeezed the urge into a tight ball of loathing as he crossed to the door.

Kyle called after him, the words growing increasingly faint as long strides carried Daniel down the hallway and toward the hospital's exit. "Oh, yeah, okay, a dramatic exit. Get over yourself,

Dan! You need me. Hey, hey, stop walking. I'm talking to you! You can have the stupid coin back if it means that much to you! D'you hear me? Hey! Come back, bastard!"

I was such an idiot. He's never had my best interests at heart. He only pretended to when he thought he could squeeze something out of me. Daniel forced cold hands into his jacket pockets as he stepped into the street. Cars in a nearby jam blared their horns, but the noise seemed muffled to Daniel. He felt shaky and lost. Kyle had lied to him, stolen from him, and sabotaged him.

But what if he's right? What if Bran has been lying to me, too?

He wanted to keep walking, but he had no place to go. He chose a street at random and followed it. Gridlocked roads and crowded stores gradually gave way to the dirt lanes and woods Daniel had grown familiar with. His quick steps slowed as he found himself at Tilbrook Street. If he continued along the path, he could be at Craven Manor in forty minutes. Or he could turn around and return to the town.

I need to know the truth…and not just from a web page or a secondhand account. I want to see proof with my own eyes. And there's one easy way to do that.

Daniel fished the remaining gold coin out of his pocket. On one side was the family crest. On the other were the coursing lines and bumps he had assumed was meaningless texture. Kyle was right, though; now that he knew what he was looking at, Daniel realized the marks created a crude map.

He held the coin up to the light and squinted to make out the details. The lines had to be roads. They led to a triangle in the center of the disk, which would represent the manor. A mushroom-like shape in the lower left area would be the massive dead oak tree at the fork in the road. Based on those coordinates, Daniel was also able to pinpoint the road Joel took to reach the house.

A multitude of smaller triangles on the coin's lower-right side were so delicate that Daniel almost overlooked them. He pressed his back to the nearest tree and rotated the coin so that its ridges and gullies caught in the light.

If one triangle symbolizes Craven Manor, a group of them must be the town. A line branched off Tilbrook Street and led to the cluster. If Daniel could find the path, he could follow it to the town without passing through Craven Manor's grounds or beneath Bran's watchful eyes.

Daniel looked behind himself. Thick plant cover butted up against both sides of the path. Vines tangled between gnarled pines. There was no sign of the road.

It might have fallen out of use at the same time as the road to Craven Manor. In that case, it would be overgrown.

Daniel hung close to the path's edge and skimmed the plants and the ground for any signs of a disused path. Two hundred years could do a lot to remove humanity's meddling. It had done a remarkable job swallowing the flagstones leading to Craven Manor, and it seemed to have been just as thorough in erasing the path to Flinton.

Daniel moved at a crawl. The woods seemed impenetrable, and by the time Daniel had covered the same ground three times, he was starting to think the path was permanently gone. He stopped to lean against a trunk and wipe sweat off of his forehead. A small fallen tree caught his eye. It didn't match its surroundings. Daniel tilted his head; the tree was narrow and strangely blocky, and when straight, it wouldn't have been any taller than his head.

A signpost. Daniel grinned as he dug leaf litter away from the post's base. As he'd hoped, a mostly crumbled sign protruded from the ground. The words were long gone, but he was certain it had once pointed to the mystery town.

There was no sign of stones among the tree roots, so Daniel guessed it had been a dirt path. He stuck out blind and hoped he was moving in approximately the right direction. *Shoot for the moon. If you miss, you'll die horribly in the void of space.*

A frightened chuckle escaped him. He didn't fancy freezing to death in the forest, but the sun was only just past its zenith. He had time to retreat back to the road if he couldn't find Flinton within a couple of hours.

Provided I can find my way back. He was beginning to wish he'd brought a ball of string or paint to mark his path.

But then his foot slipped into a hollow. As he straightened himself, he realized the ground wasn't perfectly even. A long, snake-like bump rose above the forest floor, an arm's length wide. He peered through the trees; the ridge continued as far as he could see. The road to Flinton had been raised to protect it from floods and snows. It wasn't more than a foot, but as long as he kept to the high ground, he wouldn't become lost.

That was easier said than done. The plants were thick to the point of being smothering. Several times, Daniel had to slide off the road to wend his way around a nasty snarl, and every step was a struggle.

He knew he had to be on the right path, but worry began to niggle at him as the sun fell lower and grim gray clouds replaced the clear skies. *When do I call it quits? How dark does it have to get before I give up and try another day?*

The answer wasn't pretty. Daniel knew he would stay out as long as it took to either corroborate Kyle's story or exonerate his friend.

He hadn't expected the word *friend* to enter his mind when thinking about the Myrickses. The relationship had been full of doubt from its early days, but when he searched his soul, he realized he'd become so invested in the family that he had started to think of them as friends.

It wasn't a close sit-for-hours-and-chat kind of friendship. But a loyalty existed, the kind that had made Daniel instinctively bristle against Kyle's accusations.

That's a dangerous path to go down. You trusted Kyle far longer than you should have. Has Bran really earned your loyalty?

Daniel hated the circular argument he'd become trapped in. He hadn't had a close, honest friendship since his grandmother's passing—and it wasn't for lack of trying. It left him feeling like a man adrift in the ocean, clutching at seaweed and sea foam no matter how many times they collapsed under his fingers.

His foot slipped, and he clutched at a tree to keep his balance.

He'd spent the previous moments fixated on the ground beneath his feet, and when he finally looked up, he saw dark shapes clustered among the trees to either side. They were large and blocky, and it took a moment to realize what he was looking at.

Houses.

CHAPTER 21

DANIEL TOOK A DEEP breath and left the trail to approach the nearest building to his left. The stone house was small—about the size of his groundskeeper's cottage—and its walls were painted black by grime. Part of its roof had collapsed, and one wall bent inward.

That, at least, proved part of Kyle's claim: there was a town, and it had been abandoned. Daniel got as close to the building as the vegetation would allow him and tried to look through the window. Everything he could see was crumbled and rotted beyond recognition.

He clambered back to the road. More houses and fences flanked him as he moved closer to the town's center. They were all relics, barely recognizable among the living trees. The stone structures had mostly survived, but Daniel also passed bare foundations and piles of decay that must have been wooden buildings.

The plants became thinner as brown, dry, waist-high grass covered the road. Daniel suspected he'd entered the town proper. The ground was too firmly packed to allow much to grow, but thin, struggling trees had still managed to put down roots. Dilapidated houses, at least a hundred of them, spread across the plane. Larger buildings gathered in a cluster fifty yards ahead to mark what had once been the main street.

Spanish moss hung from rooftops, and their long tendrils shifted in the wind. Most of the stones were covered in lumpy moss, and all but a handful of windows were broken. One house had a dozen metal birdcages strung around its front door. They still clinked together, though rust had muffled and deepened the sound. Daniel rose up onto his toes to see inside the cages and found a cluster of tiny bones buried in the grime.

Many roofs had partially or fully collapsed, disguising the house's contents, but what he could see was broken by age. Tables, chairs, even support beams were collapsing under the weight of time.

Daniel stopped by one of the more intact houses and rested his fingertips on a windowsill. The moss was spongy under his touch, and flakes crumbled away. He stretched to see over the remaining glass fragments and caught a glimpse of a lumpy blue shape in the room's darkest corner. It felt out of place in the derelict room. The object was large—maybe as large as he was—and propped against the wall at a strange angle.

He couldn't see it properly from the window, so he skirted around the building. A stone step led to the front door, which hung at an angle, supported by one hinge. A quick yank wrenched it free.

A musty, bitter smell assaulted Daniel as soon as he entered the room. It was like inhaling the aftermath of a fire, but instead of soot, he tasted age. He gagged and bent over until the nausea faded, then pressed deeper into the house, toward where the strange shape had been.

Remnants of life were buried among the decay. What might have once been a doll had become a gray lump, half-sunk into the floor. Teacups lay broken on the wood, fallen from their shelf, which had cracked. The curtains had fused to the walls.

He found the blue shape in the dining room's corner. The room was dim, and Daniel had to squint as he approached the object. It was some kind of mold-smothered cloth, covering…

"Oh—oh no—"

Fingers curled out of folds in the fabric. Strands of dry brown hair poked free. As Daniel circled the shape, he saw the face. Skin had turned back and sunken into the bones. The eye sockets were empty, but their shadowed pits seemed to stare at him.

Black fungus spilled out of the body, exploding from any nick or tear in the skin, to give it a horrific bulging shape. The fungal growth held a bizarre bubbled texture, like freshly poured tar or over-whipped cream.

Daniel pressed a hand across his mouth and backed away. His thighs hit the corner of a chair, and the structure broke apart. With a yelp, he leaped around it, then he ran for the door.

He didn't breathe deeply until he was back outside, panting

and gasping in the cool air. The image of the dead woman being swallowed in billows of black mold was still clear in his mind.

She was just left there. No funeral. No burial. She hasn't even decayed properly. Kyle was right. Something unnatural happened in this town. Something evil.

Every building was crumbling with age. Daniel hadn't thought it was strange before, but as he straightened, he realized the decay wasn't as far advanced as he would have expected from two centuries of neglect.

Morbid obsession drew him deeper into the network of buildings. He kept a forearm covering his mouth and nose any time he leaned through a window or open door. Two houses on, he found another cluster of bodies. A woman lay in bed, two childlike shapes cradled in her arms, and a figure wearing men's clothing sat in a chair beside her. He'd inclined his head to rest it next to hers, as though the family had been embracing one final time.

Their skin was darkened and stretched tight, but it still bulged strangely in places. A watermelon-sized lump had grown on the man's back then ruptured, and the sticky fungus spilled out and ran in a tendril to the floor. Where it touched the stone, it seemed to absorb into the building and spread through its structure.

The buildings aren't covered in moss. They've been infected. Daniel felt sickened that he'd touched it. He scrubbed his fingers on his jeans, although he knew the paranoia was likely coming too late. If the black substance was still infectious, he'd been thoroughly exposed to it.

The farther he went, the more bodies he found. Some had

perished in bed. Some sat in chairs or collapsed across the floor. Daniel found a human-sized lump of the ichor in the street. Weeds had grown around and through it, and their stems had been distorted into a grisly mottled color.

These deaths weren't natural. The fungus has preserved them, somehow. He stumbled on, simultaneously not wanting to see any more and unable to look away. Larger buildings marked where the main street ran. Daniel recognized what he thought would have to be a bank, a general store, a farrier, and a church. Signs of death were more common there. Clumps of the black gunk collected in doorways, on steps, and in the street. A strip of leather cord ran from a large mass to the railing beside the bar, and Daniel suspected it had once been used to harness a horse. Animals apparently hadn't been immune, either.

The church was affected worse than other buildings. The fungal growth spread up its sides and across its peaked roof, almost like a blanket. Only the cross poked free. Daniel approached cautiously. His nerves were wound tight, and sweat beaded over his skin despite the cold day.

The church was one of the largest buildings in the town. He thought it must have once had stained-glass windows, but they had long been broken out of their frames. Its doors were missing, and the interior was a nest of shadow. Daniel crept closer, past the rusted metal bars that had marked the church's fence, and up the two steps to see inside the building.

Bodies had littered the rest of the town, but it was nothing compared to the church's insides. Everywhere he looked were white teeth, bony hands, and matted hair. Daniel keeled over and clutched his hands around his chest to shield against the shock and nausea. There had to be more than a hundred corpses inside the building. Some seemed to be reaching for the windows, as though trying to crawl through. Others were grouped at the back of the building, at the altar, and behind the pulpit. Still others had died in the pews and become permanently affixed to the decayed wood.

Daniel closed his eyes and turned to face the town. He visualized how it must have once looked—sturdy, humble buildings, clear dirt roads, and gardens full of life. He imagined hearing wailing shrieks and broken yells as something evil moved from building to building, striking down life wherever it existed. Some would have made a stand with pitchforks and kitchen knives. Others would have fled for the only place they felt safe—the church.

He opened his eyes. The church doors were missing from their hinges. He retraced his steps down into the weedy yard and found them—two massive, heavy blocks of wood, lying among the weeds. Massive claw marks scored the doors. Daniel's mouth dried as he looked across them. The scores were longer than his arm and at least two inches deep.

The monster tore the doors off their hinges and threw them aside like they weighed nothing. He tried not to imagine the terror the townspeople must have felt as the creature stepped across the threshold and claimed the lives inside.

He couldn't stand being in the wretched town any longer. He ducked his head and jogged through the scene of a centuries-old slaughter. Questions warred for space in his mind. Why hadn't he ever heard of Flinton or its fate before? Why had the bodies just been left to rot in their houses?

A path to his right disappeared into the forest, and Daniel knew it had to be the road leading to Craven Manor. He turned away from it and toward the path he'd arrived on. He didn't feel as though he could breathe properly until he was back inside the smothering plant life and away from the horrible, overwhelming decay.

He had the answer he'd been seeking, at least. Kyle had told the truth about Flinton. And he'd likely told the truth about the cause of death, as well.

Bran had shown Daniel only his cat, crow, and dog forms, but Daniel shuddered as he imagined what other beasts Craven Manor's owner was capable of creating. A bear made entirely of shadow. An oversized wolf. Or perhaps something Daniel had never seen before. Some otherworldly nightmare full of hatred and cruelty, breaking windows and crushing roofs as it swept between houses.

He admitted to bashing his mother's skull in with a rock in the garden. I should have taken that as a warning that he has no compunction about murder in cold blood.

It was growing too dark to see the path clearly, but Daniel refused to slow down. He had a desperate, itching need to get away from both the town and Craven Manor, and he didn't care how many times he tripped over exposed roots or got snagged in scratching vines.

Bran had lost his strength in the last two hundred years. His animal forms were all desperately thin and old. And most of the time, his human body could barely lift anything heavier than a flower.

The small bouquet of wildflowers outside Annalise's crypt gave Daniel momentary pause. It was hard to reconcile the image of a bloodthirsty killer with the man who had stayed to care for his sister. And Annalise clearly trusted him. When Daniel had asked her about her brother, she'd smiled.

Maybe Annalise doesn't know what Bran did to the town. If Kyle's story was accurate, the incident in Flinton had happened after her death. She could be ignorant of Bran's true nature, and maybe that was why he was so kind to her. Even killers wanted to be thought of as heroes.

It made a lot of sense. Bran was polite and considerate toward anyone who was on his side. He only showed his crueler aspect if his morals were questioned or his secrets challenged. Like what Kyle had done.

Daniel felt sick. Once again, he'd put faith in a person, only to find out he'd picked the wrong side.

It wasn't too late, though. He was away from Craven Manor. With the gold coins, he could travel somewhere Bran wouldn't ever find him. He could rent an apartment, maybe even buy a cheap car, and finally be able to get a job and straighten out his life.

Daniel staggered as he stubbed his toe against a fallen log, and frowned as he hopped around it. The plan sounded good, but it left him feeling uneasy. He'd earned the first two coins with the work he'd done around Annalise's tomb. But the second payment had been in advance, for the week of labor yet to come.

His eyes were sore from stress. Daniel wanted to rub at them, but he still couldn't forget the feel of the bubbling black fungus under his fingers. He blinked furiously instead.

You can't give up the coins. They might be the difference between having a normal life or becoming trapped on the streets again. Besides, it's not like Bran needs them.

Keeping the money still felt wrong. Daniel tried shrugging, but the uncomfortable twinge wouldn't go away. He was taking money that rightfully didn't belong to him. The fact that he was taking it from an evil man didn't make his conscience any lighter.

I'll sleep on it. Tomorrow might bring a clearer idea of what I need to do.

The vegetation finally cleared, and Daniel found himself back on Tilbrook Street. He turned left, toward the town. Indecision and loneliness ate at him. He wished he had someone he could talk to, a kind ear that would listen and give honest, unselfish advice. Someone like his grandmother.

Daniel stared at the moon slowly rising above the trees. There was someone in his life who matched that description…in a way. She wasn't the most conventional place to look for help, but she might be the best. After all, Daniel remembered her telling him about the years she'd spent in the local historical society.

He pulled up his collar to shield against the wind chill and quickened his steps toward Mrs. Kirshner's apartment.

CHAPTER 22

DANIEL SHUFFLED HIS FEET as he stood on the doorstep of apartment 612. He felt painfully self-conscious. Leaves and grime had gathered in his hair, and brushing his fingers through it hadn't done much to improve the situation. His jeans were in dire need of a wash, and thorns and sharp branches had nicked holes in his jacket.

The door rattled as the occupant unlocked it, and a second later, Mrs. Kirshner's wrinkled face was squinting up at him. "Daniel! You are back, Daniel! I have been missing you."

A smile came easily, and some of the tension left Daniel's muscles. "I've missed you, too, Mrs. Kirshner. Have you been well?"

"Yes, yes, come look!" She seized his sleeve and tugged him into the apartment, even though she was short enough that he could easily see over her fluffy white hair. "Someone give me gift. Money under the door. Look!"

Daniel followed her finger, and a laugh burst out of him. Mrs.

Kirshner had invested part of his money in a gigantic cat climbing tree. It was a maze of tunnels, boxes, and ledges that reached almost to the ceiling. She'd placed it in the room's corner, where it clashed hilariously with her old-fashioned, sparse furniture. Her gray cat lounged on one of the highest ledges.

"Alonzo looks happy," Daniel said as the magnificent creature blinked down at him.

"Yes, Alonzo is happy, and I am happy." Her eyes sparkled. "My cookies have cranberries in them tonight. You can stay for a bit, yes? Have tea with me?"

"I'd love that." Daniel cleared his throat and shuffled his feet. "And, uh, actually—this is going to sound very rude—but I need somewhere to stay tonight—"

"Daniel stay here." She patted his shoulder on the way past and made herself busy in the tiny kitchenette preparing tea. "Daniel is good boy."

"Thank you. So much. I'll pay you back when I can—"

She made shushing noises as she dropped tea bags into two cups. "Daniel keeps me company. He is like grandson. He is always welcome."

Daniel sank into the small wooden chair beside Mrs. Kirshner's recliner. The cat tree wasn't the only change he saw. She'd bought curtains for the windows and new cups to replace the chipped ones. Both looked like good quality but not expensive brands. Except for the cat tree, she seemed to be using the money carefully.

Alonzo slipped out of the seat and thumped onto the ground. He stretched, back arching, then reached a fluffy paw up to tap at Daniel's leg. He knew what it wanted and moved his hands out of his lap. "Up you go."

It leaped up then bumped its head into his chest. He sank his fingers into the long gray fur and enjoyed the feeling of rumbling purrs as he scratched around the cat's chin.

"Hot, hot, very hot," Mrs. Kirshner murmured as she set the teacups on the floor beside them. She'd stacked four of her cookies on the saucer beside his cup. They looked as though they had more cranberries than batter, but Daniel was starving and picked one up.

"Mrs. Kirshner, you used to be a part of the local historical society, didn't you?"

"Ooh, yes." She settled back into her seat and adjusted a knit blanket around her shoulders. "When I move here, I have no friends. I meet lady on street, tell her I am lonely. She say, 'Come join club! Learn about country!' So I do." Creases built around her eyes as she smiled. "They were so kind. It did not matter that I did not know the country or could barely speak the language! They wanted to help me to learn. They are still best friends. It was happy times."

Daniel nodded and adjusted his cup of tea. He knew Mrs. Kirshner and her husband had emigrated from Germany nearly fifty years before, and they had been a core part of the local historical society until death and illness had caused it to finally disband. He went out on a limb. "Mrs. Kirshner, have you ever heard of a place called Craven Manor?"

"Ooh." She made a series of muttering tsking noises. "Bad house. Bad family."

"And Flinton?"

"The lost town. Yes. You have been learning history, Daniel?"

Her smile was so genuine and sweet that Daniel couldn't bring himself to tell her he'd been living at Craven Manor. He didn't want her to recoil from him.

"A little bit. Can you tell me about them?" he asked, digging his fingers deeper into Alonzo's fur.

"It is all very old stories now." She picked up her saucer. The cup wobbled, and for a second, Daniel was afraid the arthritis in her hands would cause her to drop it. But she stabilized the cup and blew on the steaming liquid. "Two hundred years old. Maybe more. Family lived in big mansion on the hill. A mother and two children. Myricks. Family had a lot of money—dead husband was duke—and their money make the town rich."

Mrs. Kirshner paused and sent Daniel a searching glance, as if she were trying to gauge how much to tell him.

He gave her an encouraging nod. "Go on."

She narrowed her eyes. "Daniel believes in science. Stories from old are myths to him, yes?"

"Uh…not necessarily." He didn't know how much to share, but at last he said, "I believe in ghosts."

She made another murmuring noise, and the teacup shook as she sipped from it. "Daniel is good boy. Has open mind. These days, people do not trust in the old stories. They do not understand, so they think it all fiction! Myricks family came from, uh, from…from…"

"Vikings?" Daniel prompted.

She bobbed her head. "Yes, yes, Viking family. Warlords. It is said a great king became a monster in battle. A beast with huge claws and gnashing teeth. Kill his enemies in one swipe!" She mimed the motion, baring her dentures and swiping a hand through the air. Her tea sloshed dangerously, and Daniel rushed to steady it for her.

"A shape-shifter."

"Good, Daniel, yes. Myricks family became very rich, built mansion, built town. Named house Craven Manor. Craven means *fear, coward*, yes? House was to create fear in people who saw it. But over time, meaning changed. People began saying it is a house of the craven. Great warlord was long dead. Myricks descendants grew sickly and strange. More and more, they hid in their house and only spoke with people through letters."

Mrs. Kirshner adjusted her blanket again and shuffled her fluffy pink slippers. Daniel noticed she'd replaced her old, holey gray slippers. She looked adorable.

"Finally, the great Myricks family is just three: a mother and two children. The husband died young. Son was strong, but daughter was sickly. Couldn't see sunlight; it burned her skin like fire." Another tsking noise. "Son went to new country for his studies. Mother stayed to look after daughter."

Daniel scooted a little closer. "Do you know what Eliza Myricks was like? Was she a mean woman?"

"Oh no, no. Very shy woman, very sweet. Afraid of everything, so stayed hidden in manor all day. Afraid of doctors, but let one visit for daughter's sake." Mrs. Kirshner huffed out a sad breath.

"Then famine came to Flinton. Crops wouldn't grow. Animals went hungry. People ask why. Back then, everyone very religious. Very, uh…very superstitious. Priest says they are under curse, that a witch killed their plants. They believe him. They look for witch. Decide it must be the little girl in the manor."

"She was so young, though." Daniel spoke before he could stop himself, but Mrs. Kirshner didn't seem to notice the slip.

"Yes, yes, only twelve. But villagers say she is ungodly. She never goes to church because she cannot leave home during the day. They think the sun sickness is a sign of demons. They say she is the witch and attack the manor. Take her back to the town. Burn her at stake."

Daniel grimaced. He hadn't expected Mrs. Kirshner to know all of the gory details, but she recounted them without hesitation.

"When mother arrive, all that is left is burnt bones. She collect them in bucket and take them back to home with her. Very sad. Lock herself in house, never come out again. Then son return from school."

Alonzo shifted on Daniel's lap. He curled his arms around the cat to keep it from falling off then resumed scratching around its head. "What do you know about the son?"

"Bran. He was not good man. Very cruel, very angry. He loved sister and thought mother was to blame for death. He attacked her. Killed her. Buried her in shallow grave. Then he went to the town." She gave him another searching glance. "Here is part people do not believe. But legend say he became great beast, like the Viking warrior in his blood. A monster and a shadow, breaking doors, killing when people tried to stop him. He left a great sickness behind him… A plague. It got into people, make them rot before they had chance to die. Some run into woods, but Bran catch them before escape. Others hide in church."

Daniel visualized the door, torn off its hinges, massive claw marks gorged into the wood. He was grateful he had Alonzo in his lap; the cat was the only thing keeping him warm.

"They thought holy ground save them." Mrs. Kirshner shook her head and murmured something in German. "It did not. All who ran to church died that night. Every last one of them. And after he left, sickness spread through town, killing people who had hidden. When they realize what happened, people from other towns send help. Send doctors and supplies. But anyone who step foot in town get the same disease. It grow in their veins, like plant, and kill them same day."

Daniel blinked and saw the corpses, bloated and bulging with the fungus. It had spilled out of tears in their skin. His fingers itched, and he wished he'd asked Mrs. Kirshner for a shower before sitting down. But by that point, he was too deep in the story to stop.

"When they see the plague spread, other towns stop sending help." Mrs. Kirshner drained the last of her tea and set the cup aside. "They not let anyone come to them, either. No asylum. They shoot them when they see them come down the road. They scared of letting it spread, yes? Don't want their own families to die."

He nodded slowly. It sounded horrible, denying help to

people who were dying, but if your life and the life of everyone you cared for was at risk…

"Flinton dead in two days." She held up two stiff fingers. "No people, no animals live. Other towns agree—they not let anyone visit for fear of more death. It becomes ghost town. Dead town. Forgotten. All around is forest, so plants grow through town. Now it is not on map. People forget it is there. If history books write about it, they talk only about plague; no mention of Myricks or great beast." She shrugged. "All that is left is stories told between friends, like this."

"Thank you." Daniel's mouth was dry, and he finished his tea. It didn't help reduce the parched sensation. "I'm glad you could tell me about it."

She folded her hands and gave a small sigh. "Is nice to talk about history. I miss it, yes? Wish historical society could meet again. But so few of us are left, and we have no money for room rental. But perhaps…perhaps we figure something out. I may visit friends again. See if we start meetings again, even just for a short while."

"That sounds nice." Daniel stared into the dregs of his teacup. His mind was absorbed in the story, and he didn't realize Mrs. Kirshner was staring at him until she spoke.

"Why Daniel curious about Myricks? When Daniel hear about town?"

"Oh! Uh, I just…"

"You say you believe in ghosts." She tilted her head to the side. "You like to hear ghost stories, yes?"

"Um..." He struggled for an answer, and settled on a lame, "Yes?"

"You hear ghost story about Myricks house." She nodded, as though that settled the matter. "And you want to know more."

"Yeah, that's, uh, basically what happened."

She reached across the space between them and patted the hand resting on Alonzo's head. "Daniel stay away from Myricks house. Bad place. Not safe. Don't want to be trapped, not like Eliza Myricks."

He frowned. "What do you mean...trapped?"

CHAPTER 23

MRS. KIRSHNER KNIT HER wrinkled hands together. Her attention was focused on the opposite wall, though Daniel didn't think she saw it. "You don't know story? Bran Myricks did awful thing to mother. He hate her so much, he trap her soul where she will never rest and never sleep. She is locked in a tower, never able to reach heaven. They say she will not be free until the seals on the door are broken."

"Oh." Daniel felt queasy. He didn't realize he was holding the cat too tightly until it began squirming, and he quickly released his hold. "Sorry, Alonzo… Shh. I'm sorry."

"They say Bran lives on at Craven Manor. He is crazy, yes? He keeps his family with him—not just mother, but also little sister. He knows hell will swallow his soul when he dies, so he lives on, and they are forced to suffer beside him. Forever." She shuddered. "Bad house, bad family. You stay away, yes, Daniel?"

"Yes." He tried to imagine spending eternity trapped in a house that was slowly collapsing around him, all because of one man's selfish, spiteful whims. Daniel had been alone with Bran so often. Did the house's master have the power to trap Daniel's soul, as well? Had he unknowingly been dancing with eternal imprisonment?

Mrs. Kirshner stood and took Daniel's cup. He offered to help her wash up, but she waved him back down. "Stay, stay. Alonzo is comfortable, yes? Daniel keep him warm."

Good old Mrs. Kirshner. The cat always takes priority. Daniel managed a smile as he scratched under Alonzo's chin. Sounds came from the kitchen as his host rinsed the cups and put them away, then with a grating noise, a rarely used drawer was opened. Daniel peered over his shoulder and saw Mrs. Kirshner returning with something clasped in her hands.

"Gift for Daniel," she said, beaming at him. "My grandmother make. Wards off bad spirits, yes? Made of salt and silver, blessed by holy man. Daniel keep close. It will protect."

"I..." Daniel blinked at the talisman she'd dropped into his hands. It was made of a series of tiny silver beads threaded around a small glass vial. A leather strap had been attached to it so that it could be worn as a necklace. "I don't want to take your grandmother's gift. It must be important to you."

She patted the top of his head as she shuffled past. "No, better this way. Daniel look after me. I look after Daniel. Good boy, good boy."

As he watched her go, a sense of disorientation swept over him.

She'd clearly understood more than he'd told her. She wouldn't have given him the talisman if she didn't think he was at risk from Craven Manor.

It's kind of her, but I won't need it once I move to a new house. He turned the talisman over in his hands. It had a nice weight to it. *I have no plans to ever return to Craven Manor.*

He put conviction into that thought, but as soon as it passed through his mind, he wavered. Eliza and Annalise's story left him feeling guilty. He'd escaped a lion's jaws, and the smart thing to do would be to keep moving and not look back. Still, he couldn't help but feel responsible for the tormented family, especially Annalise. She'd become like a friend.

The guilt continued to niggle at him during his shower. As he scrubbed his hands in Mrs. Kirshner's poky, blue-themed bathroom, he looked at the issue from every angle. The manor and its occupants were all but forgotten. The police wouldn't help. *If I don't do something, no one will. They'll be trapped there, forever.* The thought horrified him, and the soap slipped between his numb fingers. He shivered and turned the tap on a little warmer.

He would be well within his right to walk away from the situation. He had no legal obligation to help the Myricks family... but he already knew he would never be able to forget them. The knowledge that he'd left them to suffer would hang over his head for the rest of his life.

You won't be missed if you disappear. He stepped out of the shower and stared at his blurred reflection in the mirror as he dried his hair. *Mrs. Kirshner will be sad not to see you, and maybe*

Kyle will occasionally wonder where you went, but society won't miss you. No one is relying on you or waiting for you to come home. That makes you the best candidate. If you fail, no one else will be hurt.

Bran's words came back to him: "Things that die here have a tendency to linger." Daniel thought he could face death without too much regret, but an eternity trapped on Craven Manor's grounds with its vengeful host horrified him. Maybe Bran wouldn't try to keep him chained on earth. He wasn't family, after all, and Bran seemed to be obsessed with his mother and sister. But the risk still existed.

Daniel spent the night in Mrs. Kirshner's living room, arranged on a bed of cushions and spare blankets. He tossed and turned, alternately staring at the streetlight's glow where it arced across the ceiling and watching Alonzo dozing in his cat tree. As he lay awake, a plan began to form. It was crude and rife with ways it could go wrong, but if he could stay calm and act natural, he thought he might be able to pull it off.

It all relied on maintaining Bran's trust. The manor's owner would be suspicious that Daniel hadn't returned that day, so he would need a plausible excuse for having stayed in town. He would also need to keep his mouth shut about everything he'd learned.

Daniel rose as soon as the sun came up. Mrs. Kirshner tended to sleep in, so Daniel moved as silently as a wraith as he made two plates of breakfast in the kitchen. He ate his by the window and watched the people on the street outside. The apartment block wasn't in a nice part of town. A child played barefoot in the gutter for several minutes before his mother found him, smacked him, and dragged him inside one of the buildings. Most of the faces that passed by looked haggard and weary, infused with the kind of tiredness that comes from a lifetime of stress.

Daniel wondered if his own face would grow that haggard if he stayed in the city. For the few brief days he'd worked at Craven Manor, he'd felt as if he'd escaped into a better life. His work had mattered…even if it was just to a ghost and a man made of shadows.

He exhaled as he turned away from the window. He left Mrs. Kirshner's plate on the table and washed his own. Finally, he took the pocketful of cash—the proceeds from the coin he'd sold the previous day—and hid it in her cupboard, behind a can of peaches. It might take her a few days or even weeks to find it, but the cash would support her and Alonzo for a while once she did. His conscience wouldn't let him spend the money on himself, but he had no compunctions in leaving it to a woman who'd deserved a better lot in life.

He picked up the talisman off the windowsill. The leather strap went around his neck, and he tucked the vial under his shirt then checked how it looked in the bathroom mirror. As long as he kept his jacket zipped, the talisman was invisible. Daniel silently let himself out of the apartment.

City sounds engulfed him as he stepped onto the street. Two men yelled at each other from inside a store, and cars blared their horns. Daniel ducked his head and thrust his hands into his pockets as he half walked, half jogged away from the noise. He stopped at a general store two blocks away and spent the last of his money on a small bag of supplies.

This is the right thing to do. He felt queasy and sweaty. Paranoia about touching the rot in the abandoned town resurfaced, but he comforted himself by recalling that Mrs. Kirshner had said the disease killed its host within a day. If he'd contracted anything, he would have felt it already. The clamminess was derived purely from stress.

City became countryside, and Daniel followed the familiar trail down Tilbrook Street. The massive gnarled oak at the end shifted in the wind, and its branches seemed to beckon him forward. Daniel turned and followed the flagstone trail into the overgrown forest.

The woods seemed noisy that day. Birds and insects clamored to be heard, and Daniel tried to clear his mind as he focused on the sounds. Looking nervous when he arrived back at Craven Manor might sink the whole plan.

The gates came into view sooner than he would have liked. He stood outside them for a moment to take in their rusted, deteriorated visage. The bronze plaque that announced Craven Manor glinted in the light.

"*A manor to strike fear into people who saw it. A manor inhabited by cowards.*" He licked his lips and stepped through the gate's narrow gap. The maneuver became easier every time he performed it, but he hoped he would only have to practice it once more...when he left Craven Manor for the final time.

Daniel left the plastic bag not far from the gates, hidden behind thick bushes. Then he turned and followed the familiar path through the garden toward the manor.

The anxiety-prompted sickness returned as the building came into view. Its dark stone walls, high windows, and insane mix of buttresses and extensions were overwhelming. He looked toward the tower and thought he saw a ghostly pale face pressed against the glass. As he stared at Eliza, she retreated into the shadows.

"*A shy woman. A woman riddled with phobias.*"

The crows had gathered in the tree and the stone supports around the front doors. Daniel searched for the huge, age-tattered bird, but Bran wasn't among them. He climbed the steps to the open front door and stepped inside.

He'd forgotten how forlorn the foyer was. The void magnified the sound of every breath and movement. The chandelier barely refracted the light that struggled through the windows. Every object—the empty photo frames and candles on the mantelpiece, the fireside chairs, the high curtains framing the windows—were all suffocated under the blanket of dust. It was too dim to see the spiderwebs, but Daniel knew they were lurking, waiting for him to walk into them.

Moment of truth. Will Bran believe me?

CHAPTER 24

DANIEL WAITED IN THE doorway for several pounding heartbeats, but the manor's master didn't swoop down from the higher floors. He tried to calm the shaking in his hands and stepped forward. "Bran?"

Two amber eyes glinted by the cold fireplace hearth. Daniel felt a pang of relief and let a natural smile grow. He liked cats. Talking to Bran in his animal form would be easier than trying to lie to the man's face.

"Hey, sorry it took me so long to get back." He moved toward the cat, trying to keep his stride natural and his trembling fingers hidden in his pockets. "I stopped to visit my neighbor, but she was sick, so I stayed the night with her to make sure she was okay."

The best kind of lie is a distortion of the truth. That was one of Kyle's favorite mottos…or a paraphrasing of it, at least. It was easier to keep a story straight when most of it was factual.

The cat blinked. It maintained its usual pose, pin-straight and with the tail coiled around its legs in a neat loop. Daniel knelt next to it. Someone had refilled the kindling and logs beside the fireplace—probably Joel. Daniel began stacking the wood in the empty grate. "Let's get this house a bit warmer for you."

Bran turned to face the fireplace expectantly. That was a good sign; he was more interested in heat than an interrogation. Daniel waited until baby flames licked over the kindling before speaking again. "I saw Kyle, but he's not looking good. He was still in a coma, and the doctors are worried about brain damage. I might go back and visit again in a few days."

He hated lying. It left him feeling clammy and dirty, but Bran needed to think he and his secrets were safe. He needed to think Daniel was on his side.

The cat looked up at Daniel, but he couldn't read the golden eyes. Its ears maintained a neutral position, but the tip of its tail flicked, suggesting Bran's mind wasn't as calm as the feline's face appeared.

"I know I missed a day of work, but I'll make up for it. If it's all right with you, I'll keep working on the paths through the garden. It will be easier for all of us if we can get around a little faster."

Bran turned toward the flames and gently lowered himself onto his side. His eyes drifted closed as he enjoyed the warmth. Daniel waited until the flames were established and had plenty of fuel to keep them burning, then he rose and dusted his hands on his jeans.

"I'd better get to it, I guess. I'm pretty tired, so I'll go to bed early tonight, but I'll catch up with you again tomorrow, okay?"

There was no response—not that he'd expected one—so Daniel made his way toward the door. It took a lot of self-control to keep his pace natural when nerves made him want to sprint out of the building. He threw a glance over his shoulder before slipping outside, but the cat remained lounging by the flames.

As he stepped into the woods, he sucked in quick breaths, simultaneously trying to get oxygen to his limbs and resist the urge to hyperventilate. He felt as though he'd just walked beneath a sleeping dragon's nose and come away unscathed.

Lying to a cat had been easier, but it had also made it difficult to gauge what Bran was thinking. *Does he believe me? Or does he know the truth and is biding his time until retribution?*

The second option was enough to paralyze him, so Daniel pushed it to the back of his mind and focused on what he needed to do. The day was still early, and to maintain the appearance of normalcy, he would have to go about his job as if nothing were wrong.

He went back to his cottage. A collection of blocky shapes had been left outside the building. Joel must have made his delivery while Daniel was away.

The largest shape had to be the generator. Daniel ran his hand over the large, box-shaped plastic-and-metal machine. In addition to it, Joel had brought the fridge, a countertop dishwasher, and a halogen oven. Crates of supplies sat beside it. The vegetables had wilted from being left outside too long, but they were in abundant supply.

It would have looked strange if he ignored the delivery, so Daniel spent an hour moving the new equipment into his cottage. He didn't bother setting up the generator since he would never get a chance to use it. But he packed the fruit and vegetables away and arranged the new equipment on his countertop, as though he intended to finish its installation later. Then he collected his shovel and gloves from the shed and returned to the garden.

He'd started progress on a path between the crypt and the house before discovering Eliza's bones. It made sense to continue that work, though he would need to scope out a new lane that had a respectful distance from her body. He found where he'd left off and spent a moment in silence beside the woman's grave. The ground, which had been heaped, was starting to sink back toward level as rain and time compressed it. The makeshift cross he'd placed at the grave's head drooped to one side, and he righted it then looked behind himself.

Eliza's tower was visible from his position, but not much of the rest of the house. The sun's angle made it impossible to see inside the shadowed window, but he wondered if she was watching him.

You haven't been forgotten, Eliza. Just wait a little longer.

He backtracked along the path and marked a new branch that would circumvent the grave by at least twenty feet. Then he started working—pulling weeds out of the ground, digging up small trees where possible, and slashing through the vines and spiderwebs that crisscrossed the area. By keeping the trail fluid, he could weave it around larger trees and take the path of least resistance, which made his work infinitely faster. He'd reached Craven Manor's front door by the time the sun was close to setting.

Bran can't complain about today's work, at least. He wiped the back of his arm across his forehead to clear the sweat that had built there. The exertion had left him drained but satisfied. It felt good to tie off at least one loose end.

The crows were coming in to roost. One at a time, they swooped down from the heavens to alight on branches or stones. Their mournful cries drifted through the cooling night air, and their feathers made a rustling cacophony as they shuffled and bickered among themselves.

Their cries followed Daniel as he took the path he'd cleared back to the crypt. He stopped outside the stone tomb for a moment to clear away weeds that had started to grow in his absence and to say a silent goodbye to Annalise. He didn't know if he would be able to help her. He had a theory that she stayed because her mother was trapped, and that once Eliza's ghost was free, Annalise would follow. If Mrs. Kirshner's account was accurate, it sounded like the mother and daughter had formed a close bond.

But if freeing Eliza didn't save Annalise, Daniel would have to play the situation by ear. There were no locks, salt, or binding runes on Annalise's door. Maybe the girl herself didn't even know why she was trapped on earth. If that was the case, there might not be anything Daniel could do for her. She seemed so friendly and curious, he hated the idea of her being left alone with a man as evil as Bran.

Focus. One step at a time. Look after Eliza first.

He cleared up a few fallen leaves from the front of the tomb then stepped back. He wished he could warn her about what was coming, but he bit his tongue. It would be dangerous to show his cards too soon. Annalise was still loyal to her brother.

Daniel returned to his cottage. He focused on keeping his routine as mundane as possible. Not much of the house was visible from his window, but for all he knew, Bran might be watching him, unseen, as a crow in the trees. He kept the window's curtains open as he washed up, prepared dinner, and ate. Then he changed into his bed clothes, pulled the curtains, and blew out the lamp.

He sat on the edge of the bed for hours. The clock's hands were barely visible in the darkness, but he watched as they crept past nine then ten. Finally, at eleven, he rose and changed into an all-black outfit.

If Bran had been watching the house, he would think Daniel had fallen asleep after dinner. With luck, he would have gotten bored of watching the cottage hours before. Still, Daniel kept his movements small and light as he turned the cottage's handle and crept through a narrow gap in the door.

There was no sign of the crow or the cat. Daniel kept his senses alert as he slipped through the shadowed garden. Day birds had fallen silent, but the bats and night animals chattered. Instead of taking the easiest routes, Daniel deliberately kept to the thickest and darkest parts of the garden as he approached the gate.

He found the bag he'd hidden in the bushes and dug through

its contents for the watch and binoculars. Then he slung the bag over his shoulder and began climbing through the trees.

He found a nook between two trunks with ferns growing around. It offered him a view of the cottage without having to get too close, and the ferns helped shield him. He leaned his back against one tree and tucked his legs in. The space was so gloomy that he felt certain anyone looking in his direction would miss him, but it was still hard to repress the impulse to curl into a ball.

He kept the watch out as he waited. Every few minutes, he shifted position to keep his legs from falling asleep. Time crept by painfully slowly, and tiredness began to make him drowsy. He pinched his arms until they were blue to keep himself alert.

Eventually, his watch ticked over to midnight, and Daniel lifted the binoculars. He could see the cottage's front door and the small cleared space around it. He panned the lens across the space, looking for signs of movement among the plants. It was hard not to feel paranoid. By ten minutes past midnight, he was sweating. At fifteen past, the paranoia morphed into a dogged fear that something was creeping up behind him. It took all of his self-control to keep his eyes focused ahead.

Finally, at twenty past midnight, a glimmer of motion darted between the trees. Annalise frisked toward the cottage, her dress and hair streaming behind her as she leaped over fallen logs. She was so fast and faint that Daniel had trouble keeping the binoculars trained on her.

Daniel was tempted to watch the girl frolic, but she wasn't his primary concern. He turned the binoculars toward the tree boughs and panned across them. A flurry of motion in a large pine twenty meters from the cottage caught his attention, and Daniel had to bite his lip to keep a cheer inside. As he'd hoped, Bran had left the mansion to watch over his sister's play. The great crow alighted in the pine tree and fluffed its feathers as it settled.

Fresh nerves shook off the last hint of Daniel's tiredness. He simultaneously felt the press of limited time and paranoia that moving too soon would attract Bran's attention. He watched as Annalise tapped on the cottage door. She tilted her head to the side, waiting for Daniel's response. When the door didn't open, she skirted around the building and began tapping on the window and walls.

The massive crow sat as still as a statue. His attention seemed focused on his sister, and he showed no sign of impatience. Daniel finally dared to pack away the binoculars and crept backward, deeper into the forest. He clutched his bag of supplies close as he wove toward Craven Manor.

CHAPTER 25

DANIEL'S PROGRESS WAS AGONIZING. He was afraid that if he moved too slowly, Bran would return to the manor before his task was finished. But if he went too fast, he risked making too much noise. He was breathless and shaking with tension by the time he reached the manor's stone steps.

Crows shuffled above Daniel as he jogged up to the front door. He didn't think they were sentient enough to communicate with Bran, but he kept one eye on them. Too much chatter or the flap of wings as they flew away would be enough to alert Bran to the intrusion.

He released a held breath as he passed through the doorway and into Craven Manor. It was nearly impossible to see without a light, but Daniel couldn't risk burning any of the candles. He had to make his way by touch and memory, helped by the thin portions of moonlight glinting through the grimy windows.

Leaf litter crunched under his feet as he crossed the foyer. The fire had gone out long ago, but its embers still released warmth into the cold night air. Daniel found the stairs and began climbing. He cringed as the aged wood groaned under his weight.

Two eyes watched him from the landing. Daniel's breath caught as they fixed on him, then he pressed a hand to his heart as he realized he was seeing the portrait. Not much of the painting was visible—just the eyes and a hint of the nervously smiling lips.

On the landing, he turned toward the stairs to the third floor. The higher he went, the harder it became to see anything. Spiderwebs made him twitch as his questing hands brushed through them. A creak echoed from deeper in the house, and Daniel had to force himself to keep his eyes ahead. *Just a board flexing as it cools. That's all.*

He hung close to the bannister as he ascended. Even before he saw the door, he heard the noise of fingers being scraped over wood. It had filled him with horror before, and its effect was no less potent that night—but for a wholly different reason. Instead of fearing what would happen if the woman was allowed out, he felt sick to think of what she'd endured. For two centuries, she'd been trapped in that tower, clawing every day to be allowed out, but never heard or seen. He risked a whisper. "I'm here, Eliza."

The scrabbling seemed to grow louder as he stepped into the landing. The hallways extended to the left and the right, swallowed in shadows. The stone pathway ahead was a pit of oppressive black. Only the noises floating out of it proved it still existed. The gasping, urgent breaths had become audible beneath the scratching.

Daniel finally dared to take the flashlight out of his bag. He turned it on and pointed it down the passageway. The beam was small and pale—he'd deliberately chosen a cheap LED flashlight to keep its light subtle—but it picked out flashes of the black door, the white cross, and the bronze lock.

"Eliza?" He hadn't heard any sounds to suggest Bran had left the gardens, but Daniel still kept his voice quiet. The clawing was definitely louder. The gasps sounded hungry…and desperate. Daniel lowered the bag to the ground and dug through it. "Just a moment, Eliza. You'll be out soon."

He found the bottle of water, unscrewed its cap, then knelt by the edge of the door. The line of salt was clear and bright in the light of the flashlight, and Daniel drenched it with water. It was the only thing he'd been able to think of to get all of the salt out of the textured stone. He spilled the entire two liters over it then used his hand to brush the liquid away.

Keening noises punctuated the gasps. Fingers scrabbled around the underside of the door, searching for an opening. Daniel threw the empty water bottle aside and took the last item out of the bag: a hammer. There was no way to keep this part of his task silent. He took aim then brought it down against the lock. The impact sent a jolt through his arm and jarred his shoulder, but the metal fell away with a clatter. Using his foot, Daniel pushed the lock out of the way, then he reached for the handle.

The noises inside had ceased. Daniel imagined Eliza waiting

on the other side of the door, knowing her freedom was seconds away. He twisted the handle. The metal made a horrific screech as it moved for the first time in two hundred years, but the latch clicked as it came free. Daniel pulled open the door and stepped back to give the ghost free passage.

Nothing moved past him, though. Daniel lifted his flashlight and directed it through the black doorway. His beam picked up two feet of stone passageway then narrow stairs climbing into the darkness. No one—ghost or human—stood on the other side.

Has she already passed over, maybe? Was opening the door enough to give her peace? He craned his neck to see up the passageway, but the circular staircase twisted out of sight.

"Eliza?" His instincts begged him to back away, but Daniel stepped through the door. The air felt colder inside the tower—and not just by a degree or two. His breath misted when he exhaled. Tiny flakes of frost grew on the stone walls. Daniel touched one of them and recoiled as the chill burrowed into his skin.

He couldn't leave without being sure the ghost had been set free. He climbed the first stair, stopped to listen, then took another step, a third, and a fourth. The tower's staircase wasn't opulent, like the rest of the building. No windows lined the twisting passage, and the walls were bare. The stairs were narrow and steep, and they curled at such a sharp angle that several times, Daniel felt afraid of missing his step.

This isn't a guest room like the other chambers in the house. It's a prisoner's abode.

The higher he climbed, the colder he felt. Wind whistling

through tiny cracks in the stone built into a mournful tune. Daniel kept his flashlight moving across the walls and steps, constantly on guard for either a ghostly figure coming down toward him or Bran coming up behind him. He began to feel as though the stairs would never stop. His leg muscles ached, and heat in his core battled the chill that was crawling into his skin. He tried to remember how tall the tower was from when he'd seen its outside. It had reached a little higher than the roof, but not so high that he thought it justified so many steps.

Then his flashlight picked up a shadowed doorway ahead. Daniel quickened his pace and burst into the room at the top of the tower. His breathing was painful, and frost prickled his lips as the moisture on them froze. He panned the light over the space, moving slowly and trying to understand each of the bizarre items littered there.

The tower room was circular and no more than ten feet wide. A bundle of blankets and a pillow made a crude bed against one wall. An empty rusted pail lay on its side against the opposite stones. Two small novels had been stacked beside it. Immensely thick curtains, so old they were barely more than rags, framed the narrow window.

The window! He turned off the light as he swore under his breath. If Bran had been looking toward the house, he would have seen Daniel's light. He could only pray the mansion's owner had remained facing the cottage.

"Eliza?"

The tiny room offered nowhere for her to hide. He would

have assumed her ghost was invisible, except he'd already seen her at the window several times.

Something about the space felt off. Daniel squinted in the thin moonlight coming through the window as he tried to pinpoint what was making the hairs rise across the back of his neck. The bed was so small that an adult would struggle to lie in it, even with their legs tucked up. He knelt beside it and plucked at the blanket. The cloak of dust covering it was just as thick as what lined the stone floor. A small object lay nestled under the pillow, and Daniel, feeling guilty for disturbing the personal space, tweaked the decayed clump of fabric and feathers back.

A small hand-sewn cloth doll had been hidden beneath the pillow. Its eyes were crooked, and it barely had any wool hair left. Even after being lost for so long, it was clear the doll had been much loved. The threads were all loose from where it had been held, stroked, and squeezed. *This was a child's room.*

He turned toward the bucket. A dark powdery substance coated its insides, underneath the pervading dust. He swiped a finger over the grime and rubbed it between his index finger and thumb. It was gritty and held a strange, almost oily texture.

Charcoal. He recoiled, wiping his fingers clean on his jeans with feverish urgency. He'd found the bucket Annalise's burnt bones had been stored in.

The two books on the floor were both small. One was a work of fiction. The other, the Bible. Daniel turned to look at the window. Wooden shutters had been left open. The curtains were bedraggled and moth-eaten, but a hundred years ago, they would have done a remarkable job at blocking out all traces of light.

So this was Annalise's room. A burning revulsion flooded Daniel's stomach and made shivers dig into him. Mrs. Kirshner had said Eliza was a kind, if shy, woman who loved her daughter. If that was the truth, why had Annalise been sequestered in a space that was barely better than a prison cell? The bed was well used. She must have spent months, if not years, in the tiny room.

Daniel's uncertainty was morphing into panic. He'd felt so confident about his purpose, convinced that Bran was the evil party, and certain that Eliza deserved to be freed. Now, he didn't know what to think—but the tower door was already open, and its lock couldn't be reaffixed.

A noise echoed in the small space—fingernails dragging across stone. Daniel's heart lurched as he turned to face the open doorway, his only escape from the prison.

The entryway was empty. Daniel swallowed as he took a hesitant step toward the door. The scratching was relentless. The source was impossible to pinpoint; the sound seemed to be coming from ahead of him, his sides, above, and below all at once. Moonlight lit the tower room, but it couldn't penetrate more than the first two staircase steps.

Get out, you idiot! Get out! He took another step forward. As he reached toward it, the door shifted. His nerves were keyed tight, and Daniel lunged for the escape. He was a second too late as the door crashed closed.

The boom was impossibly loud. Daniel yelled, but the door's

reverberations drowned out his cry. He pressed his hands to his ears and staggered back, tripping over the bed and hitting the wall.

Eliza isn't gone. Terror clenched his insides. It felt like a vice squeezing his chest until his heart felt ready to burst and every inhale threatened to crack ribs. He looked from the door to the window and back. The door had no lock or handle on his side. It had been designed to prevent escape. He imagined himself as the tower's new victim, hidden away and trapped there for an eternity, spending his years pacing at the window and scratching at the door. Craven Manor's pet, its dark secret, he would never be discovered again.

No. No. No. The word bounced through his head, loud enough that he had to open his mouth to give it a way to escape. "No!"

Daniel crossed to the window. The flashlight felt cold in his shaking fingers. He knew his cottage had an uninterrupted view of the tower, but he couldn't see it in the wan moonlight. He didn't even know if Annalise had stayed by the house when he didn't reply to her knocks, or if Bran continued to watch over her. But he had to try.

He turned on the light and guessed a direction. The beam was weak. He could barely see the circle it cast, but he prayed it would be enough to catch Bran's attention as he panned it across the trees.

Making a deal with the devil to save my soul. His grandmother had said the phrase to him once, when she'd signed the papers authorizing the chemotherapy. The words had never felt more real, or more awful, to Daniel. He was begging a killer to save him from death.

The scratching, scrabbling sounds had grown closer. Stress made Daniel's skin prickle as though a low electrical current ran through him. He kept the light moving, searching for the cottage among the trees, hoping against hope Bran would turn to look at the tower. Underneath the scratching came the rasping, dry breaths.

Terror rooted Daniel to the spot. His fingers shook so badly that the light jittered until it was practically useless. The urge to turn and scan the room was overwhelming, but he couldn't lose focus. Something deep in his gut told him turning away from the window would be a very dangerous move.

Shhhhhhk. The nails scraped over stone, grinding inexorably closer. An undercurrent of desperation rippled through the gasps. *Shhhhhk.* He could almost feel the reverberations through the floor. Sweat trickled into Daniel's eye, but he didn't even dare blink. *Shhhhhk.* It was just behind him, so close that…

Air ghosted across the back of his neck as the stranger exhaled. It was like a razor blade of ice scraping over the already-chilled skin.

He couldn't stand it any longer. He turned.

CHAPTER 26

DANIEL PRESSED HIS BACK against the window. The flashlight's beam jittered as it tried to cut through the shadows.

It wasn't this dark before. The window's curtains were wide open; the moonlight should have been able to illuminate the space. It brought back memories of the afternoon in Bran's study, where multifaceted shadows crawled across the walls and smothered the fireplace's flames. Only this time, the shadows were crawling up Daniel's legs.

Daniel gasped as he saw the black marks writhe over him. Wherever they touched, ice spread over his skin. They were growing higher, over his hips, and clinging to his torso.

A block of thick shadows had gathered before him. They were solid, independent of any surface, and seemed to grow on top of each other in a writhing, struggling mess.

He turned the flashlight toward the creature. The darkness

pulled the light in, swallowing it. Tendrils reached toward the flashlight. When they touched it, the bulb flickered and died. Frost coated the plastic cover, and Daniel choked out a cry as he dropped it.

He was alone with the darkness, trapped in the tower. He could see nothing except rioting layers of shadows. He could feel nothing except the cold.

The shadows were at his throat. The muscles constricted, strangling his breath. Daniel clutched at the vulnerable skin. He could feel the cold radiating from the shadows but couldn't get under them. As he scrabbled, he touched the leather strap hung from his neck.

Daniel pulled out Mrs. Kirshner's talisman. He could see the silver-wrapped vial. It wasn't quite glowing, but the darkness couldn't swallow it the way it had everything else in the room.

The shadows recoiled. Daniel lifted the talisman higher. The pressure around his throat relaxed, and he dragged in a ragged gasp. Moonlight filtered through the glass once again, and it revealed the creature that lived in the attic.

Part human, part monster, the figure was all horror. Black hair coursed around a woman's twisted face. Her eyes flashed black, and when her lips parted, vicious teeth glinted.

"Move on, Eliza." Daniel took a half step toward her, the vial held ahead of himself. He had no idea if the specter could understand him, or even had the ability to follow his instructions, but it was the only thing he could think of through the stress. "Your time on earth is over. *Move on.*"

Terror and anger twisted the face. She flinched back from the talisman, retreating an inch at a time as Daniel crept forward. Then her body seemed to bulge. The inky shadows swirled like smoke, billowing and growing until she filled half the room. Her features distorted until they were unrecognizable as a human, and the bared teeth expanded into fangs.

"Move on." Daniel's words came out as a gasp. Every muscle in his body shook as freezing air radiated over him. He ignored his screaming instincts and inched closer, until his outstretched arm was inches from the swirling black mass.

Eliza exploded toward him. The impact slammed into Daniel's chest. He heard glass break. Everything was darkness, motion, and fear, then he was falling. His limbs struggled for any kind of purchase, but they thrashed through empty air. Glimpses of the tower's outside walls rushed past his eyes, followed by a flash of the nearing ground.

Then he was wrapped in the sound of feathers and the sensation of plucking talons. He felt pulled in every direction. There was no breath left in his body to scream. The motion and sound felt as though it would never end, but then he slammed into the ground, and lights burst across his vision.

Daniel blinked. He lay on the mossy earth below the tower, half-tangled in stunted shrubs and vines. A ringing noise echoed in his ears, and his vision had grown blurry. He gagged when he tried to breathe, and twisted to the side.

His first thought was that he'd gone insane. A massive black bird fluttered across the ground as it tried to right itself. It was easily as big as Daniel. He gaped at it, horrified, before understanding clicked into place. Bran had caught him.

The bird flapped, and the massive wings gusted dirt and dead leaves over Daniel. Then suddenly Bran was in the bird's place. His black hair hung in disarray, and his gray, papery skin looked nearly transparent in the moonlight. He crawled to Daniel and clutched his shoulder.

"What have you *done*?" More accusation than question, the words were wheezed through bared teeth. Bran's blackened fingers carried no more weight than the feathers he'd just worn.

Daniel opened his mouth to answer, but his tongue felt numb. He rolled away from Bran and threw up.

"Well. You are not dead, at least." Bran's rasping voice was clipped and tight. "Can you sit up?"

Daniel tried. His head swam, but his muscles were starting to respond to his commands. He wiped the back of his hand across his mouth as he pulled his knees close to his chest. "I opened the tower door. I'm sorry."

"Did she get out? Has she escaped?" When Daniel didn't immediately respond, Bran snarled, "Answer me!"

For the first time, Bran was showing real anger. *No,* Daniel corrected himself as his fuzzy vision captured the man's wide eyes and flared nostrils. *Not anger. Terror.*

"I washed the salt away. Broke the lock." Admitting it hurt, but he sensed that hiding anything from Bran would be a mistake. "I don't know if she's out. She slammed the door behind us then threw me through the window."

"Damn it." Bran grimaced as he ran his hands through his hair. Then he reached toward Daniel. "Show me your hands."

"What?"

"Let me see your hands!"

Daniel obediently held them out. They were sweaty and still shaking. Bran took them in his own, the touch no more solid than a breeze, and Daniel had to suppress a flinch at the sensation. What he could feel of Bran's skin was cold and unnervingly spongy. *A corpse's fingers.*

Bran turned Daniel's hands over then exhaled and released them. "You are not infected. That is some small luck, at least."

"Infected. Like...the people from Flinton?" Daniel thought he knew the answer to his question, and it filled him with sick horror.

Bran's glance was sharp. "You discovered our lost town, did you?"

He was afraid that Eliza *had infected me.* Daniel's mind reeled as he tried to piece together the puzzle. He felt like he might be sick again. "A supernatural plague spread through the town. But you weren't responsible for it, were you?"

Bran stood and turned away, but not before Daniel glimpsed his mouth twist with grief. "No. Flinton was dead before I even knew it was in danger. Can you stand, Mr. Kane?"

Daniel's legs may as well have been made of rubber, but he willed them to lift him to his feet. He staggered, and pressed a hand to the mansion's wall as dizziness crashed through him. "What exactly happened? I saw the corpses and the doors torn off the church. It looked like a monster had run through the streets."

"That is not far from the truth." Bran crossed his arms over his chest. His sunken, vein-mapped cheeks looked grayer than normal. Multiple shadows coiled away from where he stood, some snaking into the forest and others climbing the mansion's stone walls. "Famine struck the town while I was away at school, and the villagers started calling for a witch hunt. It put the idea in my mother's head that Annalise was filled with demons. She locked my sister in the tower. Partially to hide her from the villagers, and partially to contain her. But months went by without rain. Eventually, Eliza's mind and will crumbled, and she brought Annalise to the church…to be killed."

Daniel struggled to reconcile the new information as his head swam. He could sense bruises growing across his back and side where he'd hit the ground, and as the shock-induced numbness faded, he felt the sting of a multitude of small cuts where glass shards had clipped him. "So she was responsible for Annalise's death, after all?"

"Yes. When we spoke in my study, I told you nearly the whole of the story, but I omitted some details that were especially unpalatable to me." Bran's smile was bleak and humorless. "When I arrived home from school, I found all traces of Annalise erased from the manor, as I already told you. I eventually discovered her bones in what had been her room and her prison, the tower. I confronted my mother."

"You didn't kill her?"

"Not immediately. I heaped blame on her head. How could she murder her own daughter? If there had been any evil in the house, it was her. I suspect my words...*broke* some part of her. She changed. Became less than human." He began pacing, the anxious motion making his hair flow as though it were weightless. "I had not known it, but she had been containing the old-world magic her whole life. She was a shape-shifter who had repressed her nature, terrified it was a curse."

Small details were starting to make sense. Eliza hadn't let the doctor examine her. She invited no visitors into her home. She had even sent the maids away. Those were the actions of a woman desperately afraid she might expose her true nature.

Bran continued, his hoarse voice cracking. "A monstrous creature of shadow escaped the house. I did not know where it was going and did not try to follow it. I only found out later that she went to Flinton. Perhaps she was trying to shift the blame for Annalise's death from herself to the townspeople. Or maybe she was simply lashing out at the nearest habitation. Either way, she spread a terrible plague through the town—a rot that grew from the inside, incurable and with no hope of survival."

"I found her bones in the garden, though." Daniel looked behind them. The night seemed unnaturally silent. His instincts said he wasn't safe now that the tower door was unlocked, but he couldn't bring himself to stop Bran's story.

"Yes. After two days, she returned home as a human. I found her stumbling and raving in the gardens. When I tried to touch her, she lashed out at me." He held up his hands, his fingers tipped with black. "She touched me with the plague. When I saw what was happening, I realized her existence created an unspeakable threat, not just for myself, but for anyone she came in contact with. I killed her to prevent her from spreading the infection further."

Bran tilted his head back to look up at the tower, and his eyes tightened. "I did not expect the shadow creature to survive after her mortal body died. It spewed out of her mouth like a vile pillar of smoke and nearly killed me before I trapped it in the tower."

And I set it free. Daniel groaned. He tried to push away from the wall, but unsteadiness threatened to topple him.

"I suppose you visited Flinton. That is what infused you with doubt, correct?"

"Yeah. I, uh…" Daniel swallowed. "I was told you were responsible for what happened there."

"Then this is my own fault, more than anyone else's." The shadows spreading out from Bran twisted like angry snakes. "With the town dead, and no one allowed to visit it, rumors about its demise were rife. I spent months spreading my own version of events. I visited pubs and wrote anonymously to influential members of society. In my tale, I was the villain. I removed all mention of my mother from the story and claimed that I alone had killed the town."

Daniel frowned. "Why would you do that?"

"Protection. I worried about what would happen to Annalise and to the creature in the tower if strangers came to the house. By spreading the report that I was an old-world monster hungry for blood and capable of poisoning a village, I could make people fear me. A handful of laborers came to loot the manor in the years after Annalise's death. Simply making my presence known was enough to frighten them away." Pale lips stretched into a ghastly smile. "I am sure my appearance aided in that effort."

"So you taught people to fear your home to keep them away."

"Precisely. As time went by, Flinton and Craven Manor grew fainter in people's memories. The forests hid them from curious eyes. Stories became myths. And now the youngest generation—*your* generation, Mr. Kane—has not so much as heard of them. And I had intended for it to always stay that way, forgotten, hidden, safe where we can cause no more harm."

"And to keep Eliza trapped?"

"She is the plague." Bran's fingers twitched. "Now that she is unchained, she will be eager to feed and regain her strength. If she finds her way to any towns, the plague will spread, and nothing can be done for those infected."

Daniel pictured Mrs. Kirshner, terrified and alone in her apartment, cradling her cat as the plague turned her veins black and bubbled her skin. He lurched away from the wall and grabbed at Bran. Touching the other man felt like clutching spiderwebs; they were real and tangible but had no substance. The sensation was alarming, but he didn't let go. "We've got to stop her."

The man's gray face twisted. "How? Salt will slow her but cannot contain her. I had used bolts from the church she worshipped at, but now that they are broken, I have no other recourse."

Daniel scrambled for the strap around his neck and pulled the talisman out. "What about this? I used it against her in the tower. She was afraid of it."

Bran bent closer. As his fingers traced over the beads and vial, his eyes lit up. "Holy water. Pure silver. I can feel the energy flowing out like heat. And if I can feel it, she will, as well. It…it may be enough."

"You think it can kill her?"

"I do not know. But we can try." He turned to examine the house. His movements had become sharp and tense. "My mother will have left the tower by now, but if we are lucky, she might still be contained within the house. Come, quickly, Mr. Kane. I will need your help."

CHAPTER 27

BRAN LED DANIEL ALONG the side of the house. His coat flapped behind him in the cold night air, and his vein-mottled skin looked almost ghostly in the moonlight. Daniel's right leg ached, and his joints were still jarred from the fall, but desperation pushed him to match Bran's half run.

They rounded the mansion's corner, weaving between dead trees and snagging vines. Bran moved with the litheness of a cat and seemed to almost float between the obstacles. That was one of the perks of being made from shadows, Daniel supposed. As they neared the front entrance, the murmur of restless crows filled the cold night air.

Bran sent a glance over his shoulder. "I have very little strength, so I will rely on you to be my hands. We must spread salt across the exits before my mother has a chance to leave the house. Once she is outside the manor, cornering or containing her will be impossible."

"Salt. Yes." Adrenaline kept him on his feet as he stumbled, half-blind, through the weeds and bushes. "Just tell me where to put it."

"Any unlocked door or open window." Bran ran a hand across the tree's bark as he passed under it, and the crows sent up a mournful cry. "Any escape large enough for a human to move through and close enough to the ground that you could survive the jump. And be careful. She is trapped in the same sphere I am, the limbo between the living and the dead. Do you understand? She will be looking for prey to feed on, and she can hurt both you and Annalise."

They reached the open door at the top of the stairs. Bran paused just inside the foyer, his back straight and chin lifted as he scanned the darkness. Daniel held his breath, and together, they listened for motion inside the building. It was deathly quiet.

Bran inclined his head toward Daniel. "Do you remember where the salt is?"

"The little cupboard behind the kitchens."

"Good. I will go ahead and search for my mother. I suspect she will be lethargic after being contained for so long. I will buy you what time I can. Keep the talisman close for now, but be ready to pass it to me once she is trapped."

"Okay." Daniel felt for the little vial under his shirt and squeezed it. "Good luck."

"To you, as well, Mr. Kane." Bran fell forward as though lunging toward the floor. The man vanished in the space of a heartbeat, and in his place was the black cat. Its amber eyes glinted in traces of moonlight as it bounded toward the stairs. It bled into the shadows and a moment later was gone.

Daniel ran his eyes over the space, trying to gauge how much salt he would need to block all of the broken windows. The foyer was oppressive during the day, but at night, he could only make out small patches of it where moonlight sneaked through the glass. Finding his way through the mazelike back rooms would be impossible without light, and he'd lost his flashlight in the tower.

He jogged toward the fireplace, where the half-melted candles stood between the empty photo frames and vases. He snatched a three-pronged candelabrum up and struggled to get it lit. The trio of flames were small, only really enough to light his face and two feet of the darkness that stretched ahead, but they were better than nothing.

Daniel kept half of his attention on the staircase and the higher floors as he crossed to the servants' area at the back of the building. It was hard to know if the silence was a good sign…or a warning. Bran seemed to think Eliza would be slow and cautious after her incarceration, but they had spent a lot of time in the yard. There was no guarantee the woman was still in the house—and if she was, which section she might be creeping through.

A board groaned above him, and Daniel flinched. He held his candles higher and scanned the barely visible chandelier and the plaster ceiling. *It might be the wind. It's an old building.*

The metal door handle to the kitchens screeched as he turned it. Daniel tried to swallow around his dry tongue. The collage of abandoned pots and dust-coated plates glimmered in his light. He slipped around the massive wooden counter and toward the door hidden in the back of the room.

Something clattered on the second floor. Daniel froze, breath held, but the sound didn't repeat. He quickened his movements as he entered the storage room and knelt beside the bags of salt.

Thank goodness for Eliza's paranoia. She probably never expected to be trapped by her own precautions.

The bags were too heavy to lift. Daniel gripped the corners of one burlap sack and tried to drag it, but it weighed more than he did. He felt tiny twitches as the fibers, weakened by age, frayed.

Another floorboard groaned, this time from the opposite side of the house.

Daniel leaped back into the kitchen and hunted through the counters and drawers for a sharp knife. He found one that was discolored with rust but still gouged a chip out of the tabletop when he stabbed it. He took it back to the pantry and used it to slash a hole in the bag's side.

Liters of fine white salt poured out. Daniel kicked the bag, encouraging it to spill its load, until only a third remained. Even mostly empty, it still carried at least twenty kilos, and that would be plenty.

Daniel heaved the bag over his shoulder and grunted as the weight taxed aching joints. He snatched the candelabrum off the floor and moved through the kitchen, knocking chairs askew in his haste.

Block any door or window a human could slip through. He

started by shutting the most obvious escape—the front door. The hinges were stiff, and he had to lean his weight into the wood to move it, but a satisfying click echoed through the space as it shut.

Daniel put the candles down and kicked the leaf litter away from the entrance. He didn't know if the salt line had to be unbroken to work, but it wasn't a time to take risks. Once the space was clear, he heaved the bag off his shoulder and, cradling it in both arms, tipped it so that a stream of the white crystals poured out. He drew the line from stone to stone, completely blocking the doorway, then stepped back.

Daniel considered the windows. They were high—he would need to stand on a ladder to reach them—and just wide enough for a human to squeeze through. They had latches, which meant they could be opened, and some were broken. Daniel dragged the sack behind himself and ran a line of salt along both windowed walls. Finally, he gave the same treatment to the doors leading to the servants' quarters and the other doors leading off from the foyer. He didn't know the house well enough to guess what kind of back doors and staff entrances it might be hiding, so it was safer to simply block them off wholesale.

Once Eliza comes down the stairs, she'll be trapped in the foyer. Theoretically. He glanced toward the staircase, but there was no sign of either Bran or the shadow creature. No more noises came from the higher floors.

Daniel retreated to his candles near the front door and tied the top of the sack to make a strap. It still held four or five liters of salt, and he slung it over his shoulders like a satchel.

Am I missing anything? I've covered every escape on the ground floor. And the upstairs windows should all be sealed. Except...

Something rattled on the second floor to his right. Daniel twitched toward it, one hand braced on the makeshift satchel, and waited. A board flexed above and to the left. Silence reigned for a beat, then one of the crows outside the door cawed, making Daniel flinch.

The house had two broken windows: the tower and the third-floor window Kyle had been pushed through. Bran believed Eliza wouldn't make any kind of jump that could hurt her, but the broken window had a tree beside it. The gnarled structure could be climbed. The chances that Eliza would find it were small, but even small chances were too risky to ignore.

Daniel ran for the stairs. He hung close to the bannister and rolled his feet to minimize the noise he made, but the carpeted steps still groaned under his weight.

Has Bran found her yet? Or is she hiding? He was tempted to call out to the other man, but advertising their locations could only put them both in more danger.

He reached the second-floor landing. Annalise's terrified, paint-rendered smile overlooked him as he crept toward the stairs' second flight. He caught a scrabbling noise coming from the hall to his right. Daniel lifted his candelabrum higher, but all he managed to illuminate were the red-painted walls and dark-wood doors.

Block her escape first. Find Bran after that.

His pulse beat painfully quickly as he climbed the second flight. He felt the tower's presence before he could see it. A cutting, cold wind brushed through his hair and made the candles flicker. The breeze had been funneled down the twisting stairs and through the tower's open door, and it chilled Daniel to his core.

He kept one eye on the inky stone hallway as he crept toward the room with the broken window. Its door was shut, and Daniel opened it as quietly as he could.

More cold air came through the bedchamber's broken window. Daniel shuddered. He held his candelabrum well ahead of himself and used it to fight back the shadows that clustered in the space. Chairs were upended, and a vase lay broken on the floor from Bran and Kyle's fight. The wardrobe door hung open, and Daniel caught a glimpse of rotting robes stored inside.

Daniel placed the candelabrum on the dresser beside the door and tipped his salt bag. The fine white grains tumbled over the carpet as he began creating a line across the doorway. His breath plumed in the frosty air.

Wait...that's wrong. Daniel pulled the bag up, stopping the line half-drawn, to stare at the white mist drifting out of his mouth. The outside was cold at that time of year but not cold enough to cause condensation. It was reminiscent of the frigid air he'd felt in the tower.

She's here. He wet his lips. *Should I call Bran? Or will that make her flee?*

Prickles crawled over his skin. He stood in the doorway, facing into the room. It left his back painfully exposed to the hallways and the stairwell. He tried to listen, but no sounds made it past the rasp of his own ragged breaths.

The candles guttered, their flames struggling to stay alive. Daniel silently begged them to hold on. Their glow made little progress against the dark, but it was better than being blind.

Where is she? He let his eyes travel across the broken furniture. The room didn't hold many places a human-sized being could be concealed. One place his candlelight didn't reach was the space underneath the sagging queen bed.

He flicked his attention toward the window at the opposite side of the room. Its curtains swirled in the cool night air. If he tried to confront Eliza, she could leap through the hole in the glass. And once she was outside, wrapped in the twisting, maze-like garden, there would be no way to get her back.

Daniel took a step into the room. He hung left, close to the wall, to give the bed the widest berth he could manage. The candles stayed on the dresser, and they continued to splutter, making the shadows dance across the walls.

His outstretched arm bumped the wardrobe. He had to shuffle a few inches closer to the bed to slink around it. The smell of rotting fabric grew worse as he passed the open door, and it turned his stomach.

A symphony of night animals and creaking branches floated through the window. Glass crunched under Daniel's feet, but he still didn't take his eyes off the bed. His chest was impossibly tight and his mouth parched as he reached a hand into the bag of salt.

Gently, quietly. He pulled out a fistful of salt. Grains ran between his fingers as he spread it across the window's casing and shards of broken glass.

A soft hissing noise spread through the room. Daniel's fingers shook as he returned them to the bag and brought out another handful of salt. The sound seemed to wrap around him, coming from all directions at once. It was simultaneously frightened, angry, and aggressive.

And it wasn't coming from under the bed. The realization made Daniel's heart skip a beat. As the last of the salt fell from his fingers, he glanced behind himself, where the wardrobe stood at his back.

Two cold eyes glared out of the darkness.

CHAPTER 28

DANIEL OPENED HIS MOUTH, but he couldn't make any sound. The wardrobe's half-open door was less than an arm's length away. Scraps of decayed fabric poked out of the opening, forced out of their usual resting place by the creature that had taken refuge inside. The eyes were locked onto him. He stared back, trapped in the stalemate, as the hissing grew harsher and the temperature plummeted. Then he managed to draw in a sharp breath and yell, "Bran!"

Eliza exploded out of the wardrobe. Daniel glimpsed the door spiraling through the air and heard it smash into the wall behind the bed. Something heavy and impossibly cold slammed into his chest. He fell, and his shoulders and back scraped over the glass shards. Gnashing teeth extended from a wolflike maw made of darkness. Froth dripped from them and splattered across Daniel's cheek. He grabbed for the talisman and thrust it between himself and the monster, and the creature arced back with an ear-splitting yowl.

Daniel rolled, trying to escape the numbing cold that pressed against him, and teeth dug into his shoulder. He screamed, and the teeth tightened. He pressed the talisman into the monster's head and felt it buck. A gurgling, wheezing noise bubbled through its jaws, but it didn't release him.

Something large flew through the room's open door. It slammed into the shadow creature, and Daniel caught flashes of talons and beady, black eyes. *Bran.* The impact scraped him across the floor, digging glass shards into his arm, but the monster finally released his shoulder.

Bran and Eliza tumbled across the floor. The crow was massive, larger than Daniel, but Eliza had grown, as well. Her body seemed more liquid than solid as the smokelike shadows coiled around her. Daniel found it hard to make sense of what he was seeing, except for the gnashing teeth and white eyes.

The monster leaped for the open window but didn't pass through. She rebounded as though the glass pane were still intact, and a whistle-like shriek made Daniel flinch. The salt line had contained her.

Bran leaped toward Eliza. Massive wings buffeted Daniel as his claws clutched the shadow monster. They slammed into the wardrobe. The wood was rotten, and the structure collapsed on top of them. A dark shape exploded out of the fragmented boards. It darted across the room and through the still-open door, around Daniel's half-completed salt line.

The enormous crow flapped once then dove toward the floor, where it seemed to crumple in on itself. The tattered black feathers became dusty fur, and the small black cat stood in the crow's place. It blinked at Daniel then leaped through the door in pursuit of the black monster.

Daniel, breathless and dizzy, leaned against the wall below the window as he struggled to replenish his oxygen. The bedroom seemed unnervingly still now that the warring shape-shifters had left. He touched his fingers to where he'd been bitten. Flecks of blood dotted his arm, but it came from where glass shards had nicked him. The bite had felt agonizingly hard, but it hadn't broken the skin. Dark bruising spread from the teeth marks instead.

She's strong and fast. Daniel tightened his uninjured hand over the talisman as he lurched to his feet. Bran would need the holy water and silver if he had any hope of winning against Eliza. Sounds of a fight came from the staircase, where screeching and beating wings combined into an eerie tempest. Daniel snatched the candelabrum off the dresser to light his way and ran down the first flight of stairs.

The first landing was empty, but as he turned its corner, he saw shadows dancing through the strokes of moonlight that striped the foyer floor. He leaped the last three steps and felt his breath freeze in his throat.

Bran and Eliza tangled in the center of the foyer floor, their inky-black forms blending together. The giant crow was trapped on its back, its wings beating futilely and talons twitching. The shadow monster tore out clumps of feathers. The plumage scattered among the dead leaves and swirled in eddies as the crow's wings fluttered. Each beat was weaker than the one before.

"Hey!" Daniel plunged his hand into the bag of salt as he ran toward the fight.

Eliza raised her head. Black liquid dripped off her bared fangs. Daniel threw the salt at her. The granules glittered in the candlelight as they arced through the air, and when they hit the monster, its snarl transformed into a howl. Plumes of black smoke burst out of her form as though she had been singed. She scrambled back, her head thrashing.

Daniel skidded to a halt at Bran's side. The crow flapped a final time, then its wings drooped to its sides. Daniel dropped the candelabrum beside Bran then lifted the talisman in one hand and a new handful of salt in the other.

Eliza circled at the edge of the candlelight. He could see nothing of her except the glint of murderous eyes and the frothing saliva dripping from her jaws. Daniel bared his own teeth, daring her to try again. Her eyes flicked between the salt and the talisman. She snapped her jaws then leaped away, toward the front door.

Daniel followed her movements and drew a sharp breath. He'd shut the door before pouring salt in front of it, but it now stood propped open. He ran past the massive crow and threw the fistful of salt, hoping it would be enough, but Eliza flattened herself close to the ground as she darted under it. She slipped through the door and disappeared into the night.

"No—how—" Daniel looked down. The salt he'd painstakingly

spread across the threshold was smudged. *By who? Bran? That doesn't make sense—*

He turned to the scene of the fight. The crow had transformed back into the small black cat. It looked horribly forlorn as it lay in a ring of shredded feathers and dark blood. Daniel took a step closer, but Bran wasn't moving.

"Lookie here, I finally found you."

The voice came from behind him. Daniel twisted. He was just in time to stop Kyle's fist from connecting with his head. He grasped the wrist, holding Kyle at arms' length, and stared at him with growing horror.

Kyle looked ghastly. He wore his jacket over the hospital pajamas, which were stained and torn from traveling through the forest. His hair was a mess, and unshaven stubble covered his sagging cheeks. He carried a yellow plastic jug in his spare hand. When he exhaled, his breath reeked of alcohol.

Daniel grimaced. "Damn it! You can't be here! You opened the door, didn't you? You must have broken the salt line."

"The what now?" Kyle took a step closer.

Daniel backed up.

Kyle tried, and failed, to twist his hand free as his bloodshot eyes narrowed. "Look, I don't want any problems, you hear me? I'm just here to claim what's mine."

Daniel refused to release Kyle's wrist as the man forced him to back up another step. "You're insane for coming back. What are you after? Your backpacks? I left them in the corner by the door."

"I'm insane?" Kyle's laugh was cracked and raspy. He dropped the yellow jug, and it made a sloshing sound as it hit the floor. "Take a look in the mirror. And I don't want a backpack, you idiot. I'm after what I'm owed. The gold. That freak threw me out of a window and screwed up my shoulder. I'm entitled to compensation. Just tell me where it is, and we can avoid any other trouble, yeah?"

They took a third step back, trapped in a stalemate. Daniel could clearly see what he'd already started to suspect in the hospital; Kyle had become irrational and obsessive. The hungry light in his eyes was unfamiliar. He would have never thrown away his sense of self-preservation before the accident, no matter how great the reward. But the fall had damaged his mind, and all he cared about anymore was getting the golden coins.

"Okay." Daniel looked over Kyle's shoulder, toward the open door. He didn't know how fast Eliza was moving. If he was quick, it might not be too late to corral her back inside the mansion. "I'll give you all the gold I have. But first I need your help. A woman named Eliza ran through the door just a moment ago. She looks like…like a monster. We have to get her back inside the manor. I can't tell you how important it is. If you help me, I'll get you everything I have as a reward."

He'd been too focused on the door. Kyle took advantage of his distraction and closed the space between them, his other fist rising. Daniel ducked to avoid the blow, but his balance had been thrown off, and his legs fell out from underneath him. They collapsed to the ground, Kyle on top of him, and Daniel gasped as the air was forced from his lungs.

"Oh, you need help all right." Kyle sneered, his mouth stretched into a demented smile. He gripped Daniel's shoulders, pulled them up, then shoved them back down, cracking his skull against the tile floor. "A whole, huge lotta help."

Daniel's vision turned black.

CHAPTER 29

DANIEL GROANED AND ROLLED to his side. Lights flashed across his eyes, and nausea made him retch, but there was nothing in his stomach to bring up. Audio distortions dug into his skull, making him shudder. It sounded like static. He wished it would stop; it was hurting his head. But as he lay still with his eyes squeezed closed against the lights, the sound only grew louder.

Not static… Crunching leaves?

He lay on the marble floor. The cold tile felt good against his flushed skin and aching head, but the dry leaves dug into his cheek. His left arm hurt. A thick, unpleasant smell pushed through the scent of dust and decay and made the migraine throb twice as bad.

Gasoline. Kyle was carrying a plastic bottle. Did he spill it when he dropped it?

Daniel cracked his eyelids open. The lights redoubled, flashing white and yellow, and Daniel's scrambled mind put the pieces together. He lurched to his knees and instantly regretted it as the migraine slammed his skull hard enough to make him gag again. This time, when he inhaled, smoke itched at his lungs.

He lit a fire. The madman's trying to burn the house down.

Daniel couldn't have been unconscious for more than a minute or two. The fire was still in its infancy but spreading quickly along gasoline trails. Kyle had doused circles through the dry leaves and led the flames to the decaying chairs beside the fireplace then tipped the candelabrum over to light it. Daniel didn't know if there was enough kindling to spread the fire to the rest of the building. He didn't want to find out. He stood, begging his feet to carry his weight, and staggered. The salt bag was still slung around his shoulders, weighing him down, but he didn't want to drop it yet.

Flames licked close to his boots. Daniel stamped on them, crushing the leaves they were consuming, but all he managed was to shoot embers out like miniature fireworks.

He covered his mouth and nose with his sleeve and tried to blink through the haze. The fire was too widespread to give him hope that he could put it out. It had already caught on two of the long, tattered curtains at the back of the room. Smoke filled the space, making Daniel cough, and the thinning oxygen left him dizzy.

I've got to get out. Daniel rotated, hunting for Bran. He tried to call the man's name but choked on the air.

The sickening odor of burning feathers built into the bitter smoke. Daniel turned toward it and found the scene of the fight, where the crow's plumage had been torn out. The feathers were melting in the flames. Daniel staggered through them and found the black cat lying on the tiles. He didn't stir even when the fire licked close to him, but his chest rose in small gasps.

"Bran!" Daniel knelt at the cat's side and nudged its head. Oxygen deprivation was making it hard to think and see. The cat didn't move. Its eyes were closed, but its jaw hung open a fraction. The tiles were splattered with the crow's dark blood, but Daniel couldn't see any sign of cuts on the cat's body. Even so, something was very wrong with Bran. Daniel eased one arm under the cat. He cradled its head in his elbow and tried to keep the rest of its body level as he held it close to his chest. Then he stood and ran through the growing flames.

Instead of subsiding as the leaves were consumed, the blaze had grown larger. Its heat made sweat run down Daniel's forehead and back, and every breath made his throat and lungs ache as moisture was sucked out of the air.

The front door was still propped open. Daniel didn't know if Kyle had left or ventured farther into the building. It seemed insane to light a fire unless he was about to leave, but on the other hand, Kyle wouldn't want to return to the town empty-handed.

Daniel ran through the open door and stumbled down the stairs to the yard. Compared to the inferno, the outside air was achingly cold. Daniel's skin smarted from the shift.

Crows shuffled in the tree. Their caws blared through the still night air as they vocalized their distaste for the glow and smoke coming through the window.

Daniel squinted as he hunted for the shadow beast among the moonlight-speckled, overgrown plants. He couldn't see any movement, but the plants to his right were darker and lumpier than he remembered, and Daniel pulled the cat closer to his chest as he crept toward them.

Patches of the trees' bark had bubbled and discolored into fist-sized clumps then frozen solid again. The effect was like melted plastic. Daniel picked up a stick and used it to prod one of the protrusions. Black liquid oozed out, and Daniel's mouth twisted. *The plague.*

He could visualize the monster lurching into the garden. It would have brushed against trunks and branches, and everywhere it touched had become deformed. The poison was spreading, too. Even in the few seconds he'd been watching, he could see the discoloration creeping across the bark. Everywhere it touched puckered in and shriveled.

Damn it. How far will this spread? He could see the trail leading farther into the woods. The trees' distortion was horrific and repulsive, but it gave him a clear path to follow.

Daniel bent to place the cat onto the ground outside the house, but stopped. The crows continued to shuffle and cry behind him. They were scavengers, and to them, an unresponsive cat would look like a carcass ready to pick dry. Daniel shuddered and held the feline closer. He did his best to ignore the nausea and dizziness as he jogged into the trail the shadow beast had created.

The woods felt more oppressive than normal that night. Branches scraped across his cheeks and snagged his clothes.

Sticky liquid—sap burst from the trees that had been damaged—dripped onto him. The crows continued to cry, but as they faded into the distance, a suffocating silence took their place. No animals or insects moved inside the gardens. Daniel was alone with his ragged breathing and pounding heart.

He didn't get far before a shape blocked his path. It looked as though it had once been a hedge. Twisted branches and dense leaves grew out of control, higher than Daniel's head. The trail of plague climbed over the structure, but there was no way Daniel could follow.

He glanced to his right. A dozen meters away, the crypt's rooftop seemed to shimmer in the cool light. Daniel turned toward it and struggled through the vines and spiderwebs blocking his path.

"Bran?" He nudged the cat's head as he broke into the small clearing he'd created around the tomb. "Bran, can you hear me? We're at Annalise's tomb. You'll be safe here. Okay?"

Daniel ducked into the small alcove at the crypt's door. The stone seats would be cold, but it was better than leaving Bran out in the open where birds or animals might find him. Daniel lowered Bran onto a clear patch of the stone bench then shrugged out of his jacket. The chill sent shudders through him as he wrapped the clothing around the cat's limp form.

His arm stung. He had aches and bruises forming across his body, but none of them hurt quite like his left shoulder. He held his arm up to the moonlight.

Dark marks ringed his upper arm where Eliza had bitten him

and burst his blood vessels. The marks seemed to have grown since he'd checked them in the upstairs bedroom, and a red flush spread down toward his elbow.

That's not good. Daniel pressed his lips together. Prickles rose across the back of his neck, and he squinted toward where moonlight poured through the alcove's doorway. It highlighted a faint, wispy figure. Annalise's eyes were huge and terrified, a perfect replica of the expression she wore in her portrait.

"It's going to be okay." As soon as he spoke, Daniel felt guilty. The words were dangerously close to a lie.

Annalise's eyes flicked from Bran to Daniel. She twisted her fingers together.

Daniel remembered what Bran had said earlier: Eliza was trapped in the realm between the living and the dead and able to harm them both. He pressed his palm into his aching forehead as he tried to think through his next move. "Annalise, I want you to stay here with your brother, all right? I'm going to try to track Eliza and kill her if I can. If she comes back to the crypt, I want you to do whatever you need to in order to stay safe. Do you understand?"

There was comprehension in the panic-filled eyes, but Annalise didn't nod or smile. The fingers continued to twist together, squeezing and wringing with anxious energy.

"If Bran wakes up, tell him where I've gone. But stay quiet and don't venture out where Eliza can see you." Daniel hitched the bag of salt a little higher on his shoulder. There wasn't much left in it, but it had been effective at driving the shadow monster back.

He gave the siblings a final parting look. Bran's whiskers were barely visible under the jacket. Annalise stood beside him, head bowed and fingers still working. She looked lost. Daniel wished there were something else he could do for her, but neither of them would be safe until Eliza was gone. He faced the gardens and stepped into the smothering vegetation.

Bran said she would be looking for prey. Will she go straight to a town, or will she stay on the ground she knows as she hunts for Annalise, Bran, or me?

As he wove toward the damaged hedge, Daniel hoped for the latter option. He tried to imagine what his city would look like a year after feeling Eliza's wrath. Would the concrete and bricks crumble under the rot like the wooden homes in Flinton had? He pictured corpses, bubbling and lumpy with the fungus, huddled inside their apartments and cars. Other cities would set up a quarantine zone, as the towns surrounding Flinton had. They would do what had to be done to keep the disease contained, even if it meant turning away refugees.

Daniel spotted a deformed tree ahead and corrected his course toward it. The plague crawled over the trunk, and black fungus had begun to ooze out of cracks in the bark. Daniel avoided touching it as he ducked around the dying plant and followed the trail. Eliza seemed to be heading toward the gate Daniel used to access Craven Manor.

He felt woefully underprepared for the confrontation. He had the talisman and the salt but none of Bran's knowledge or experience. He didn't know what he needed to do to kill or even contain Eliza. If he was lucky, tying the talisman around her neck would be enough. If he was unlucky, he might need to find a way to make her eat it or break the glass and sprinkle the holy water over her. He didn't want to contemplate what would happen if none of that worked.

The plants thinned, and Daniel stepped into the clearing ringed by stone statues and benches. A dozen agonized faces seemed to glare at him, the discoloration highlighting the folds of their clothes and painting tears down their cheeks. The basin in the circle's center looked deeper than it had before, and its filling of leaves and dirt seemed darker.

Daniel came to a stop. He was breathing heavily, and his legs, taxed to their limit, shook.

Which way did she go? It was hard to see the trail of destruction when shadows disguised it so well. He huffed, trying to replenish the oxygen in his aching limbs, and a cloud of condensation gusted away from his lips.

She's close. When he searched for it, he felt the unnatural chill cutting at his skin and digging into his bones. He reached into the bag of salt as he turned in a slow circle. Mist had appeared out of nowhere, spilling between the statues and swirling around the dry fountain, and thickened with every passing second. As Daniel hunted among it, his eyes began to register bizarre shapes slinking through the white.

A featherlight touch breezed across the back of his neck. He reacted quickly, twisting away from the sensation and pulling out a handful of salt. The space behind him was empty. He blinked, then the mist shifted, and Daniel gasped as he recognized the outline of a figure.

Annalise peeked out from behind one of the statues. The girl was shaking. Her hair flowed around her face like a river, but hardness had replaced the fear in her eyes.

Daniel released the salt and took a step toward her. He kept his voice to a whisper. "What are you doing here? It's not safe."

She gave her head a small, quick shake. Daniel frowned. *Eliza didn't find the tomb, did she? No, there couldn't have been enough time—Annalise must have followed me. Why? To help?*

"You need to go back and hide." Daniel was hyperaware of the way each word created a tiny plume of condensation. Sweat on his forehead stung as it froze. "Quickly, Eliza's here. I'll be fine—go and stay with Bran."

Annalise raised a hand. Her long, near-invisible finger pointed over Daniel's shoulder. He tried to swallow as he turned.

Mist grew thick in the space between a headless faun and a weeping Grecian woman. Among the swirling white glowed two wide, hungry eyes.

CHAPTER 30

DANIEL TOOK A STEP back. He reached into the sack tied to his side and grasped a fistful of the coarse grains. The shadow creature drew out of the mist, its writhing, smokelike form pushing the white fog aside. Its eyes had latched on to the girl behind Daniel, and he shifted to block Eliza's view.

How much does Eliza remember? Annalise is technically the reason she became this monster. Does she want revenge?

Eliza took another step forward. Her monstrous maw gaped open, dripping strands of saliva onto the leaf litter. Her claws, each one as long as Daniel's forearm, flexed and dug up clumps of dirt. She'd grown larger since he'd confronted her in the foyer. He didn't know if she was feeding off the environment or whether Bran's blood had nourished her, but she towered above him.

How on earth am I going to get the talisman onto her without being ripped apart? Terror squeezed Daniel's insides, but he couldn't afford to feel it. A single moment of weakness could carry an unforgivable cost.

Motion made him flinch. Annalise darted out from behind him. She leaped toward the creature that had once been her mother then danced back.

Eliza reacted instantaneously. A snarl ripped through the cold air as she lunged toward the girl. Daniel threw the salt with a yell. He'd hoped it would stop the monster, but Eliza's momentum carried her past it, her jaws reaching toward the girl's throat—

Annalise ran into the statue of an elegant woman holding a vase. The ghost morphed through the stone like smoke through a fly screen, and a second later, she appeared on its other side. Eliza hit the sculpture. A scraping, crunching noise rent the air as the impact crumbled the stone. The woman's head tumbled off, the tear-streaked cheeks catching in the light before it smashed on the ground. The vase flew away, half of an arm still attached to it. Chips and dust billowed out in a small cloud, and the shadow monster yowled.

Trapped in the space between the living and the dead—like Bran, not quite tethered to the real world but still too solid to walk through walls. We can use this.

Annalise's huge terrified eyes met Daniel's. She looked as though she wanted to speak, but he understood her glance and nodded. "Keep her distracted. I'll get the talisman around her—somehow."

The girl's lips twitched, and for a second, a smile lit her expression. Daniel grabbed clumps of salt out of his bag, trying not to notice how much his left arm ached, and scattered them over the ground between the nearest statues. The leaf litter was too uneven to let him make unbroken lines, and there was no time to clear it away, but Daniel hoped the salt would still give some protection. He stepped behind the lines he'd created as Eliza rose.

Black blood dribbled from the wolflike skull where she'd impacted the stone. She turned toward Daniel, but before she could move more than a step toward him, Annalise dashed in front of her.

"Be careful!" Daniel ran forward. A swipe from the immense claws grazed the tips of Annalise's hair. The girl was fast and light on her feet but too reckless. She twirled to face the monster as she darted through another sculpture.

Eliza had learned from her first mistake. Instead of chasing blindly, she swiped at the statue. Stone fragments sliced through nearby vegetation as she obliterated the dancing faun.

Daniel tossed another handful of salt behind himself, finishing a poor barrier around one-half of the circle. Then he ran forward, keeping his steps as light as he could and weaving behind the fountain to avoid drawing too much attention. The black creature prowled around the basin's other side. Its eyes were fixed on Annalise, and it didn't react to Daniel as he approached from behind.

Annalise toyed with the beast, dancing forward and then leaping back. Her movements kept Eliza's attention fixed on her, but it also brought her dangerously close to the snapping jaws. Daniel took a breath to steel himself then pulled the bag off his shoulder and lunged forward. He threw the sack into the air, launching its salt across the congealed shadows. At the same time, he threw himself onto the monster's back.

Eliza reacted as soon as the salt touched her. She arched, eyes blazing, and a sound somewhere between a roar and a human's scream ripped out of her. The shadows thrashed as plumes of smoke billowed off them. Daniel hit her back and dug his hand and legs in. It was one of the most bizarre sensations he'd ever experienced, like clutching air that refused to give under his fingers. She was colder than the arctic, and tremors ran through his skin as though he'd landed on a live wire.

It was working, though. The salt had distracted her enough that his presence wasn't her priority. She bucked and thrashed, but the motions weren't intended for him, and no claws dug into his side. Daniel clung on with all of his strength and reached one hand into his shirt for the talisman.

His fingers touched skin. Daniel's heart lurched as he fumbled for the leather straps and silver-wrapped vial. He came up empty.

No! He couldn't breathe, couldn't think. *Did I drop it? Where?*

Eliza's scream boiled down into a rumbling growl. The plumes of smoke thinned as the salt ceased to burn her. She twisted her head, and one of the electric-cold eyes latched on to Daniel. He could feel its intensity like poison in his blood.

Daniel pushed away from the creature and grunted as he hit the ground. The impact jarred his head, still sore from the fight in the foyer, and a spark of understanding hit Daniel. He wanted to scream. Kyle must have taken the talisman. He would have seen the vial while Daniel lay unconscious in Craven Manor's foyer. Kyle wasn't the kind to ignore a trinket that might be valuable, especially not when its owner wasn't in a position to guard it. He would have snapped the cord off Daniel's neck and carried it away. *Where? Deeper into the house, which is now being consumed by flames? Or into the garden and toward the town?*

Both options carried it far beyond Daniel's reach. The monster twisted toward him. It had grown impossibly large. As its jaws widened, the stench of rot and evil flowed out of them.

A glint of light appeared beside Daniel. Annalise's open palm smacked the monster's head as she leaped past it in a desperate effort to distract it. The attempt worked a little too well. The monster twisted after her, and the maw snagged her hair.

Annalise tumbled to the ground. Her mouth opened in a scream that no one heard. She tried to crawl backward, away from the beast, but it kept its jaw locked on her hair. A flick of its head dragged the girl forward, and Annalise's face crumpled in pain.

"No!" Daniel beat at the wolflike head, but his fists seemed to cause it no more pain than a gnat. The closest glowing eye locked on to him. It seemed to be laughing. Eliza knew she had won. A massive claw-tipped hand rose and pressed into Annalise's back.

A high-pitched shriek came from the sky. Daniel, trapped in a whirlwind of horror and fear, couldn't identify the sound. Then the cry was joined by a flurry of beating wings, and he was buffeted back.

Daniel lifted his arms to shield his face, but he didn't need to. The crows paid no more attention to him than they did to

Annalise. They were focused on one object alone: the beast made of shadows. The birds—at least two dozen of them—swooped at it in waves. Each time they descended, they pecked. Some came away carrying threads of shadow. One fluttered out of reach with something round and moist glistening in its beak. Daniel gagged as he recognized the object as an eye.

Eliza's scream was loud enough to make Daniel's ears ache. Her head whipped as she tried to fix her jaws around the birds. Gore oozed from the plucked eye, and when she jerked, globs flew out and splattered across the mud.

Daniel scrambled back. It took a moment to find Annalise among the motion; the girl was cowering behind the empty fountain. She held both hands above her head and pressed her face into the ground. Daniel called to her, but she didn't respond.

One of the pecking, flapping birds was larger than the others. It was struggling to stay in the air, each beat labored, and its wings were missing plumage. It seemed to be leading the flock and ventured closer to the frothing teeth than the others dared.

"Bran!" Daniel's voice was hoarse. He scrambled closer, hand stretched out. "I don't have the talisman! Be careful!"

If Bran heard him, the bird didn't show it. Black writhed over black as shadows and crows tangled. It was impossible to see what was happening. Then Eliza let out a final, screaming howl and plunged away from the mass. The crows followed as she darted between two of the statues. She crossed over a salt track, and a billow of smoke rose from her back as she lurched into the forest. Within seconds, she and the crows had vanished.

Daniel gained his feet. His arm, the place he'd been bitten, no longer hurt. Instead, it felt numb. He touched it and recoiled. The flesh had turned cold and lumpy.

"I am sorry." The wheeze sounded barely human.

Daniel staggered around the fountain. Bran lay in the scuffed dirt and shredded plant matter where the fight had unfolded. The man's breathing was rapid and shallow. He tried to roll onto his side but flinched and slumped back.

Daniel knelt beside Bran. He reached toward his friend's shoulder but didn't touch it for fear of hurting him more. "Can I do anything?"

"No." Bran's smile devolved into a grimace.

Daniel felt ghastly. The fight had taken all of his remaining energy. Even in the wan moonlight, he could see something was seriously wrong with his arm. The red flush had vanished, and black lines ran out from the bite wound. They extended as low as his wrist, and he suspected they ran across his chest, as well. "I'm infected, aren't I?"

Bran didn't reply, but there was sadness in his eyes.

Daniel ran his good hand over his face and sighed. He was glad it was night; darkness helped hide the growing bulges as the fungus writhed through him. He hoped he would succumb to it quickly, before dawn. "I screwed everything up. Everything. I never should have—"

"To err is human." Bran's eyes drifted closed. "She would have found a way out eventually, with or without your help. My containment was imperfect and was slowly decaying."

"I sure didn't help, though."

"If anyone is to blame, it is me for withholding my family's past from you. Pride is truly a deadly sin, and I let it cover up the darkest parts of my history. And now we all pay for it."

Daniel stared toward the forest. He could no longer hear any sign of Eliza or the crows. Even if he'd had the strength to run, he doubted he could catch up to her. And he was helpless against her without any weapon. There was nothing he could do except wait.

Annalise curled up at Bran's side. She was trying to hide her presence, but Daniel caught glimmers of her outline when she moved. He wondered if she would stay after he and Bran were gone. He imagined her spending a century among the trees and crumbling walls, alone and forgotten, and he understood why Bran had put his own afterlife on hold for her.

Daniel tilted his head back. An orange glow lit the tops of the trees to his right. At first, he thought it was dawn come prematurely, but then he tasted smoke on the air and realized its source. "The house is burning."

"Good." Bran's inhale was like sandpaper over wood. "It is tainted ground."

"Still, it feels wrong, doesn't it? So much history bundled up in one building. And not all of it bad." Daniel wrapped his good arm around his knees and rested his chin on their tops. He was freezing cold. When he focused on it, he could feel the plague spreading through him. His arm felt too large, the skin stretched tight, as fungus crawled through his veins like fuzzy, repulsive caterpillars. He knew he would break into a screaming, crying mess if he watched it, so he fixed his eyes on the orange glow and began talking, almost desperately. "All of those bedrooms. Your family must have been big when the place was built. Even with the dust and dirty windows, it was still a magnificent home. I bet it would have been amazing with the candles all lit and full of guests."

"If you care for the damn building so much..." Bran lifted a hand toward the sky. He spread his blackened fingers then contracted them into a fist and pulled it back toward his chest.

Daniel blinked at the treetops, but it took a second for him to taste the change in the air. The stars began to disappear. Then a speck of cold water hit Daniel's cheek. It was followed closely by more, then a flash of lightning brightened the scene for a moment as rain clouds swarmed the area. The rain came thick and hard, smothering them. It plastered Daniel's hair to his face and washed the dirt, salt, and dust off him. The stone statues looked even grimmer with rain saturating their forms, but it also softened them in a strange way. They no longer seemed judgmental, but merely sad. In the distance, the glow from the fire began to abate.

"That's a cool trick." He gave a shaky laugh. "Must make watering the gardens easy."

Bran was silent. His pallid face had become slack, and the pained crease between his eyes was gone. Daniel watched the raindrops ping off his skin for a moment then buried his face in his knees. He couldn't see Annalise any longer. He felt wholly alone. It was just him and the hideous growths spreading through his body.

Rain washed over him, filling the fountain and turning the ground to mud. Daniel clenched his teeth as he tried to keep his cries silent. Something moved through the plants ahead. Daniel made himself lift his head. The sounds came from something large. It snapped branches and crushed leaves underfoot, and beneath the churn of motion was an undercurrent of harsh breaths.

Has the shadow beast come back to finish what she started? Let her. I have nothing left, so my death may as well buy the people in town a few more minutes.

The shape paused between two trees. With the clouds blocking the moonlight, it was perfectly hidden in the shadows. Daniel could see only a pair of wide eyes.

CHAPTER 31

DESPITE DANIEL'S FOG OF exhaustion and grief, something about that shape skulking between the trees seemed wrong. Daniel focused on its eyes. The crows had plucked out one of the shadow beast's, but the figure ahead of him had two.

"Hello?" His voice sounded awful, as though he'd screamed until he was hoarse. He tried to rub his wet hair out of his eyes but accidentally used the infected hand. The spongy, bulging flesh was horrifying.

The shape took a step forward. It was too small to be the massive beast Eliza had become. In the cloud-dampened moonlight, Daniel caught a glimpse of human skin. The gait was familiar. Bile rose in Daniel's throat.

"It's a bloody labyrinth here." Kyle spoke in a stage whisper, one projected so loudly that Daniel had no problem hearing it through the drumming rain. "It's cursed. It's got to be. He won't let me leave. Which way is out, Dan? You've got to tell me. Just point in the right direction. There won't be any more trouble from me."

He carried a bag. It looked heavy. The idea that he might have actually found Bran's coins flitted through Daniel's mind, but it was drowned out by cold, burning resentment.

Kyle took a step closer. The splotchy color from earlier had drained from his face, leaving it gray and mixing sweat into the rain that coursed over him. He raised a hand to shield his eyes. Daniel could feel his cousin's gaze skipping from him to the crumpled body at his side. He shuffled forward to hide Bran. To let Kyle gawk at him felt wrong. Irreverent.

"Tell me how to get out of here." Kyle still spoke in a whisper. He had probably heard the fight, Daniel realized, and had been spooked. The alcohol was wearing off, and with it went the bravado. He was probably desperate to get to the safety of his home again, but he'd spent more than an hour lost in the living maze surrounding Craven Manor. In another life, Daniel would have felt pity for him. But all he had left was burning, boiling frustration.

"You're to blame for this!" He couldn't keep the angry tremor out of his voice. "I've got blame on my shoulders, too. So does Bran. And Eliza. And the people who killed Annalise. We're all at fault here, but you were the lynchpin. If you hadn't tried to rob the house, broken the tower door, told me about the town, taken the talisman—"

"The way out!" Kyle's boots squelched in the mud as he lunged forward. His face contorted in fear and anger, he raised a fist. "You've got to know where it is! Show me, you bastard!"

Daniel raised his infected arm to point behind himself. Kyle gagged and staggered back as he saw the blackened, bulging flesh. What little color had been in his face bled away. "What the hell?"

"This is on your head." Daniel dropped the arm. He could feel the infection crawling through his chest and creeping up one side of his neck. He wondered if he would suffocate when it reached his esophagus. That would be a mercy. "It's on my head, too. Why couldn't we have left well enough alone?"

"You're not making any sense, man." Kyle's eyes didn't leave Daniel's arm. Gripping the bag with a shaking hand, he backed away, his steps unsteady. "Just…just stay there, all right? I'm gonna get out of here and…and I'll send someone back for you, okay?"

That was a lie. Kyle clearly had no intention of looking back once he was out of Craven Manor's bounds. Daniel tilted his head back to feel the rain across his face. The anger faded as though the water washed it away. Instead, he felt numb. His infected arm was prickling, but he didn't want to see how bad it had gotten. He dreaded seeing the skin split, the fungus spilling out to cement him to the ground beside Bran's body.

"Just…don't try to follow me, all right?" Kyle was at the edge of the clearing. The shadows behind him seemed impossibly dense, like a wall of black that would swallow him up.

Daniel's heart missed a beat. The darkness had blinded him, and the rain had deafened him to what had been going on around them. He tried to call a warning. "Behind you!"

"Stay—stay there—" Kyle's eyes flashed as they watched Daniel and the blackened arm. He didn't hear the grating, gasping breaths. He didn't see the shadows beginning to coil around him. He couldn't feel the single eye trained on the back of his head.

Daniel reached forward, but his legs refused to lift him. Kyle responded to the motion by taking another step back, right into Eliza's open maw.

The scream was one of the worst things Daniel had ever heard. He threw his good arm over his eyes to block out the sight of the carnage. The wail only lasted two seconds, then Kyle gurgled and abruptly fell silent. The sounds of snapping bones and wet chewing noises followed.

Daniel moaned. He'd hated Kyle, but he'd never wanted the other man to die. He kept his head down, sickened by the slippery chewing noises. Eliza would come for him next, he knew. He inclined his head toward Bran's side, where he'd last seen the ghost. "Annalise. Run. Hide."

A flicker of movement illuminated her. She was sitting with her knees drawn up under her chin, arms wrapped around them, and head bowed so deeply that her hair hid her features. She shook her head vigorously.

"Please. You still have a chance. I can keep her occupied for a few minutes."

The chewing noises fell quiet. For several painful heartbeats, the only thing Daniel heard was the rain rushing through the foliage. Then a low, slow whining noise came from the shadows. Daniel had been trying not to look at it, but as the sound grew louder, he couldn't stop himself.

Eliza had grown immense. Her shoulders brushed some of the

trees' higher branches, and her sides pressed against the trunks surrounding her. Bright-red gore sparkled on her teeth. Her single eye seemed to shine as it rolled back in her head. A shudder ran through the writhing shadows, then she thrashed her head to one side.

Daniel scuttled back and bumped into Bran. As another keening, screeching noise escaped the monster, the need to hide overwhelmed him, but there was nowhere to go. Instead of trying to run, he ducked down and pressed his good arm across his face.

The wail grew in pitch and volume. Trees creaked as Eliza lurched into them. Her massive claws dug into the ground, and as they twitched, they tore up chunks of earth.

Flecks of something dusty brushed over Daniel's cheek. They felt like moth wings, and he impulsively swatted at them. One of the shapes stuck to his hand and crumbled when he flexed his fingers. Like a scrap of burnt paper, it was thin and fragile, and the rain made it disintegrate into soot-gray clumps.

More of the shapes brushed past Daniel. They clung to his hair and clothes, and he shuddered at the sensation. He knew where they were coming from, but it was horrible to watch the monster, Eliza, disintegrate. She threw her head back, the neck twisting farther than should have been possible, and as she screamed, the muscles in her throat rippled then tore. They billowed away, and the shadows became soot as they left her body. It clumped on the ground, in the branches, and over the grim statues.

She's dying. Daniel squinted against the rush of black fragments. Eliza seemed to be crumpling in on herself, as though someone had put a magnet inside her chest and her body was being sucked into it. Claws broke into shards. Her face collapsed. Her limbs twitched a final time, then a billow of black smoke exploded out from her. Daniel gagged as it washed over him. It seemed never-ending, as though the world had been swallowed in the heavy, cold dust. Daniel squeezed his eyes closed and tried to hold his breath, even as he convulsed with coughs.

As the rain beat through it, the air gradually cleared. Daniel's lungs stopped burning. He blinked his eyes open and saw the scene had been blanketed with a layer of soot. A mound of it rested where Eliza had last stood. Rain was turning it into a clay-like mud, and a bright, metallic shape emerged in the heap's center as the soot was washed away.

Daniel scooted forward and used his good hand to pluck the talisman out of the charred fragments. It felt warm. *How about that. Kyle must have put it in his pocket. And Eliza swallowed it when she consumed him.*

There was nothing left of either Kyle or Eliza. Daniel slumped back, his chest aching and his head foggy. He should have been elated or at least relieved, but instead, he just felt numb. He clutched the talisman to his chest.

The horrific, crawling sensations had stopped moving through his veins. Daniel glanced at his damaged arm but grimaced and looked away again. The skin had turned shades of mottled gray and black. He couldn't bend the fingers. But the fungus had stopped spreading. He supposed he was grateful for that.

Bran had been coated by the sticky black soot. Daniel returned to his side and pressed his fingers to the man's neck. The thin skin felt as cold as marble, and there was no sign of a pulse. For all Daniel knew, Bran might not have had a pulse for decades. The man's face was slack, though. He looked peaceful. Daniel pulled up the corner of his T-shirt and tried to wipe the grime off Bran's face. His own clothes were covered in the same soot, though, and he only succeeded in rubbing it around. He exhaled and dropped his head.

Annalise appeared at his side. He could feel an icy chill rolling off her, worsening the shivers he'd developed, but he didn't pull away. She was frightened and lonely. She needed friendship.

"I won't leave you," he murmured. "You won't have to be alone."

She made no indication of hearing him.

Daniel sat there, surrounded by the broken statues, for what felt like hours. The fire's glow had disappeared from the tops of the trees. The rain slowly eased into a trickle. Eventually, dawn touched the edge of the sky with the promise of light. It wasn't much, but after being nearly blind for most of the night, Daniel was relieved to see his surroundings again.

He lifted the bloated arm. It was impossible to recognize as a part of him. His legs still shook, but he thought they would carry his weight. He shuffled onto his knees.

"I'm going to get inside," he said to Annalise. "Did you want to come?"

She stayed sitting, her arms wrapped around her knees and her face hidden under the mane of fine hair. Daniel swallowed and looked back at Bran. He needed to get somewhere dry. As the rain thinned and dawn broke, a horrific chill burrowed into him, and hypothermia became a serious threat. If he didn't move soon, he might never stand again.

He imagined walking away and leaving Bran in the garden. He pictured the crows coming back and pecking at the body. Insects teeming over him. The soot running under his eyelids, between his teeth, into his pores. He couldn't stomach it.

Daniel dug a hand under Bran's shoulders and lifted. He hadn't expected to be able to carry the man, especially not when his muscles were so drained, but he'd forgotten how insubstantial Bran was. He weighed no more than he had as the thin black cat. Daniel reached his damaged hand under Bran's knees and hoisted him up, staggered, then stabilized himself.

"Are you coming, Annalise?" He couldn't see the girl. For all he knew, she might have retreated back to the crypt as soon as light danced along the horizon. He took a deep breath and tried not to let the shivers bring him to his knees as he pressed into the forest.

The rain was no more than mist-like flecks, but fat drops continued to run off the trees. Daniel barely felt them. His clothes were sodden and heavy, and his shoes squelched in the mud. He felt as though he would never be warm again.

The groundskeeper's cottage emerged from between the trees. *Home.* It meant warmth, dry clothes, and a bed, but he was too tired to feel more than a dull anticipation. His legs moved faster as he drew nearer, until he was stumbling through the weeds to reach its door.

He struggled to keep Bran in his arms as he blindly felt for the door handle. When he'd left the building, he hadn't expected to ever return to it. He was glad he hadn't locked it on the way out.

The room was quiet but not as warm as he'd hoped it would be. He carefully placed Bran on the ground beside the fireplace then scooted onto the hearth to light it. His fingers shook so badly that it took him two minutes to coax sparks out of the flint. When the kindling finally caught, he threw the stones aside and held his fingers so close to the flames that he would have burned if he weren't so cold.

The plague-infested flesh in his right hand was like something out of nightmares. In the soft glow of the fire, there was no way to avoid looking at it. He prodded at the back of his hand, and shudders coursed through him at the spongy sensation.

He tried flexing the fingers again. They were still stiff but curled a little farther. He didn't want to think about the limb being amputated, though that was probably what a hospital would do.

Am I even safe to go to a hospital? The damage had stopped spreading when Eliza died, but that didn't mean it was harmless. He didn't want to risk infecting other people…especially patients with compromised immune systems.

But what's going to happen to me if I don't get it treated? Will it kill me? Turn to rot and poison my blood?

Two soft taps echoed from the house's front. Daniel turned. In his rush to light the fire, he'd left the door open, and he thought he saw a glimmer of flowing hair. The sun was just starting to breach the horizon and soften the pitch-black sky, but there were still a couple of minutes until dawn proper reached Craven Manor. Daniel managed a thin smile. "Did you want to come in? I'll shut the door and leave the windows closed so you'll be safe from the sun."

He hadn't even finished speaking before Annalise ran through the doorway. Her form took on enough solidity to be clearly visible. She stopped beside the fire, hands clasped ahead of her, and looked down at her brother.

"I'm sorry," Daniel said. He forced himself to leave the growing flames to shut the door. Annalise folded herself onto the hearth beside Bran then faded from sight again.

His wet clothes were leaving puddles across the floor. Daniel cleared his throat. "Could you face the wall for a few moments, please?"

He couldn't see the girl anymore, so he hoped she had listened. He grabbed a towel and dry clothes from his bag then hurried to change. Getting the shirt over the swollen arm was a challenge, especially with numb fingers, but he managed it after a brief struggle.

The soot still stuck to Bran. Daniel hated seeing him like that, coated in the residue of his insane mother. He fetched a tea towel, wet it, and did what he could to wipe the grime off Bran's face. As he worked, he tried to swallow the aching lump in his throat. He hadn't yet thought about what would come next. He would need to bury the house's master. He thought he could dig the grave beside Annalise's tomb, as long as the girl approved.

At least for now, he can sleep here. I'll worry about his final resting place later.

Daniel threw the grimy cloth into the sink. He knew he should eat something, but he'd run out of energy. He compromised by drinking deeply from the tap then stumbled back to the fireplace and dropped two new logs onto the growing flames. Then he crept to his bed and curled up under the layers of blankets as the fire began to spread warmth through the room.

Even after the physically exhausting night, sleep eluded Daniel for more than an hour. Every time he started to drift under, nightmarish images shocked him awake. He kept accidentally touching the damaged flesh on his right arm. And it was impossible to forget the body sprawled on the hearthside rug behind him.

Finally, weariness dragged him under. His dreams were strange. At one point, he imagined he saw Bran standing by the fire, hands clasped behind him as the firelight danced over his gray features. Daniel stared at his profile for a moment then mumbled, "I thought you were dead."

"I am. And I have been for quite a while." Bran's mouth twitched into a smile. "But I've found that death and I don't agree too much. Go back to sleep, Mr. Kane."

"You need to start calling me Daniel. Figure we've been through enough to be on a first-name basis, haven't we?"

"I suppose so. Daniel."

When Daniel next woke, the fire was dead. There was no hint of light around the window or under his door, which meant he'd slept through the whole day. He sat up and rubbed his hand over his eyes as he waited for his head to clear.

His left arm ached. He shambled out of bed and searched for the candle on the desk. He managed to light it one-handed and lifted the growing flame to see his damaged arm.

Someone had tied the silver talisman around his hand, strapping the vial and silver beads against his skin. He was surprised to see the swelling had gone down. It was still discolored, and mottled red-and-purple bruises ran through the slate-gray undertones, but he could curl his fingers into a proper fist.

He lowered the arm and turned to face the room. The space in front of the fireplace was empty. Daniel let a smile grow. "Well, how about that."

CHAPTER 32

Three Days After the Fire

DANIEL APPROACHED CRAVEN MANOR. The storm had doused the flames, but the sour scent of burnt wood and fabric still lingered in the air. Three of the trees growing closest to the building were scorched black. A sense of gratitude crashed through him. Without Bran's storm, the flames could have easily spread through the long-dead vegetation filling the gardens and burned Daniel alive in his cottage.

The flock of crows complained behind him. They'd abandoned the blackened tree beside the front door but still lingered close to the house. Daniel made a mental note to bring them some fresh meat later. They deserved a treat for their efforts in the fight against Eliza.

He climbed the wide stone steps, where a layer of soot had

replaced the usual coating of dried leaves. The smell of smoke became stronger as Daniel stopped in the space where the wooden doors had once stood.

The thick dark-wood slabs were almost completely gone. Clumps of charcoal lay across the top step, and he could see the melted remnants of the hinges. Daniel swallowed and looked through the hole where the doors had been.

Craven Manor's insides made for a depressing sight. It had never been especially welcoming or cozy, but he'd grown to appreciate the massive hall and its antique fittings. The chandelier lay in a tangled wreck in the center of the foyer. The marble floor was invisible under thick ash. The high windows had exploded in the heat, and parts of the roof had collapsed. The rotted furniture surrounding the fireplace was gone, as were all of the trinkets on its mantelpiece.

One element upset Daniel more than any other: the dramatic wooden staircase had been consumed, and only an ugly stub remained. Without it, the room felt unbalanced and wrong. He couldn't see Annalise's painting on the landing, but the damage to the lower level didn't bode well for it. He exhaled and folded his arms across his chest.

"Sometimes, a drastic loss can herald a new start. A *fresh* start."

Daniel turned. Bran stood on the patch of ground outside the manor. He gave Daniel a short nod and climbed the stairs to stand at his side. Together, they stared through the charred remains of the door.

Daniel's throat was tight, and it took him a moment to speak. "Are you all right?"

"As well as a dead man can be, I suppose." He looked better than Daniel had expected him to; his skin was still paper-thin and gray, but the awful mapping of black veins was less pronounced. "I feel drained. Scraped thin. But I hope time will return some of my strength, as much as is left." Bran's glance was sharp. "I'm surprised you returned."

Daniel shrugged. "I didn't really have anywhere else to go. I spent a night in the hospital waiting room and a second night with Mrs. Kirshner—she's my old neighbor—but I needed to come back eventually."

"Were my coins not enough to afford you new quarters?"

Daniel tactfully avoided the fact that Mrs. Kirshner was spending them on cat toys. Instead, he told the truth. "They would have. But nowhere else feels like home."

"I am grateful." A smile was audible in Bran's voice. "It was lonely without you. And rebuilding the manor will be easier with someone who can lift objects heavier than a pen. How is your arm?"

"Uh, sore." Daniel flexed the fingers. The flesh was still blotchy shades of gray and black, but the swelling had subsided. He'd wrapped it in bandages, partially to protect against infection and partially to avoid horrifying people he passed in the streets, and kept the talisman tied against the skin. It seemed to help. "The doctors had no idea what it was or how to treat it. I left before they could suggest any crazy experiments. Do you know if it will get better?"

"Truthfully, I have no idea." Bran held out his own hands. The fingertips that had once been mottled black were a dark gray. "Now that Eliza is dead, my own affliction seems to be receding. The plague must have been tied to her will. Without her anger to fuel it, it is dying. But I am not mortal. I do not know how the infection will impact a living organism. I suppose we must take each day as it comes."

Daniel tilted his head back to examine Craven Manor's ceiling. "You said something about rebuilding."

"Yes. It is perhaps foolish and more than a little vain, but I do not like seeing my family's home brought to such a level of disgrace. If I can borrow your talents, we might see what some time and effort can repair." Bran nodded over Daniel's shoulder, toward the forest. "We can begin by retrieving the bag of coins your cousin attempted to abscond with."

Four Weeks After

"NO, I'M JUST SAYING, it doesn't make sense."

Daniel's attention picked up at the words. He was in the dining room, working through a budget for Craven Manor's repairs. The words floated through the dining room door, and he put down the pen and crept closer to the opening. Two men were working on the fireplace, removing the scorch marks and repairing the mantelpiece. They spoke in subdued voices, but the words still carried easily through the manor's empty foyer.

"I mean, the house catches fire within a week of him moving in. That's insurance fraud 101, right?"

His companion snorted. "Or maybe he just doesn't know how fireplaces work. This Kane guy is barely more than a kid. It's no different than my cousin on his learner's license buying an expensive car and crashing it."

"Exactly. He's young. Twenty, maybe twenty-two. How'd he get this house? Where're his parents? It's just this kid living in a burned-up mansion in the middle of nowhere. I'm telling you, something's fishy."

"Keep your voice down, idiot. Fishy or not, we're getting paid up front and in cash. As long as I don't have to chase down overdue invoices, I'll gladly turn a blind eye to a bit of weirdness."

"Still, though—"

"I heard him telling Terry he inherited it. Apparently some great-great-great-aunt or something took a shining to him as a kid and wrote him into her will."

"I wish I had a rich aunt."

"Don't we all."

Brief laughter broke the tension, but the reprieve didn't last long. The first man spoke again, his voice so quiet that Daniel had to tilt his head close to the door to make out the words.

"There's something else. This house is weird. All of these instructions to not come until after dawn, not to explore the garden, not to stay after dark—"

"He likes his privacy. Rich people usually do."

"And I keep hearing footsteps and doors opening, even when

Kane is out of the house. I'm thinking maybe we're not alone here—"

"You're getting paranoid, man."

"Don't you feel like you're being watched? I mean, hell, just look at this place! It's like it walked out of Halloween Town. If any house was going to be haunted, wouldn't it be one like this?"

"Are the ghosts going to get in the way of me doing my job? Because unless they do, I honestly don't care."

"I think the cat…laughed at me."

There was a very long pause. Daniel folded his arms across his chest and bit down on a smirk.

Finally, the first builder spoke again, sounding defensive. "I'm serious. That cat has been following me everywhere. This morning, I hit my thumb with the hammer, and its mouth opened right up. I swear it was laughing."

"All right, you've officially gone around the bend."

"Shut up!"

"If the house bothers you that much, put some more energy into your bloody work. The sooner we finish, the sooner we can get out."

"Fine."

Daniel, keeping his feet light, crept back to the table and settled into the chair. Although the foyer's damage was extreme, the stone walls had hindered the fire's progress deeper into the house, and most of the rooms were still structurally intact. He'd had to scrub soot off the dining table, but then, there'd been so much dust on it that it had needed a deep clean anyway.

The scruffy black cat sat pin-straight on the tabletop, overseeing Daniel's work. They made eye contact, and Daniel couldn't repress his grin any longer.

He kept his voice to a whisper. Bran's ears were good enough to pick it up. "If I'd been there, I would have laughed, too."

The cat's jaws opened, and he exhaled a soft, hissing imitation of a chuckle.

Six Weeks Later

DANIEL SHIVERED, DESPITE FOUR layers of clothing. He leaned his back against one of the lichen-crusted trees. Tendrils of mist coiled around him, but they were thin that night and didn't obscure the crypt ahead of him.

The flowers and bushes he'd planted had taken root. Most were dormant in the latter half of autumn, but come spring, Annalise would be surrounded by a carpet of color.

Bran emerged through the trees to his right. Daniel was gradually getting used to the man's silent appearances and departures. For the first few weeks, it had been incredibly unsettling to look up and see the tall figure in the doorway when no footsteps had heralded his arrival. Now, it was just another quirk he'd adapted to.

Daniel raised a hand in greeting but couldn't manage a smile. "The police stopped looking for Kyle today."

"Ah." Bran came to a halt beside Daniel and leaned against a tree. "I'm sorry."

Daniel shrugged. He was glad Bran hadn't been happy at the news. He knew it was better for them and for Craven Manor if the police inquiry died, but at the same time, it seemed horribly final. Kyle hadn't even had a funeral. There hadn't been anything left of him to bury; all that remained were Kyle's bag—stuffed full of coins from Bran's study—and black soot staining the statues and mixed in with the dry mud.

No one except Daniel and Bran knew that Kyle had traveled to Craven Manor that night. He'd left the hospital without checking himself out. The police's main theory was that he'd sustained more damage to his brain than the doctors had first assumed and wandered away in a delirium. They thought he might have perished in an abandoned building—there were plenty of those in his city—or strayed into the woods and died of hypothermia. Kyle didn't have any family beyond Daniel, so no one was hounding the police to prolong the search. He would live in their database as a missing person, albeit one who wasn't actually missed.

Except by Daniel.

He kept replaying the events surrounding Kyle's death again and again. He alternately blamed himself for enabling his cousin, and for not showing enough compassion. Kyle might not have been a shining example of human goodness, but Daniel believed he wasn't inherently bad, either.

"Daniel?"

He startled at Bran's rasping voice then managed a grimacing smile. "Sorry. Stuck in my head."

Motion caught his eye. Annalise had emerged from her tomb. She stood twenty paces away, swaying, with her hands clasped behind her back. She grinned, and her excitement eased some of Daniel's tension. He smiled back at her as he pulled a small metal tube out of his pocket. "Ready?"

She nodded. He turned the laser pointer on. The red light cut through the mist and appeared on a tree several feet to the tomb's left.

He'd come up with the idea after trying to play hide-and-seek with Annalise. He could never keep up with her, and her transparent form gave her a distinct advantage. The laser pointer solved both problems. Daniel could rest, and it gave Annalise a challenge.

Annalise vanished into the mist. Daniel tried to track her movements, but she was good at hiding herself. He took a guess and turned off the laser pointer. Annalise's hand appeared on the tree a second afterward.

Bran laughed. "Almost."

Daniel turned the light on again, this time pointing at a different tree. He tried to guess how long it would take her to reach it, but was a moment too slow as her hand appeared under the red dot. She twirled in triumph then danced back into the mist.

"Nice job," Daniel called then turned out the light again.

Annalise vanished as she waited for him to pick a new target.

Daniel tilted his head toward Bran as he flicked the beam on again. "I spoke to Joel this morning. He can bring us a generator to power some stuff in the manor, if you want. Lights. A radio. Or any other kind of entertainment you want."

Bran rolled his shoulders. The movement reminded Daniel of the way the crows would ruffle their feathers. "I'm sure that isn't necessary."

"Don't you get bored, though? During the day, I mean, while I'm working?"

"I have been alone for nigh on two hundred years. You would be amazed at my tolerance for it."

Daniel chuckled, and his moment of distraction cost him a point as Annalise caught the light. He switched it to a new location, on the crypt's wall. "Fair enough. But you don't have to be alone. Not anymore."

"Hmm." Bran glanced behind them, to the behemoth of a building rising over the treetops, and his expression softened. "Perhaps some lights in the house would be nice."

Daniel had let his attention wander from the game. Annalise appeared at his side to startle him. She brushed her fingers across the laser pointer, turning the metal ice-cold, then frisked away, her face bright with mischievous laughter.

Five Months After

Daniel flexed his shoulders as he jogged up Craven Manor's wide front steps. Winter was on its last legs, and premature bright-green leaves were beginning to sprout from their trees. He wore a thick jacket, but he doubted he would need the wool gloves that were tucked into his pocket much longer.

The mansion's front door stood ajar. He rarely closed it. The habit was part sentimentality by that point; he was so used to the door waiting open for him that shutting it felt wrong. The gap let leaves and dust blow through the opening and made sweeping a job that never ended. But it also provided extra illumination for the foyer, which still felt gloomy, even after the modern lighting had been installed.

Daniel shed his coat and hung it on one of the metal hooks beside the door. The high ceiling was empty; he and Bran hadn't replaced the chandelier after the fire, and Daniel found he preferred it that way.

Repairing the building had taken months. The flames hadn't spread far from the foyer, but whatever they'd touched had been a lost cause. He and Bran had salvaged as much as they could, though, and mimicked the house's original design with the new installations. They'd managed to repair Annalise's scorched portrait, and it continued to look over the entrance from its place above the stately wooden staircase.

The foyer was cozier now. A thick rug cushioned the floor around the fireplace. Steady flames crackled in the grate, radiating warmth across the space and lighting the stone walls.

Bran never ate or slept, but heat and cold were two sensations he could still feel. Daniel lit the fire when he woke every morning, and he made several trips back to the building through the day and evening to restock its wood. Under his watch, the fire was never allowed to fully die unless the grate needed cleaning.

"Good evening." Daniel rounded the plush red chairs and slid into one. The fire felt amazing after the biting cold outside. "I finally cleared up that fallen tree to the east of the crypt. We've got a whole six functioning paths weaving through this maze now. And enough dry wood to last us until next year."

"Look." Bran, reclining in the chair next to Daniel, nodded to a small, furry shape at his side. He seemed to be trying not to move. "She's asleep."

It had taken five months, but Daniel had finally convinced Bran to let him adopt a cat from the shelter. He'd picked out a young gray girl, and it was snoozing beside Bran, its fluffy head resting on his leg.

Daniel grinned. "I told you she'd like you."

Bran's long fingers scratched behind the cat's ears. Its whiskers puffed out, but it didn't stir. "The poor creature is too foolish to know she ought to be afraid of me. Much like you." Bran's expression was deadpan, but laughter sparkled in his eyes. Daniel snorted.

With Eliza dead, the plague was slowly receding from both of them. Daniel's arm had regained sensation and most of its dexterity, though the lingering discoloration meant he either wore long-sleeve shirts and gloves or wrapped it in bandages when he visited town. Bran's features were becoming less nightmarish, as well. Daniel thought that, in a few months, the other man might be able to visit town as a human without getting more than a couple of wary glances.

"We've got the historical society meeting here tomorrow." Daniel stretched his feet toward the flames. "Do you want to join us this time? I'm sure you'd be welcome."

"Perhaps another day." Bran continued to scratch behind the cat's ears. *Baby steps,* Daniel reminded himself. He couldn't rehabilitate a recluse overnight. Simply agreeing to let Mrs. Kirshner and her friends spend the evening in his parlor once a week was a large concession.

Daniel and Bran generally only used a few rooms in the mansion: the foyer, the parlor, the library, and the dining room. They had closed up nearly all of the second- and third-floor bedrooms, including the tar-painted tower door. It was easier than trying to keep them maintained, though Daniel hoped Bran might eventually open up a few of the rooms to guests. He suspected Mrs. Kirshner and Bran would get along well, once they both got over their wariness, and it would be good to know his neighbor was looked after and comfortable in her retirement.

Daniel had asked Bran to reduce his pay to something reasonable, but an envelope with two gold coins still appeared outside his door each week. It was far more than he needed. Some of the money had gone into a car. Some was invested. And he spent the rest on antique books about spirits and the supernatural, which were gradually filling out the decimated library's shelves. He still didn't know if it was possible to release Annalise's spirit from the manor. But if there was a way, he wanted to find it and at least give Annalise the choice.

Daniel couldn't hide a smile as he watched Bran lavish

affection on the sleeping cat. Wind whistled through gaps in the stonework, but it seemed distant and comforting as he bent forward to add more wood to the fire.

Bran had said something shortly after Eliza's attack: "We will take each day as it comes."

That was the motto Daniel was living by. He didn't know if his arm would ever fully heal, and it was still possible that Kyle's death could be connected to him. Life might eventually carry him away from Craven Manor and its unusual owner.

But none of those eventualities felt threatening, not when compared to what he'd gained. His home was comfortable. His work was rewarding. And for the first time in years, he had a genuine friend. The job was unorthodox, but he felt as though he'd found his purpose as Craven Manor's custodian. And so he would take each day as it came.

ABOUT THE AUTHOR

Darcy Coates is the *USA Today* bestselling author of *Hunted*, *The Haunting of Ashburn House*, *The House Next Door*, and more than a dozen other horror and suspense titles. She lives on the Central Coast of Australia with her family, cats, and a garden full of herbs and vegetables. Darcy loves forests, especially old-growth forests where the trees dwarf anyone who steps between them. Wherever she lives, she tries to have a mountain range close by.

SHE'S ALWAYS WATCHING...

When Guy finds the deed to a house in his mother's attic, it seems like an incredible stroke of luck. Sure, it hasn't been inhabited in years and vines strangle the age-stained walls, but Guy's convinced he can clean the building up and sell it. He'd be crazy to turn down free money. Right?

But there's a reason no one lives in Rookward House, and the dilapidated rooms aren't as empty as they seem. Forty years ago, a deranged woman tormented the family that made Rookward its home. Now her ghost clings to the building like rot. She's bitter, obsessive, and fiercely jealous...and once Guy has moved into her house, she has no intention of letting him go.

For more info about Sourcebooks's books and authors, visit:
sourcebooks.com